LOVERS

Fran Clark

Island Dream Books

Book Cover by Rima Salloum

New for February 2024

The Island Secrets Complete Series

Holding Paradise – Book 1
A Prayer For Junie – Book 2
The Long Way Home – Book 3
When Skies Are Grey – Book 4

Join my mailing list and get the prequel to Book 1 free

If love makes the world go round
And love's such a wondrous sound
Why can't we give our lives to love?

To Live To Love
Fran Clark 2008

1

Ione

I thought if I prayed hard enough, there might be a let up in the rain. It began two days ago, a fine spray on the window pane, as I packed my life away in cardboard crates. I look over at Mrs Baxter's garden from my patio windows. For her, the rain continues, her roses smiling to the heavens as if the rest of our prayers don't count. Very soon, though, all the gardens will have fallen leaves collecting on patchy lawns, flowers will be deadheaded, patio furniture locked in sheds but I won't be here to watch it happen.

This rain, today, falls hard and fast as if every drop was a pent-up emotion, crammed inside a cloud of fury, waiting to burst out. There are angry stabs on the decking, purposeful splashes on the leaves of the geraniums. I wonder if I should grab my pot plants and take them with me to my new flat, after all, but I have nowhere to put them now. My car is full, and the movers are almost finished loading. The small items of furniture I kept are all on board, and the boxes marked *Misc* are mostly stacked in the van. There are several boxes marked *Misc*. It wasn't until I'd sat in the stark living room yesterday and noticed how many that it occurred to me I should at least have written *Misc Kitchen* or *Misc Bedroom* just so I knew where everything went when I got to the new place.

I decide to leave the geraniums.

The removal men, when they arrived two hours ago, looked at me with pity. They probably wondered why I was leaving a three bedroom house in Manchester and travelling all the way to London to a two bedroom flat on my own. What was my reason for downsizing? Had I lost people along the way? Had I been too hopeful about filling the house with a husband and children? Maybe I'm overthinking this. I'm just another job for them. They'd been efficient and matter-of-fact, but not in an unfriendly way.

On the floor next to the living room door, along with my handbag, is the box. Mum's ashes. I'd kept them in the dark wooden box on a shelf in the top of my wardrobe. David complained that it was freaking him out, seeing them in the living room every time he sat down. Like the house was haunted. I moved them—couldn't handle another argument—so they were out of sight. Mum was never out of mind, not for me. Although she'd left it to me, this would always be Mum's house. Being haunted by her wouldn't be so bad—I missed her with every fibre of my being.

I'm not looking forward to the drive: four hours with just one stop. Maybe I'll take two stops if I feel tired. I didn't sleep much the night before. Tossing and turning, worried I'd done the wrong thing, moving to a completely new city, one I really only saw through Mum's eyes. She'd refused to go back there, not even for a visit. I'd wanted to stop the moving process many times, take the For Sale sign down, call the school in Holland Park and tell them I'd changed my mind, something had come up. But I'd had a long and successful interview and a new job was part of the big change I'd convinced myself I needed.

Two nights before, I'd gone for a farewell drink with Jeannie. She left her husband, Oliver, to sort the twins out by himself for a change and had taken me out. I wasn't really in the mood. I forced myself to go. Of course, I wanted to say goodbye or *au revoir* to Jeannie. She is my best friend and has seen me through some difficult times. Jeannie helped me escape from my whole situation. One that had gone on for long enough. Any longer and I would have ended up on the psychiatric ward of Manchester General after yet another spell in A&E. Jeannie hadn't meant for me to go as far as London, maybe just the next town or city.

'You know I'm going to miss you like hell, Ione?' she'd said in the trendy bar we'd found ourselves in after Jeannie said The Angel had the atmosphere of a wake. A wake in which the deceased had an assortment of morbid-looking friends who enjoyed a drink but were lacking in conversation. Jeannie said it was far too sad, and we should go to Grainger's, ignoring my protests about not being dressed right and being the wrong side of thirty. Grainger's played their music loud. All the tables were high and the stools were tall. I'd have felt as if I was on display, and there wouldn't be a dark corner to hide in. I was still working on the coping mechanisms the counsellor had given me for that sort of thing, but I wasn't quite there yet. I didn't mention the part about not wanting to be noticed to Jeannie because I knew she'd lecture me about how beautiful I was. How she wished she had my thick hair and complexion. Exotic, she once called me. A Jamaican mother and Greek father equals exotic to Jeannie, and I couldn't argue with her.

'I'll miss you, too,' I'd said. I did all I could to choke back a sob. I promised myself I wouldn't make a scene. *Leaving Manchester would be the making of me*. This was my mantra. 'But I do have mixed feelings about leaving the house. He ruined it for me.'

'Don't think about the last few years. Just try and remember the time before.'

'I'm trying. My childhood memories, the teenage years. They were the best, but it was hard to hold onto the memory of me and Mum. The times we had. I know I've told you this, but it broke her heart when I moved out to go to uni.'

'Funny, isn't it? When I left home, I told my parents, you'll never see me again. I'm travelling the world, starting with New York. I'll be rich. I won't miss Manchester for a second. I told them I'd send them the odd Christmas card and that would be it.' We both laughed at the reality of it all. 'Two years in Leeds—didn't even make it to an airport—and I'm back. Pregnant. Married to a slob and moving into a three-bedroomed semi round the corner from the flipping folks.'

Despite what she said about them, Jeannie was close to her parents. They'd helped her with Benjie, now fifteen, and when she and then Oliver had been out of work, they had paid the mortgage. Though she groaned non-stop about her husband, Jeannie was in total agreement whenever I reminded her how lucky she was to have found a man like Oliver.

I, on the other hand, had found a man who would kick me down a flight of stairs, then step over me to go out and play cards with his friends. As if seeing his wife's legs lift from under her and hearing her cries as each part of her body jammed into a wall or banged into the banister as she careered down the stairs was perfectly acceptable. Like it happened in every household. The first time David was violent, physically that is, is a time I still have etched in my memory. I'd made some comment about not having anything nice. I was looking into the wardrobe at the time, referring to its contents and the fact I needed something for the baptism of Jeannie's twins. I remember how, in a flash, out of the corner of my eye, I saw a dark figure lunging towards me. At first, I didn't know what I was seeing. His eyes were wide; bulging from his head. His hands, outstretched as he came at me, were not like hands but savage instruments. David leapt at me to attack, but I couldn't understand why. I didn't move. He was on me, forcing me to look at him, spitting angry words into my face.

'David. What are you doing?' I kept screaming for him to stop, but he battered me around the bedroom, screaming obscenities, telling me I was ungrateful, he'd given me so much. I remember the pain as he beat my arms, my back. I tried to run from the room. He grabbed me again, clawing at my neck, wanting, as I realised in the next second, to pull me back into the room by my hair. I screamed, but there was no sound. I could feel the hot sting of his nails as they ripped into the skin on my neck and the cold feeling of exposed flesh. From halfway under the bed where I cowered and pleaded for him to stop, I saw the drops of red on the cream rug. Blood fell from open wounds, and I was trapped. I didn't think he would stop there, but he did. He looked down at me, sneering, his eyes telling me I got what I deserved. That I was ungrateful. That I was wrong. That I should apologise to *him*.

At the baptism, I held one of the twins as I stood by the altar with Jeannie holding the second twin and Oliver standing next to his brother. The priest, highly spirited, performed the ceremony. Jeannie knew something was wrong. There were questions in her eyes as she watched my fingers moving to the scratches on my neck. I couldn't stop touching them. It became an involuntary twitch I couldn't shake for years to come. If I touched my neck and the scars were gone, then maybe the beating never really happened. The scars left their mark forever. From that day, many more wounds would appear on my skin. They'd come and they'd heal. At the time, I had no idea how hard it would be to heal the things you cannot see. At the baptism celebration party, Jeannie hardly left my side. *If you want to talk to me.* She kept saying it, over and over. I should have talked to her. I should have told her from that first incident. I wanted to.

'Here's to your lovely folks, Jeannie,' I said above the din at Grainger's. I raised my wine glass. 'If it wasn't for them, I wouldn't have you as my best friend.'

'Are we really talking about my parents having sex?' Jeannie pulled a face.

We clinked glasses and laughed again.

I'd met Jeannie when I was teaching music at a local high school. I had taken a small flat instead of moving into Mum's when I came back to Manchester after uni and teacher training. I was an independent woman who'd left home over ten years ago. Mum got to know Jeannie and loved her as much as I did. In the years to come, after Mum died and I married David, I began to see less and less of Jeannie. David saw to that. Always in my head, telling me I was hopeless, that I was useless and why the school made me head of music, he had no clue. He kept vowing to come to the school and tell them what a bad wife I was. He berated me for not knowing the first thing about love and affection. Said I was a lousy lover. I couldn't cook. Everything I gave him made him gag. That was not true. He cleared his plate most evenings, coming in late and complaining the food was cold. Throwing things around the kitchen, watching me cower in a corner, afraid to look at him, afraid to move in case he kicked me into another corner of the room.

Jeannie noticed how I changed. How I stopped talking in the staffroom. Afraid to look anyone in the eye. How I lost weight. How I shouted at the children at school and demanded their very best, never allowing for one single, solitary mistake on their part.

'Here's to you, Ione.' Jeannie raised her fourth gin and tonic double. She clinked her glass to mine so loudly, the dark images shattered before my eyes and dissolved into the highly polished floorboards in the bar. 'You're only a video chat away. You can show me round the new place, virtual tour and all that. But seriously, I know I say I'll miss you, and I will, but a clean slate is going to make all the difference. Wow. Is that a smile I see? At last.' She put her hand on mine. 'Take good care. Enjoy the new school and don't, whatever you do, take any shit from anyone. You are an amazing woman. A good, kind and sensitive person. You were there for your mum when she needed you.'

'Jeannie, I'm all she had. Of course I was there.'

'It doesn't necessarily follow that children have to look after their parents, you know? I'm not looking after my folks when they're old or on their last legs. Nursing home. The pair of them, and I've got the place with the cheapest rates bookmarked in my Favourites.'

'Jeannie!' Tears that pricked at my eyes welled as tears of laughter. It wasn't a night for sadness, just joy, my forever memory of my best friend. We reminisced about how we first met. Jeannie was a special needs assistant who joined the school around the time of my promotion. I'd warmed to her straight away. No one could resist Jeannie, her loveable nature, her full smile and her sparkly eyes that crinkled at the corners. It felt as if we'd known each other forever. As it turned out, we'd not grown up that far apart. As if that wasn't enough of a coincidence, while I was at the University of Leeds, Jeannie had moved there and was living with a chubby roofer and tiler called Oliver. He stroked her long hair and called her *My Jeannie,* telling everyone at their wedding that all his wishes had come true.

At my wedding, I'd stood in the Register Office, knees trembling. I had a strange feeling at the backs of my legs. I thought the bottom half of my body was going to give way and I'd fall to the floor, drop my bouquet. The whole day was surreal. Jeannie had rubbed my back in the toilets of Franco's Restaurant at the reception, saying, 'Don't worry, love, you're just missing your mum.' Mum had died before having met the man I fell in love with and married within eight months of meeting him.

I turn on the car radio just as I hit the M6. It's too quiet. Just the squeak of the windshield wipers and an occasional sigh from me. I take deep breaths in and out as I drive. Deep into my belly as my counsellor described, yet I'm not quite relaxed. The black tarmac miles roll on as I follow the flow of traffic, changing the speed of my wipers from fast to intermittent and then back again. The rain can't decide if it's a shower, fine or gusty. Can rain be gusty, or is that just the wind? The music on the radio and the voice of the DJ are my company. It's the same station I listen to in my kitchen when I bake and plan and look things up on my laptop. For the entire journey, I'm trying to calm the nervous energy I have about moving so far and starting a new job.

By the time I reach the M1, I begin to wonder if the removal people will find the flat. They come from Manchester. How well will they know Shepherd's Bush? How well did I when I looked at the Rightmove website day in and day out, searching for my escape home. My start-all-over-again home that will obliterate the lingering memories of my life with David.

I saw him again. David, my ex-husband. He walked straight up to me in the High Street and pleaded with me to take him back. 'I'll be good this time.'

'You were supposed to be good the first time round. That was the time to be good. You ruined my life.'

I'd turned and walked back in the direction I came. A ridiculous thing to do, I realised a split second after. That was the direction David was going. I crossed the road without looking. The cars in the busy street tooted and swerved.

'What are you doing?' David said. He ran at my side to keep up, gluing his body to mine, walking as if we were close again. Like we were lovers. Smiling as he talked to me the way he used to smile when we were out and he was telling me how ridiculous I looked and that I looked cheap in that dress. 'You could have got yourself killed.'

I stopped. Stared into the eyes of the man I'd instantly fallen in love with and thought I could never live without. I wanted to say to him, 'You killed me. *You*. First my soul. You took it clean away with your disgusting words and the way you looked at me. We'd only been married a month. Mentally, you killed me, and if that wasn't enough, after you'd alienated me from the handful of people I could call a friend, made it so I could no longer hold down a job, you tried to stamp out my life with your fists and feet and anything close enough for you to throw. Traffic is the least of my problems.'

I didn't say any of this; in fact, it was the last time I would ever think like that again. I remembered all the work I'd done to get me to the place I was that day. I would never have looked David in the eye the way I turned and did right then. Not blinking, remembering the power of positive thought and definite action. He couldn't bend or break me, and he could see that clearly in my eyes and something shifted in him.

'Stop following me,' I said.

'I'm not following you. I live here now. I'm back. Can't get rid of me that easily.' It was a threat he left hanging, and I would never be sure, when I walked away, if he would ever come after me again.

London, thirty-six miles. I'll be there by early afternoon. It won't take long for the removal people to move my things in. Most of my furniture, I'd got rid of. Casting out the old and starting something new. Shepherd's Bush is an hour away, and all of a sudden, I can feel the calm rising in me.

2

Marta

Marta wasn't crying because the little boy looked sad. He was happy, actually. Large eyes. The whites of them so white, she couldn't help but notice them as she looked into the window of the music shop. She thought she saw grey flecks in the blues of his eyes, wondering if she was imagining the detail. After all, how could she be so sure, looking at him through a veil of tears and a shop window that reflected her pale face straight back at her.

The boy turned his head towards her, and Marta's breath caught in her throat. She hadn't meant to stare. The man at the counter rang up the sale and handed the hard case of a violin to the boy. Both he and his mother smiled and nodded as the man jumped from his stool and hurried to open the door for them. The boy clutched the violin case to his chest, chirping to his mother. Marta acknowledged that, like her, they were Polish. She heard the mother say, '*Chodźmy,*' to her son. 'Let's go.' Unlike his mother, the boy sounded very English, like any boy who'd grown up in London, she supposed.

As Marta watched them walk away, she felt a hand touch her arm. Turning, she saw the man from the shop beside her.

'Are you okay?' he asked.

That's how Marta met Elliot, the first person who'd shown any kindness all day, though this wasn't the first time she'd seen him. This rangy black man, skin the colour of a sweet chestnut, often sat next to the window behind the counter.

Sometimes he fixed the shelves, sometimes he read a book, sometimes he played one of the many guitars on display in the shop. He only smiled when he had a customer. Otherwise, he looked sad.

'Would you like to come in?' he asked her. His voice was soft like honey spread over warm bread; it gave her a feeling of nostalgia. She welcomed images of a place she once loved, though in reality it was a place she would never go back to.

She stepped into Val's Music Shop for the first time, but Marta knew, as she wiped the dampness of her tears away, that it wouldn't be the last.

'Come round the back,' Elliot said, leading the way. 'I'm making tea. Or coffee, if you'd prefer?'

'Is it all right? I wouldn't mind, actually.'

She followed him through a small dark corridor that led directly into a brightly lit storage room where the smell of polished wood, leather cases and something sweet greeted her. Not for one moment did Marta hesitate, walking into a back room with a man she'd never met, not officially, anyway. Something about Elliot made her feel safe, secure. She hadn't felt like that in a very long time.

Without being asked, she removed the long purple cardigan she was wearing and shook out the fine sprinkles of rain from her dark hair. Marta had quickly combed her hair that autumn morning, dressing in flared jeans and a seventies style floral shirt with a large collar. Her wardrobe was filled with brightly coloured clothes. Items she'd picked up in the charity shops she loved to frequent, and where she'd spend hours trying on clothes. Every day she wore a dress or blouse, ablaze with colour. Like the bright coloured wings of a butterfly, she thought her clothes hid the aura of grey and blue that shadowed her for the entire day. She no longer had a job, and her rent had just gone up; in fact, she'd spent that very morning asking in the pubs, cafés and restaurants along the busy Shepherd's Bush streets for work. Not being able to pay next month's rent was not the only reason for the dark shadows. They were ever-present because of the things Marta couldn't talk about. Things that were the root of her sadness and the reason why she'd wake from a dream she couldn't remember, exhausted, haunted and ashamed all at the same time. Every morning she woke up empty, and every day she'd add more colour. Brighter. Louder. A scarf, a hat, strings of beads, some bangles.

Without interrupting her thoughts, Elliot boiled a kettle and put two mugs onto the large workshop table at the back of the room. He turned and held up a packet of PG Tips tea bags and a jar of instant coffee. Marta pointed to the coffee.

'Black, no sugar,' she said and settled onto a drum stool, the closest seat she could find without disturbing the chaotic structure of the room. The deep shelves on two sides of the room rose to the ceiling and were stacked with boxes, instruments and recording equipment for studios. There was a low rail behind her, next to the door, lined with acoustic guitars. In the centre of the room were more boxes and a few piano stools covered in cellophane, placed carelessly on the balding carpet. On the back table, where Elliot made her coffee and a cup of tea for himself, there was a classical guitar on its back. It had no strings on the fret board. Beside it were various tools, open boxes and pieces of recording equipment.

'I'm Marta by the way,' she said across the room, slightly raising her voice over the buzzing of the overhead light fitting, the hum of a small fridge, a radio playing quietly on one of the shelves and the clink of a teaspoon as Elliot stirred his milky tea.

'Elliot.' He put down the teaspoon and picked up the mugs.

'I like the way it smells in here,' Marta said.

Elliot handed her a coffee. 'I like your accent. Where are you from?'

'Poland. I'm Polish. That's my accent. Is it strong?'

'No. You mean, do I understand you?'

Marta nodded.

'Of course. I'm a Londoner. You get used to accents. Especially around here. Shepherd's Bush is a real mixture of cultures nowadays.'

'Maybe that's why I came.'

'Where were you before?' Elliot moved a piano stool closer to her and sat.

'Ealing. With my sister. My sister and her husband, actually. Then Tottenham and around North London. Then west again to here.'

'That's quite a bit of travelling around. You probably know London better than me.' He smiled, blew into his mug and sipped some tea.

'Have you always lived here?' she asked.

'Mostly. What do you do, Marta?'

'For a job? I'm looking at the moment. I was working at Primark, but it was only temporary, so now I have to start again.'

Elliot put his mug on the floor beside him. 'I could use someone. Someone here. You've got shop experience.'

'Here? I don't know anything about musical instruments.'

'I do. You just have to be at the front and be nice to people, let them look around and help them. Just call me if you need me. I don't like being out there.'

'Why did you open a shop, then?'

He got up, abruptly, walked back to the workshop table and put his tea next to the body of the classical guitar. 'Wasn't my idea.' He said it so quietly, Marta wasn't sure she'd heard right.

'Is it full time?' Marta asked. Elliot turned round.

'The job is, yes. If you want it. I don't open on Monday, so Tuesday to Saturday?'

'You don't even know me. I'm a stranger to you, and you offer me a job. Just like that.'

'Well, you need a job, don't you? You can't go up and down the Uxbridge Road, looking into shops and crying all day.'

Marta raised her mug. 'True. But that isn't what I was doing. That only happened here.'

'Well, lucky me because I need you. An assistant.' He'd been leaning against the table but brought his tea back to the piano stool. Marta cradled her hot mug. 'Why were you crying?'

Her eyes turned downwards, long lashes brushing high cheekbones.

'You don't have to say,' Elliot said. 'It's just that I don't think it's a good idea to cry in front of the customers. I tried it a few times, and people ran a mile.'

They both laughed. Marta's a high-pitched sound, like a bird singing in the morning. Elliot's was deep, unrestrained.

As he showed her around the shop, Marta learned that Elliot was forty-two. He had a seventeen-year-old daughter who wouldn't be home from school yet, and that he was a widower. He'd owned Val's Music Shop for ten years.

'I think I can smarten up this shop,' Marta said.

'You mean, just by being here?'

'No, by reorganising a bit. It's too dull and a bit lumpy. You need it to be smooth so that people relax. If people relax, they'll buy more. Would it be so bad to play music in here? Just quietly, in the background?'

'It doesn't really work. Not if people want to try out, say, a keyboard or a guitar.'

'Or a violin?'

'Is it violins that make you want to cry?' he asked her.

Marta stopped buzzing around the shop. Stopped rearranging sheet music and music books so that they were upright, brushing dust off shelves and wiping it from her hands with quick flicks. She turned to face Elliot, looked deep into his eyes. She wondered how much she could trust herself to say to someone she'd only just met. He was friendly and kind, but really, Elliot wasn't a friend. Not someone she could trust with a secret so big it consumed her, nudged her awake most mornings at three, sometimes keeping her awake until sunrise. Maybe one day she'd tell him. And she would. But today wasn't that day.

'It's memories that made me cry,' she said. 'I think you'd say bittersweet memories.'

'Only if I was singing a song. But I understand if you don't want to tell me. You're smiling now, and it's a smile this place needs. That's what matters. Right?'

Marta nodded.

The door opened, and a young girl walked in. A teenage girl with thick black hair, light brown skin and a serious expression.

'Can we help you?' Marta said, rushing to her.

'Don't think so,' the girl said. She brushed past them both and headed to the workshop.

'Your daughter?' Marta asked quietly.

Elliot nodded.

Marta liked the look of the girl. Just as she'd liked the look of Elliot. On a day that started with more shades of grey and blue than she'd like to carry, Marta felt a weight lifting and welcomed the idea that Val's Music Shop was going to be home to her.

3

Elliot

Elliot didn't tell Katey, but he liked it when she popped into the shop after school. There was a time when she would go straight home and get down to her homework without even being asked. But that was when Val was there. Right after Val died, Elliot collected Katey from school for weeks until she complained that at fourteen she should be coming home herself, the way she had since she was eleven. Elliot remembered the way her friends giggled behind their hands when they saw him. They said, 'Oh, hello Mr Smith. You're here.' But he hadn't heard the sarcasm behind the words or realised that his daughter was embarrassed to have him, the only parent, standing outside the gate of a high school, coming to pick her up.

'You want people to think you're some kind of saddo?'

At the time, Elliot wanted to ask Katey not to be so disrespectful, to watch her tone. His Trinidadian mother would have clipped him round the ear if he'd been so sullen. But her Nan forgave Katey the short, cool way she spoke to her dad. She had just lost her mum. And when time went on, Nan didn't reprimand her granddaughter for not meeting her father's eye when he spoke to her or not wanting to eat with him. A few months later, Katey was all but ignoring Elliot and still Nan didn't tell Katey, *She better mine sheself.*

Katey had started coming to the shop after school before the summer break. This autumn, the first year of her A levels, she came to the shop after her first day. In all honesty, Elliot expected to see less and less of her, but he'd had the sense to not comment on it. One wrong word and Katey would stop coming, and he didn't want that.

'Everything all right?' he asked after seeing Marta out. He'd found Katey pouring out the dregs of Marta's coffee mug down the tiny sink and rinsing it out. The kettle boiled, and Katey made herself a coffee.

'Who was that?' she asked her father.

Elliot turned back towards the shop, hooking a thumb towards the small corridor.

'Yes, her,' Katey said. 'The weird woman that was just here.'

'She's not weird. She's really nice, actually.'

'Is she your girlfriend?'

Elliot sniffed.

'You're allowed to date you know, Dad? It's been three years now.' Katey scooted up onto the workshop table and began swinging her legs, hands under her thighs. Elliot thought again about how alike Katey was to her mum. She and Val had the same skin tone, faces the colour of light agave, framed by a mane of black curls. She even smiled like Val, but she hadn't acquired Val's light, easy-going nature. Val laughed every day. Saw the funny side of everything. She sang, she danced in the kitchen. She had been the glue of that family.

While his daughter was the image of her mother, Elliot wished she hadn't inherited his mood swings, his need to stay quiet and separate from people, to demand a lot and give very little. Did he teach her that? He wished he could have been more like Val when it all happened, when they lost her, but his heart was shattered. How could he laugh and keep Katey as happy as Val could? That sort of thing came so easily to her. Not to him.

'There isn't a '*time's up, you must have a girlfriend now*' date for these things,' Elliot said as he began working on the broken guitar next to Katey. 'I don't want a girlfriend.'

Katey jumped off the table and picked up her coffee.

'Dad, you're so miserable sometimes.'

'So are you.' He didn't look up. Elliot had bent over the table and was looking along the fret board of the guitar, one eye closed, fine lines appearing at the side of his face. 'Haven't you got any homework?'

'For crying out loud.' She poured the contents of the mug into the sink, grabbed her bag and jacket and stormed out of the store room.

'What?' he said straightening up and swinging around.

The shop door closed and Katey was gone. Elliot folded his hands in front of him and looked down at the broken guitar. It wasn't the first time Katey had stormed off when he'd thought they were in the middle of a good conversation.

He left the store room, went into the shop, hoping to catch a glimpse of Katey before she disappeared up the Uxbridge Road to their four bedroom house around the corner. All he saw was an image of the shop, the way it looked ten years ago: a shell of a place, dim, in need of love and repair.

'We can do this,' Val had said, spinning around on the dirty wooden floor in a long floral skirt. Her skirt lifted the dust from the floorboards making it spiral helplessly upwards. Why was she always spinning? Like a child who couldn't sit still, she was. He loved that about her, the innocence and the passion that came from her ideas. She had great ideas, but he hadn't been sure about this one.

'Who'll come to a music shop?' he'd said, pushing and pulling at a metal shelving unit precariously attached to the ceiling by a flimsy metal pin. He could see cracks in the plastering above his head and hoped it wouldn't fall in on them.

'People like us,' Val said, 'people who love music.'

'What I mean is…' Elliot caught her hand before Val could complete another revolution. Posters had been pasted to the windows from the outside, and only slivers of sunlight poked through the gaps between them.'What I mean is that it's all programmed music these days, greasy kids sitting in their bedrooms making beats and sampling loops.'

'Everyone loves music. And there are real musicians out there, just like us. Kids are still learning to play instruments, even if our one never wanted to. People will come. Even if they don't know it yet, El. Look. I can see it. Even if you can't. I've costed it out. We can do this. I'll be out front, greeting the customers. Running the show. You can hide out back, here.' She pulled him by the hand and guided Elliot to the storage room. She'd tripped over empty crates and broken chairs when the estate agent had first shown her around. Even through the debris, the dust and remnants of the disused clothes shop, Val had a vision. Elliot could do nothing to stop this. Once Val was on her creativity and production train, it was non-stop until she reached her destination. He could only be there for the ride. Grab a window seat and enjoy the view.

At home, they'd talked about the possibilities. Katey brought out a note book and started quizzing her mother about the pros and cons. Elliot remembered how Val laughed at that, told Katey that she was just like her father.

Too much like me, he thought as he stood in the shop, Katey long gone. Her long legs had marched off in anger, just as his had done on a day he could never forget. For good reason, he'd thought. After Val's last diagnosis, all he could do was march away. Away from the doctor's office, away from the hospital and down a street lined with blossoms. Beautiful pinks and whites fluttered around him on a fine spring day. He marvelled at how normal the rest of the world seemed, right after he'd received the most devastating news of his life.

Now, changing the *Open* sign on the shop door to *Sorry, We're Closed*, he remembered how he'd returned to the hospital to find Val sitting on a bench by the entrance. Her sweater was black and gold, her jeans had a paint stain on them from when she'd been painting the kitchen. She was smiling. She was smiling at him and waving, and he wanted to march away again, stand in front of the grey hospital building and shout until he was hoarse. Val took his hand that day, and they walked silently to the car park.

'It'll be okay, you know?' she'd said.

'This is the end of my world, Val,' he'd said.

'Don't forget our daughter.'

He shook his head. 'Of course not.'

After he turned off the lights in the music shop, set the alarm and locked up behind him, he thought of their daughter.

'Did I forget you?'

4

Ione

It's three thirty-seven. I used to wake up at this time in the morning no matter when I got to bed or how many times I'd already woken from a restless sleep. I thought I had freed myself of this cycle. Jeannie called earlier and asked if I was okay and how everything was. I walked her around the flat and the garden while we were on a WhatsApp video chat. I was grinning. I showed her every nook and cranny. I talked about the new school, the street I lived in, how easy the garden would be to manage. I used the word happy. And I genuinely felt completely happy.

So why can't I sleep?

Either I haven't moved far enough away from my past or the memories have seeped into my dreams again. An unnerving feeling comes over me as the thought of seeing David just before the move enters my head. He said he was back in the area. I hope he won't meet up with Oliver and get him talking about me and where I've gone. Jeannie would die before telling David where I am but Oliver, I'm not so sure he can go a round with David and not falter.

I roll onto my left side, my settle-down-and-fall-sleep side. It faces away from my bedside table where my phone, tablet and my digital clock taunt me. I don't know why I kept a digital clock that silently announces slow-moving time: green digits that relentlessly flash an ungodly hour. Another hour of sleeplessness seems to go by, but the clock tells me it's three fifty-seven.

I pick it up now, take it into the kitchen and turn it face down onto the kitchen table. In the morning, I'll recycle it, get it out of the house. I listen as the kettle boils, my leg crossed, foot jerking back and forth as I look at the string of a camomile teabag hanging down the side of a blue mug. I learned to become an expert housekeeper while living with David. Not a thing out of place before bed. I look around the kitchen. The mug I'm using was turned upside down on the sink tidy, resting next to one plate, a knife and fork, one saucepan and a stirring spoon. One of everything. Like the time before David, the time when I felt so alone, so out on a limb after watching my mother die.

David had been a saviour, and I loved him without question, completely and instantly. Jeannie always said that I'd been vulnerable and had I got to know the creep better, I would never have married him. She'd been right about that, but I loved the feeling of being in love. My love had a future; it could grow and live on for many years. When Mum passed away, I had all of this love inside me that I couldn't give to her anymore. I had no one to whisper, 'I love you' to. No one to love me back. David loved me back, he promised that he did.

The kettle clicks off and I jump. It's a loud click that echoes in the high-ceilinged kitchen, and I look at the condensation it has caused on the window. My mind shifts backwards and forwards between images of Mum and images of the violence I suffered at David's hands, and I wish that I could separate the two and banish all thoughts of David. I miss my Mum so much it hurts my heart. I saw Mum's face with every beating David gave me. I saw it contort with tears. I saw her hand reaching for me, and I knew, I knew every time I saw her that she couldn't help me. When it started, the violence, I used to get angry at Mum for not being there, resentful that I gave up everything I had in my life to be at her bedside and she wasn't there when I needed her the most. I knew I was being unfair. When I was with her, I thought nothing of being Mum's nurse, knowing that the last thing she wanted was to end her days in a nursing home, in a strange bed. That wasn't the ending I wanted for her.

If I could have documented Mum's life and everything she told me about it, I could read through it on a sleepless night like this. Mum had no time for regrets. She was always wild at heart. She married young, divorced young, fell in love with a woman painter who broke her heart by returning to Germany. Then Mum met my dad. She was thirty when she met him. He was over twenty years her senior. He was married with children.

It had taken years to learn as much as I now know about my biological father. Though there is a lot I don't know, so much she wouldn't say. For example, did he ever look for me? From the age of fourteen to the time I left for university, my mother drip-fed me little pieces of information about him, mostly about their love, nothing that could help me find him. All I had was his first name. I knew he was Greek, and like Mum, he lived in Shepherd's Bush. I couldn't be sure if Mum gave me his real name.

The fact remains, my parents were lovers, not a happily married couple. I could never come from a family for that reason. My mum, me and a father who'd never seen me didn't equal family. I always felt there was no real category for us. Mum said that was rubbish. We were a single-parent family, that was an accepted term, but it was never enough for me.

Tell me everything. It was the thing I always said when I came home in the holidays from university and I wanted to hear about Mum's life and anything she could tell me about my biological father. Especially about how they fell in love.

'I *have* told you everything,' Mum would say with a sigh. 'I've got so much to do.' She'd hurry out of the room, and I'd follow, insisting she could talk and do things at the same time.

'So, you were thirty, right? And…?'

'I was thirty … and … I worked in the dry-cleaner's off the Uxbridge Road in the day, and at night, I used to sing in a band. A blues band. The coolest one in London at the time.' Mum wiggled her hips and held an imaginary microphone to her mouth, nodding her head as if she could hear the music playing. 'West End. We played the best clubs. I tell you, your old Mum was something.'

Mum was always beautiful. Stunning when she was young. I'd seen the photographs in the albums she kept under her bed. I would point to the men in her band and ask their names, but none of them was called Charlie, none of them my father.

'So he came to a gig?' I'd urge her to tell me more.

'Yes, but Ione, you already know this.'

One day, after I'd pressed her and pressed her to hear the story again, Mum sat down, suddenly tired. The chemotherapy was still in her system, and it took the wind out of her sometimes. That day, one of the last times she talked about Charlie, I'd felt a pang of guilt for not allowing her to rest but I was hungry for information. Hungry to know my origins and to make sure that even though my parents' affair had been a secret, that they did love each other and that I was not the result of a family being pulled apart by two uncaring people who created me by mistake, my father leaving my mother alone to cope with the consequences.

'Tell me anyway.'

'So, there was this man. Really tall, thick black hair, very broad shoulders. He came up to me in the break. I was at the bar getting a drink before we did a last set. I always had a rum before the last set, and I always took it outside while I smoked a cigarette. Ione, never smoke, okay? Please.'

I shook my head.

'Then, there he was. Standing next to me. He looked surprised to see me at the bar and he smiled. He asked me if he could buy the drink, and I said I didn't have to pay anyway. He asked if one day he could buy me a drink, and I said yes.'

'Just like that?'

'What do you mean? He looked kind. He looked gentle. He had these enormous hands that looked like they could hold you really tight and make you feel really good.'

'Mum!' I always faked shock at this point. I was shocked the first time Mum implied she had a sex life. In all the years we were together, I'd never known her to have a single male acquaintance, let alone a love life.

'I gave him my telephone number, and he called me the next day. I couldn't believe we'd been living just streets away from each other for years. Anyway, I met him for a drink. We fell in love, and that was that.'

'Mum, don't miss everything out. Come on.'

'I don't want to talk about it anymore, Ione. I'm tired.'

I'd let her rest then, close her eyes and sleep. She said a word under her breath just before she fell asleep. It was a word in another language. Possibly Greek, I thought; maybe Charlie had taught her some Greek words. When she woke later, I asked if she could speak Greek and she said, no, not a word.

In bed now, with a mug of cold camomile tea on the side table, I lie on my back and I see the time of the digital clock in my mind's eye. It says four o'clock, but I know that's a lie because it's light outside. I'll have to get up very soon, be on my way to school. I suppose I'll be haunted by thoughts of Charlie and of David all day if I allow this to happen. Just as I'd gone to bed haunted by the word Mum whispered which did in fact turn out to be a Greek word. Charlie hadn't taught her the word, but he told her what it meant. If he taught her any others, I would never know. The one thing I still don't know about my father is where and if I'll ever find him.

5

Marta

Every day, she chose something she'd never worn to the shop before. There was a lot to choose from. Like the charity shops that arranged all their clothes in order of colour, Marta's wardrobe was just the same. A rainbow had exploded behind its double doors. Doors which couldn't quite close because of the bulk of sweaters and boxes on the bottom shelf. The boxes held the overflow of clothing. The hangers were doubled and tripled up with garments, and the top shelf in the wardrobe and all the drawers in the small chest beside it were full to overflowing.

Despite the clothing, Marta's bedroom was neat. It smelled of lavender incense some days. On other days, Marta burned white sage, others, sandalwood. Her bed covers were burnt orange, the pillow cases yellow, the sheet patterned with flowers. She had put up fire red curtains that were splashed with swirls of orange and purple. She'd found the fabric in Shepherd's Bush Market and toiled for days to make the curtains by hand.

In the living room, the long cream curtains were splashed with cerise flowers. The sofa and chairs, she decorated with multicoloured throws and stripy cushions. In the middle of the room and onto the wood laminate flooring, she'd put a large rug with a tie-dye pattern. There were house plants in red, gold and purple ceramic pots. These sat on all the sills, shelves and table tops of every room. Aloe, busy lizzies, orchids, spider and money plants grew at varying stages of life. Marta loved to water them, talk to them and rotate them to make sure they grew evenly.

During the day, she worked in the shop with Elliot, and during the evening, she cooked all her meals from scratch, listening to world music. She painted her toenails scarlet and practised meditation. Every day, she walked into the music shop with a large smile and a dazzling outfit. Elliot responded with a smile and hurried to the back room while Marta hummed, fixed things and waited.

It became apparent, during that first week, that Marta wasn't actually needed in the shop. Most enquiries were by telephone. Did they have this, did they stock that, did they have a late-night opening? But hardly anyone came in. Not even the little boy and his mother. Surely he'd need new strings or something one day or he might need Elliot to mend the violin. Not likely when it was still new, but Marta looked out for him all the same.

One day, the door opened and a woman walked in. She had a similar complexion to Elliot's daughter. Her hair was also thick and curly, like Katey's. She could be her mum or her aunt or something. Marta smiled at her and called, 'Good afternoon.' She seemed to shake the woman from a deep reverie.

Marta had noticed the woman as she walked towards the shop, eyes straight ahead, entering the shop as if her feet took her there and not her intention.

'Oh, good afternoon,' the woman said. 'Sorry to bother you.'

Marta thought that a strange thing to say. How could you bother a person in a shop, they were there to serve you. Maybe she hadn't been welcoming enough. She smiled wider.

'I'm a local music teacher,' the woman said. 'My name is Ione and I give piano lessons. I wondered if I could put a card up. I noticed you had a board. With cards. Cards and adverts.' Ione gestured to the board by the door as if Marta had never seen it before.

'Of course you can,' Marta said. She sprang down from the stool behind the counter and put out a hand. 'Let me see.'

Ione gave the postcard-sized handmade advert to Marta. 'How much is it to advertise?' she asked.

'Nothing at all … um …' She tried to read the name on the card. 'I-Own? Is it like iron?'

'It's pronounced I-O-Knee.' Ione grinned. 'It's okay. I get called all sorts of things. How long will you display it?'

'Oh, only for forever. Until it looks really old. I'll put it so it's noticed from the window.'

'That's really kind of you. Thanks. It's a nice shop.' Ione looked around as Marta fixed the card to the board.

'Where do you come from?' Marta asked over her shoulder. 'You don't sound like a Londoner.'

'I'm not. I'm from Manchester. I moved here a month or so ago.'

'There, it's up.' Marta faced Ione. 'I hope you get lots of students.'

'Oh, I don't think I want too many. I just want to put my piano to use. I hardly play these days.'

'Well, it's a great thing to do. Teach. I wanted to be a teacher once.'

Marta thought back to her days in Katowice. Her stern father with his thick black moustache telling Marta that teaching was an unappreciated profession. Besides, why spend all those years training when you'll end up married and running a home for your family. Marry a rich man, that's all you need to worry about. She had married a man with a good job, but there was a lot more to worry about than her father would ever realise.

'And you're a musician?' Ione asked.

Marta laughed aloud in a high pitch, a sound that could almost be a song. She wagged a finger. 'No, not me. I don't play a single instrument. But I sit here and I read all about them. I can tell you all the instruments in an orchestra. List all the brass, woodwind, drums. You name it.'

'Oh, I just thought, since you work here. I thought this was your shop. That you were Val.'

'No, no. The owner took pity on me, and here I am. Learning all about musical instruments and how to sell them, of course.'

They walked back to the counter, Marta propping herself back on the stool and Ione looking at the flyers on the counter.

'It really is nice here,' Ione said, eventually. 'A nice atmosphere. Peaceful. Anyway. I should go.'

'Come again,' Marta said. The bangles around her wrist jangled as she waved. She'd bought them from a shop at the back of Shepherd's Bush Market from a woman in a bright green Salwar suit, a thick cardigan over it, who sold rows of sari fabric, shelves of jutti and other accessories. Marta smiled as Ione walked away. She liked Ione and hoped she would be back again.

6

Ione

'Tell me everything.'

There was a park with a long path through the middle. We both used to walk along it. A special time in the day when it was okay for him to be away from work. He came from one end, I came from the other, and we'd pass messages, love letters. He started it. Our arms would brush together and he'd pass me a note. Folded up small so that no one noticed. He'd write things like, I love your skin, or, I love your eyes, I can't wait for the day when we can be together. I never rushed into sleeping with him or anything. It was months before anything like that happened. That's how I knew he was serious about me. He kept coming back to the park because he knew the time I walked home from work.

So, one day, I pushed a note into his hand. It said there was a party after a gig. I told him where the gig was, and I gave him the address of the party. I told him I'd look out for him. After the gig, I was all hot and sweaty, but I made sure I brought a dress to change into afterwards. I brought perfume. Cheap, but it was okay. I had my hair relaxed at that time, but it was all flat, none of the curls lasted in that club. Low ceiling, everyone dancing. It just got so hot. So when I got changed, I put on this hat. A red beret; it wasn't even mine, but it suited me all the same.

He didn't come to the gig. I hung back for ages in case he showed up, but the last car was leaving, and I had to go or

I'd be stranded. The party was in Paddington. Then, when he didn't show up at the party, I got really sad. I got angry with everyone for having a great time. I started drinking the first thing I could get my hands on. Gin. And I hated gin. I knew the reason he wasn't coming had something to do with his wife. She wouldn't let him go out so late. What wife in their right mind would?

I know it was selfish of me. Encouraging him like that. He was married. So when he didn't come, I took it as a sign that we shouldn't be together. At least I hadn't slept with him. Then, of course, he showed up, looking pale and wired. He spotted me straight away, made a b-line for me and grabbed me. He kissed me. Kept saying, I'm sorry, I'm sorry. He told me he and his wife had had a massive fight. We were in a bedroom, upstairs, everyone was making a racket below us, music playing loud, someone screeching a song at the top of their voice. Then it happened. We started kissing. I could feel his love. You have to believe that. He loved me, I loved him and we wanted each other. We made love in that bedroom, the walls damp, the floorboards vibrating with bass and drums. But nothing else mattered when he touched me. Held me. He wasn't a married man when I was in his arms. He wasn't old enough to be my dad, like everyone kept saying. He was mine. My Charlie. And from that day, I only ever wanted to be with him.

I call Jeannie as soon as I come back from leaving my card with Marta. I tell Jeannie that the girl in the shop wears bright clothes, just like her.

'There is only one Jeannie Roberts. I'm an original, don't you know?'

'Of course there's only one of you.'

'You sound odd.'

'No, I don't. Well, maybe I do. I just got an odd feeling when I was in that shop just now. Val's Music Shop. But the girl I spoke to wasn't Val. I got a weird vibe from the place, like I was being watched. Or I could feel this energy coming from there or something.'

'Creepy. Speaking of creepy. Not sure if I should tell you this, but I ran into your ex. I'd like to say I ran him over, but then I'd end up doing time, and I can just see the twins turning into the Krays because their Mum got a double life sentence for running over and reversing back onto that piece of shit.'

'Jeannie.'

'Yes, sorry, I'm rambling. What did he say? Oh yes. That he wants to go to London. Had a gut feeling that's where you'd be. Knew your mum was a Londoner.'

'Damn. I didn't think he'd remember that. But he won't know where in London. I never said.'

'And I flipping well didn't tell him. Don't worry, I didn't give away anything. You would've been proud.'

'What did you say?'

'I just looked him up and down and said, Ione didn't tell anyone where she was going or if she was staying in the country. I haven't even heard from her.'

'And?'

'You know that slimy, smarmy smile of his? Well, that's what he did. He smiled. Smiled and walked off like he had something over me.'

'Shit, Jeannie, do you think he knows where I am?'

'He's bluffing. Trying it on to see if I'd open my mouth. But don't worry, I was so cool. Look, the Gestapo, the Spanish Inquisition and a stint at Guantanamo Bay couldn't get me to blab. You were careful not to give anyone any details, right? What about anyone from your old school?'

'Well, they wrote a reference, but they're not likely to tell *him*. Confidentiality and all that.'

All the same, I'm walking around the house, my stomach in a knot, tying to tap into the positivity I felt at Val's Music Shop, trying to return my mind to Mum's stories about

Charlie. I want to think about love, I don't want to think about David.

He used to come over to my flat. I lived next to a school. In the afternoon, if the window was open, we could hear the children in their playtime, running around the playground, screaming, chattering like little monkeys. I used to get Wednesdays off from the dry-cleaner's because I worked Saturday, and he knew I was home in the day. He told his wife he was going to the wholesalers, but he'd do a detour to my place first. I wore a red dress, anything red that I had because after he'd seen me in the red beret, he said red suited me more than any colour. He always wanted me to sing to him. I was a blues singer, and after a while, he confessed he didn't even like the blues. He loved Gladys Knight and the Pips. His favourite song was Midnight Train to Georgia. *I'd sing it over and over to him. Sometimes he would cry. He said it was the best love song in the world.*

Mum's story about how she met and fell in love with Charlie was so different from my story. Hers and Charlie's was a valid love, despite him cheating on his wife and their not having a happy ever after. I never had a happy ever after; I also never had the kind of heat and passion that Mum talked about. David was good-looking, had lots of money, a bit like Charlie in that respect. David was single, tall, intelligent and very quiet. I was surprised when he strung more than two words together and asked me out. Jeannie and I used to see him at our Friday night session at The Boscombe Arms. He was mostly on his own. Actually, he was always on his own, but he seemed to be friendly with the publican. I'd never been a pub-goer, not a regular drinker at all. I went because I couldn't resist Jeannie's arm-twisting. She had a way of winning me over, always had. She was the wildfire girl I wished I could be but never had the courage to become. At the time, I'd moved back in with Mum, to look after her. I was teaching during the day, just about keeping it together, constantly ringing Mum's nurse and asking her to put Mum on the phone. In the evenings and weekends, I never left Mum's side. Between Mum and Jeannie, they cooked up this Friday night drinking session. They could see my stress levels skyrocketing. If Mum hadn't convinced me otherwise, I would have given up the teaching and stayed with her 24–7. Mum talked me into staying with the job, and if Jeannie had not insisted on The Boscombe Arms, I would never have met David.

When I first met David, I felt relaxed. Considering how things turned out, at the start, I felt as if I was in control. I was taking the lead in our relationship, making decisions about where we should eat, and later, about where we should shop. David always asked my opinion about anything he bought. His shirts, his suits, his shoes. I'd never been in that kind of relationship. When I was little, I was led around by the nose by my best friend Stacey. A bossy girl with frizzy hair and a larger-than-life personality. She did all my talking for me. Even in university, my closest friend was the life and soul of every party. Other students would come up to me and say, 'You're Emma's friend, aren't you?' I'd say yes, a big smile on my face, and they would invariably say, 'Do you know where she is?' They were never interested in me, I was just the nexus, albeit temporary, so that they could get to the real deal. David didn't allow me to be the dormouse: he boosted my confidence. Even Jeannie commented on how she thought I'd become bolder somehow. I liked how he made me feel. David was gentle, like me. I thought we would be a perfect match. With Mum becoming so ill at the end, when there was pain and vomit and crying in the night, I needed a gentle man to embrace me. To stroke my cheek and tell me that everything would be all right.

Just weeks after my first date with David, Mum died. She never got to meet him. He supported me through the funeral arrangements, always by my side. In a matter of months, he'd built me up and had proposed marriage. On our wedding day, months after Mum's funeral, I had conflicting emotions. I was the saddest and happiest I'd ever been. I couldn't explain how I felt to anyone. Jeannie told me I should have waited a while longer before we got married. She said David loved me and he would wait. I was the one who couldn't wait. After Mum died, with all the crying, not eating and the feelings of depression, I was afraid I would lose David. I needed him to be there, to hold me. Mum had left the house to me and he would be there with me, and one day, I'd be happy again. Weeks after the wedding, I realised I'd made the worst mistake of my life.

I push open the patio windows. It's not a warm day—the sun disappeared behind a grey cloud about the time I returned from the music shop, and I pull the thick cardigan closer around my arms. It's quiet in the garden. The last owner kept the lawn tidy. The geraniums around the borders, lilac, bright red and white, still have blooms. In the corner by the fence is a sprout of sunflowers that face away from me. They seem somewhat of an afterthought. I wonder if the seeds flew in from the garden next door. I realise I don't know my neighbours. I realise that, apart from teaching and going into the music shop, I haven't spoken in person to anyone. The flat has been silent of any conversation and, though I could never tell Jeannie this, I feel lonely and I miss Mum more than ever. I think about the advert for piano students, and I imagine one day having a conversation with someone in my flat at last.

7

Charlie

The house on Sundew Avenue was small. The red bricks went up in the seventies, and the wooden frames around the windows looked as though they hadn't been painted since then. Charlie had lived there, on his own, for twenty years. He'd moved straight after the divorce. He didn't want to leave the area. Shepherd's Bush was where his children lived, his grandchildren, too, although he had no idea which school they attended, whether any of them had gone on to university, or if any of them remembered him. His three daughters had disowned him. His ex-wife continued to speak badly about him to every member of the family, including Charlie's side, with as much vitriol as when she first uncovered his secret life.

There was a mist over Charlie's eyes now, a blueish tint over the dark pupils that once were alert and shone. A network of tiny pink veins starting from the corners of his eyes, spread their way across the yellowing whites. Silver tufts of hair sprang from where lustrous dark hair had crowned his regal head. Jowls wobbled with pockets of fat where once there was a proud chin. When he lay on his back in bed, the distended mound of his stomach rose and fell slowly, his eyes stayed closed most of the day and his mind was closing down by increasing degrees every week.

He heard the beep and tap of the key pad on the front door, and someone let themselves in. *Who was it this time*? he wondered, unable to turn himself in bed. Carers were the only people to visit him now. His daughters all had a key, but they only came to stock up the fridge and the cupboards, to make sure the carers were doing their job and that the cleaners were doing a reasonable job at keeping the dust at bay.

Whoever had come to the door was humming. She made a pleasant sound, and he wished she would sing the words to the tune, a tune that reminded him of music he'd heard a long time ago.

'Brenda? Brenda, is that you?'

'Not, Brenda, Charlie. It's me, Louise.' She leaned over his bed and smiled. 'Remember your Louise? I'm here. I'll get your lunch, okay?'

Louise was raising her voice, much to his annoyance. The carers spoke in loud voices. He didn't know why. He could hear them perfectly. The louder they spoke, the more he retreated into his world, back to a time in the past where his memories played out before him. Those times were tangible. He could quite happily stay in a past where he was tall, handsome and he knew a woman who sang, who adored him. He saw those days so clearly, and his heart broke every time he remembered that the woman who sang, the one he loved with all his heart, ran away and disappeared without a trace. Her name was Brenda.

To Louise, being the only one of his carers he spoke to, Charlie spoke a lot about Brenda. He talked about a blues club and about some letters. The letters, the letters, he kept bringing up the letters. He'd had Louise spend a whole afternoon going through every drawer in the house to find these mysterious letters, but she hadn't found a single one. All she found were some Christmas cards and a few postcards. They were worn and tatty, nothing recent.

Charlie ate very slowly now, keeping the food in his mouth for so long, sometimes he forgot he was chewing. He'd sit and stare into space until Louise rubbed his throat, stimulating a swallowing reaction from Charlie. He'd swallow, close his eyes and Louise would dab his lips with a terry cloth.

'Brenda, dance with me.'

'I bet you were a good dancer, Charlie,' Louise said. 'I bet you showed the other men a thing or two on the dance floor, had the women lining up to dance with you.'

There had been only one woman Charlie wanted to dance with. He'd given up long ago trying to coax his wife onto the dance floor. At a wedding or a family party, Charlie would be there, hand on her elbow, saying, 'Ana, come on. One dance before we get too old.' She'd shake his hand away, dive back into a conversation with her sister-in-law about their children, their lazy husbands and finding fault with the decorations in the hall or the dress the mother of the bride was wearing.

He wondered where the love in his relationship with Ana had gone. He knew he no longer loved her, and he couldn't be sure if she still loved him. They had worked hard to get the restaurant off the ground, and when it was doing well, they could relax and enjoy each other's company again. They had established Saturday as their night off. On those Saturday nights, Charlie would cook, Ana would join him in the kitchen. They'd laugh and Charlie would play his Motown records and turn up the volume on the record player in the living room. Years later, when neither of them noticed it happening, they became too tired to laugh. Charlie became too tired to cook for Ana, and she began to hate the sound of his records. In the restaurant, Charlie felt he was surplus to requirements. Ana had a newfound energy in middle age that led her to take the reins, become the organiser and planner of all restaurant matters. He'd thought of opening a second restaurant. He'd run it while Ana stayed at The Lantern, then they would have things to talk about again, the way they used to talk on Saturday night. As it was, they barely spoke. Now, Charlie had something happening in his life, something that was separate from The Lantern, but it wasn't something he could ever talk about with Ana.

One time, when Ana turned down his invitation to dance at a party, Charlie looked at his watch, wondering if he could escape, if he could somehow steal away, go to see Brenda and return without having been missed. Ana wouldn't miss him, he was sure of that. But he'd changed his mind about leaving when he looked across the hall, saw his youngest daughter, Athena. She looked at him seriously and nodded. He nodded back. She was the one most like her mother, quick to judge and slow to forgive.

Charlie had run into Athena, once, one day on Shepherd's Bush Green. She'd walked out of the hairdressers. They'd hugged for a brief moment, mostly from a knee-jerk reaction because Athena hugged no one in public, not even her own husband. She'd commented on her father's cologne. Pausing, Athena decided it wasn't cologne but perfume. Women's perfume. Not her mother's because Mama only wore perfume at the weekend for church or for parties.

'Of course it's cologne.' Charlie shrugged. 'Is it too feminine, do you think? Should I pour it into Mum's perfume bottle?'

His daughter didn't laugh. Her expression was stern, just like his wife.

'What you doing around here, anyway?' Athena asked, crossing her arms. 'Shouldn't you be prepping for dinner? You can't always leave it to Mama. She's not supposed to be running the whole restaurant on her own.'

'I'm not. And there's no reason you kids can't help out sometimes. You'll be inheriting the place one day. Besides, she sent me on an errand.'

'Where to, Pops?

'Look, what are you? The police? I have to go. Your hair is wonderful, by the way.'

He hadn't liked the way Athena stood silently outside the salon on Shepherd's Bush Green watching him head in the direction of the restaurant. Before bumping into Athena, Charlie had been going to pick up his van, not going to the restaurant. He'd just come from meeting Brenda. Brenda had moved flat recently because of dry rot in the place she'd previously rented. She was living above the dry-cleaning shop where she worked, and he'd had to park the van miles from her flat because it was impossible to park in front of the parade of shops. Ana thought he was home looking at the books as he'd said he would be. But he'd stolen an hour or two to go and see Brenda.

Two hours before bumping into his daughter, he'd let himself into Brenda's flat and found her in the kitchen making her West Indian soup. Her hips swayed to the loud music coming from the radio. She hummed to the music, unaware of Charlie's presence. She sang 'la, la' over the lyrics and then sang the words so that the singer on the radio was barely audible. Brenda would never refuse to dance with him at a party. He wished it could happen one day, that they could be open, dance at a party that wasn't a secret to the rest of his family. But how to tell his three children, his grandchildren or Ana that he was in love with someone else?

'Not bad,' he said and watched Brenda jump. She put the spoon she was using to stir the soup down on the table. She ran and leapt into his arms. 'Is that for me?' He sniffed the air in the tiny kitchenette.

'I wasn't expecting you,' she said. 'I'm cooking for the boys in the band. They're coming round to bless the house. Meaning they're coming round with bottles of booze and they'll expect me to cook.'

The food smelled nice. So different from the aromas in The Lantern restaurant. Brenda's cooking made him feel as if he had come home.

He swung her around, then felt her body against his, sliding gently to the floor until her toes touched the linoleum tiles. Her face was turned up to his, so he kissed her lips. He looked at the clock on the wall, wondered if there was time to make love to her, spend a few moments talking and finding out what had happened in her life since he last saw her two weeks ago. Two weeks he'd pined and grown impatient with everyone around him. Ana couldn't say a thing right, so they were bickering constantly. He barked at the chef, he barked at a waitress. He'd driven his wife so mad one evening, she'd pushed him into the alley behind the restaurant and demanded to know what he was so sore about.

He'd stormed away to the main road, smoked two cigarettes and tried to cool off. He came back minutes later with a smile on his face, worried he would arouse suspicion. Ana had a nose for deception, and she boasted she could read Charlie like a book.

'Can you come back later when the boys get here?' Brenda asked.

'I wish I could. One of the cousins is having a birthday party at the restaurant. I can't get away. You can tell me all about it. Don't dance with anyone else.'

She kissed him and swung him around. They danced that afternoon, danced until he really should have got going, and then she kissed him goodbye.

'Brenda, sing our song.'

'Charlie, it's not Brenda. It's me, Louise. Now come on, finish your lunch. I have some studying to do. I can read you my assignment, and you can tell me if it's any good.'

He chewed until he was too tired to continue. Eating made him tired. The bustling carers that washed him in the morning and put him to bed at night made him tired. All their chit-chat, chit-chat in a language he didn't know. The noise from the street made him tired. The constant buzz of his motorised bed, whose mattress vibrated to discourage bedsores, made him tired. Now he only looked forward to this nice girl, skin the same colour as Brenda's and the memory of the time when she was the love of his life. A time that kept coming back with increasing frequency until one day, he would never come back to the present.

8

Elliot

Mostly, it was quiet in the house. Elliot and Katey locked themselves in their individual bubbles of confinement and kept the other out with music. Katey used one of her many devices to play her tunes, usually with earbuds in. Elliot played a full album of instrumental jazz, the kind Katey hated. Sometimes Elliot sat and played his guitar, close to his wife's harp. This elegant instrument took pride of place by the patio windows in the study room where the acoustic piano was also kept. He'd sit on the stool next to the piano and play intricate riffs and rhythms. He'd strum tirelessly, sometimes closing his eyes, as he nodded in deep concentration.

He hadn't touched Val's harp, save for dusting it. He hadn't moved it because Val always wanted it positioned just so. An almighty row had erupted between Elliot and Katey when his daughter suggested that maybe they sell the harp. Neither played and the proceeds could go to a cancer charity, she kept insisting. It was worth a lot of money. Elliot reacted badly—he realised that afterwards—shouting and screaming at Katey for being heartless. How could he have said such a thing to his daughter? He loved her more than life itself but, at the time, Val had only been gone a year. Elliot wasn't aware he was living half a life: half in the present and half in the time when the three of them were happy. A time when Val was there, and all she had to do was appear and the world was instantly a wonderful place.

Elliot looked down at his guitar and began to play a tune. He was hunched over the body of the guitar, a large black instrument, his chest pressed firmly onto its waist. The fingertips of his left hand were firmly on the fret board, yet they moved deftly from chord to chord. He plucked the strings with his right and tapped the pick guard as if it were a drum. He played the tune over and over, and everything in the house seemed to melt away, except a memory of Val.

He had met her at university at a time when his parents were going through a rough patch and, as an only child, found himself in the middle of a war zone with no idea how to negotiate two parents who insisted he take sides. Because of what his parents went through, Elliot was against marriage or relationships of any kind. He'd met Val, by chance, on a stairwell at the university. He was rushing to a lecture, and Val was lost in a world of score sheets and compositions, seeing tiny notes dancing in front of her on a stave rather than the tall student whose arms she fell into on the stairs.

'I'm sorry,' he'd said.

'My fault, I wasn't watching where I was going.'

That same night, they made love in her bedroom in the house she shared with five other students. It rained all night. It was very late, and Val asked if he'd stay.

'Of course I'll stay. I don't want to go out in this weather, anyway. Not keen on rain.' He laughed.

'So if it was sunny, you'd leave me?'

'Probably not.'

'I don't understand why you don't like rain. I love it.'

They were lying on their backs. Val took his hand and held it up. Moonlight poured in through the window, the rain was heavy and loud. As their fingers interlaced like dark brown and light brown vines wrapping around each other, Elliot listened to the thrum of raindrops on the window. He could feel his heart, slow and steady, beating in a corresponding rhythm. Val sighed a slow warm breath into the air that was scented with her perfume, and Elliot turned to her.

'Tell me you love the rain,' she said.

'I don't love it, but I think I like it a lot better now.'

When he opened his eyes, his daughter Katey was standing just inches from him. Her arms were folded.

'You know I was calling you for hours?' she said.

'I haven't been playing for hours,' he said, looking up at her and having to shake himself so that he could settle into the present.

'Dad, I swear you've lost your sense of humour. I didn't literally mean hours.'

'Well, why don't you say what you literally mean?' He stood up and put the guitar on its stand next to the harp. 'If I don't have a sense of humour, then you should be literal all the time.'

'Anyway,' Katey shrugged. 'I just came to say that I'm going out.'

'What, now? No, you can't.'

'What?'

It was late afternoon, and Katey was dressed in slippers and pyjama bottoms under a large sweatshirt. She followed her father to the living room door, where he picked up the Sunday paper from the coffee table and sat on the sofa, not looking at her.

'You're not serious, right?' she said, holding the door frame.

'I told Marta we'd come for dinner.' He shook out the paper and started to read.

'You did what? Today? What, seriously?'

Elliot turned to her. 'Katey, I'm seriously being serious and in the literal sense. Marta invited us, and I said yes.'

'But on my behalf and without even asking me if I wanted to accept this invitation from a complete stranger?'

'You've met Marta.'

'Once.'

'And she's nice, right?'

'I have no bloody idea.' Katey sat on the arm of a chair. 'She's worked there a week, and she's already asking us to dinner?'

'I don't know. Yes. What's wrong with that?'

'What's wrong with it is that it's sad on so many levels. Like, first of all, how much do you know about her? She might be a serial killer, or she might live with an axe murderer. And that's just for starters. It's Sunday, a religious day for some people, right? What if we're walking into some religious ritual? A sacrifice.'

Elliot turned to her. 'I think she's Catholic. She wears a cross and chain.'

'Which could be a front for anything.'

'Seriously?'

'Does she know I'm vegetarian?'

'Are you?' His brow creased.

'Look, I'm not going. I promised Maisie I'd go round. I didn't know you were springing this on me. I just wanted to chill, listen to music and stuff. I don't want to go round some strange woman's house.'

'Katey, I told her we were both coming, and she'll be cooking for three.'

'Bring me back a doggy bag.' Katey got up and left the room. She'd spend the next hour in the shower and getting dressed.

Marta had told Elliot to come at six. It was four o'clock, and he doubted he'd change Katey's mind. But he thought he'd try anyway. He waited until she was out of the shower and then tapped on Katey's door.

'What?' she said angrily. 'I'm not interested.'

'Please, Katey. We don't do anything together anymore. I promised … I promised your Mum that I would do stuff with you, look after you, and I know I haven't done a very good job.'

She pulled open the door, standing with a bathrobe around her, crossing her arms immediately after she pursed her lips.

'I've been a crappy dad to you, Katey, and if you let me, I'd like to make it up to you.'

'What? By taking me to your girlfriend's house for dinner?'

'Again, not my girlfriend.'

'Well, she must fancy you or something. Dinner?'

'She asked you to come.'

'To sweeten you up. God, Dad, don't you get it? This woman is into you. She wasted no time inviting you round to hers when she's been at the shop one day.'

'Over a week, actually.'

'That's no time at all. I don't want to sit there like some idiot while you guys are on a date.'

'For Christ's sake, Katey, if she'd meant it as a date, she wouldn't have asked me to bring *you*.' He raised his voice which made him sound angry. He wasn't angry, just exasperated.

'Wake up, Dad.' Katey was just as loud, and so was the door as she slammed it in Elliot's face. 'And I'm not coming.'

Elliot went back down the stairs. He picked up the newspaper and tried to read, shuffling the sheets, licking his thumb and flicking over a page before he'd even taken in a headline. He went back to the study and picked up his guitar. He sat on the stool and played the song again. He played and played. When Katey left, she didn't say goodbye. Elliot continued playing until he felt cramp in his hands.

9

Marta

She was just twenty then; she felt like a child in so many ways but was about to become a married woman. It was a solemn ceremony. Her mother cried all the way through as if she were sending her only child off to war. Marta's older sister was already married. She was living in London at the time but came back for the wedding to see her younger sister marry in the church she'd married, wearing the dress she wore for her own wedding. It fitted perfectly. They were like twins in that respect: three years separated them, but they could easily be mistaken. The only difference between the two marriages was that Marta's sister was in love with her husband and Marta had no idea what it felt like to be in love. She stood at the altar, her hand in Tomasz's as he trembled and tried to push the simple gold band onto her finger. She prayed that she wouldn't disappoint him.

When they'd met at the tall office building on a busy street in the middle of Katowice, she liked him. She liked him a lot —as a friend. He had a good sense of humour, he was quite liberal in his thinking, he liked the same kinds of music as Marta and, like her, he loved to watch old films. Though Marta had never been in love, she knew enough about love to know that when it happened, it would not happen with a man.

Her secret burned inside her like a hot flame, eating away at her insides as she tried to wish away the all-consuming knowledge that she wanted to share her life with a woman.

She hadn't met the woman, but she knew this was not a thing she could discuss with her staunchly religious parents. Neither could she dissuade her father from the constant lectures about husbands and settling down, which began when she'd turned sixteen. He would have cast her out if he'd known her true feelings about men and marriage. If she was cast out, she would no longer have a family. She wasn't even sure she could confide in her sister—she was bound to give her away, tell her father. Her parents would feel the shame of having a daughter like that, there would be no amount of prayers to save her. Marta would never be welcome in their home, and the memory of a girl who smiled a lot, who did very well at school and was pretty, too, would be wiped from existence. She would have no one and nowhere to live.

As she got to know Tomasz, it became very obvious to her that he was falling in love with her. She went to his flat after going to the cinema one evening. Practically tripping over the bed, she pulled him onto her, tugging his shirt out of the waistband of his trousers. She kissed him with the kind of urgency a couple who only had one night together before they were torn away would kiss.

'Marta, slow down. What's your hurry?' Tomasz said, laughing.

'No hurry, I just want to do it.'

'You make it sound as if you're crossing something off your to-do list.'

'Well, don't you think we should?'

'I want to, but can't we slow down? Just a little?' He held her face between his hands, his skin soft, his eyes smiling as if he were appeasing a young child.

'Don't laugh at me,' she said, closing her eyes and feeling the blood rush to her face.

'Never,' he said. 'But let's do it like this.'

He kissed her. She liked his kisses. She liked his arms around her. She watched the way he pulled the rest of his shirt free, sat on his knees above her and slipped it off slowly. He had a broad chest, the skin smooth with one small mole on his shoulder. She stared at it while he bent to undress her. She looked up to the ceiling as he kissed and caressed her neck, her breasts. She felt a warm sensation between her legs, but it didn't feel right. Their bodies fitted together perfectly, him above, moving steadily and intently, there was nothing wrong with that part. It was afterwards, when she rolled over and he stroked her back and asked if she was all right; she'd said yes because, physically, she was. Mentally, though, she was building up the strength to live her whole life like this. Having someone love her and treat her so kindly, so gently and to know she could never love him in the way he loved her.

'I'm fine,' she said. Marta rolled back to stroke Tomasz's cheek. 'You know this means you have to marry me.'

'I want to marry you, but could you at least wait until I can propose?'

She looked at him, seriously, as he laughed. Then she laughed with relief, happy in the knowledge that in Tomasz, she'd made a good choice. She would be good to him. She wouldn't let him down, and he would be her means of escaping her father's house while remaining a part of her family. In this good man, she had secured a future. Without a husband, Marta had no idea where she fitted in the world. Her world, after all, was no bigger than the distance between her office building and her father's house.

Marta looked around the room again. She hadn't had a visitor in such a long time; every little detail was of the utmost importance to her. She was excited and nervous all at the same time. She chastised herself, several times, because she knew Elliot well and had seen his daughter at least twice. The two had exchanged a few words, but Marta got the impression that Katey was a nice girl. She might come across as sullen, but didn't all teenagers?

Putting on some music now, Marta began to relax. She'd made a rice dish and a vegetable curry—having not checked if either was vegetarian, she went for the safest choice. She had baked an apple sauce cake topped with oats and had bought two bottles of red wine.

When the doorbell rang at five minutes to six, Marta opened it to see only Elliot, holding a bunch of flowers from the supermarket and a bottle of white wine.

'Katey wasn't well,' he said very quickly.

Marta nodded. She could tell from the way Elliot avoided looking at her that this was a little white lie. She knew lies, knew them very well. She was happy that if all Elliot had to lie about was his moody teenager not wanting to come to dinner then he was very lucky.

'It's fine,' Marta said. 'Come in, come in. It's good to see you.'

He followed her up the stairs. 'Well, I did see you yesterday, so…'

'I know,' she said, 'but that's what you say, isn't it? When someone comes to visit?'

'Have you been reading books on etiquette? Because I don't know what people say.'

'Here we are.' Marta opened the door to her flat. It was filled with the aromas of Indian spices intermingled with a heady fog of incense sticks burning in both the living room and her bedroom.

'These are yours, by the way.' Elliot handed her the mixed bunch of roses, carnations and chrysanthemums of blazing orange, red and pink, with splashes of green fern and baby's breath. She noticed him looking at the price sticker: £12.99.

'They're lovely,' Marta said. 'Very bright. I'll put them in a vase.' She turned to head for the kitchen.

'And this,' he said, holding out the wine bottle. 'I hope you like white. I'm really into lager myself but…' He shrugged his shoulders.

'You could have brought lager, but you really didn't have to bring anything. I mean, I love the flowers, though.'

'Good.'

'So.'

'So.'

'I'll put these in water, and I'll put this in the fridge.'

Marta shook her head at how awkward she was being, speaking too fast. Was she even making sense? She worried that Elliot wasn't relaxed, either, and wished Katey had come; it might have been less like hard work. She and Elliot got on so well at the shop, and she couldn't understand why an invitation to dinner should feel so odd. She'd invited him as a way of thanks for taking her in and being so kind and for giving her a much-needed job.

When Marta returned to the living room, she found Elliot looking at her small collection of CDs.

'I didn't think people still had these.' He was bent over a compact CD player which was on the bottom shelf of a book case. There was a line of CDs next to it. Elliot had one in his hand: John Coltrane's *Giant Steps*. 'I wouldn't have taken you for a jazz fan.' He turned to her with a big smile on his face.

'I'm not, really. I bought it in a charity shop. Really, I like all kinds of music.' She came to where he was kneeling and crouched beside him. 'People still have CDs, I bet you do.'

He nodded and turned back to the small collection. 'I do. Most of them were my wife's, though. I've boxed a lot away. They're hard to part with, and some of them have great artwork, like vinyl used to. Katey downloads everything she listens to. Not that she's missing out on album covers, anyway, because the art isn't much to look at these days. Well, that's what I think.'

Marta smiled to herself. It was probably the longest he'd spoken to her since she'd started at the shop. He gave short, exact sentences when he talked to her about where things were and what she should do. He made brief comments about the weather or about how her day had been. He disappeared the second anyone came to the door of the music shop and then shut himself in the storage room most of the day. Once there, he'd play guitar or piano in between repair jobs on instruments and equipment. The back room of Val's Music Shop was where most of the real work took place. Elliot was, apparently, the go-to guitar repair man in the whole of West London. Marta spent a lot of time on the phone booking in acoustic guitar pick-up fittings, restringing, fret dressings and set ups. She noticed that Elliot was most talkative when musicians came in to have Elliot take a look at their amps or instruments. As the week progressed, Marta discovered he taught private guitar lessons in the back room, too. She'd counted eight students, three of them school children after a day at school.

She stood up.

'I like CDs,' she said. 'I'm like you, I like to see the cover, and when I move, if I move, I can take them with me. Much easier than an album.'

'Did you have a big album collection in Poland?'

'Not really.' They both sat on the sofa, sinking into an ocean of cushions. 'My sister and I used to listen to music a lot on the radio. She took me to a nightclub once, but my parents were furious with her.'

'How old were you?'

'Oh, about eighteen. It wasn't as if it was against the law or anything.'

'They were strict, then?'

'Like you wouldn't believe.' She put her head down. 'I never had much of a life.'

She'd left Elliot tongue-tied, she realised. What could he say to that? His life would have been so different from hers, and yet she only knew a few fragments about his. He was widowed. She had no idea how his wife died. He was a single parent. His daughter, at an age at which she didn't want to be seen with him. And he had a constantly sad look in his eyes. His brow was knotted as each of them searched for a way to lift the burden of the simple sentence, 'I never had much of a life.' Loaded as it was with several interpretations and possible truths, Marta kept the real truth locked somewhere very deep. Elliot could never find it, and then again, Elliot wasn't the sort of person who would ask.

Still, the words hung in the air until Marta's ever-present smile broadened.

'Let's eat,' she said. 'If Katey can't make it, we should start now to get through the amount I made.' She made to get up but somehow managed to slump back into the cushions. Elliot, already standing, extended a hand. She took it. He made a comical grunt to signify how heavy she was which made her laugh. 'Looks like I need to build your strength up, Elliot,' she said, leading the way to the kitchen.

After the meal, they drank more wine, sitting in the living room, lit by a floor lamp now that the darkness of night had taken over the grey evening. The evenings were wintry, a hint of autumn's end coming early. There was no heating on in Marta's flat, but the colours of the soft furnishings in the living room created the illusion of warmth as the two sat listening to John Coltrane at a low volume.

Marta read more than sadness in Elliot's eyes now. His emotions ran deep. She knew how to keep secrets, but it was clear that Elliot was holding something in, too. She quietly searched for hints of the root of this sadness. The obvious thing: he'd lost his wife. Maybe he wasn't over her. During their conversation at dinner, one in which he'd revealed Katey was actually at a friend's, he'd made several references about his wife. They'd met at university. After they'd left, Val got a place with the City of Birmingham Symphony Orchestra as second chair cellist, though harp was her first instrument. As a couple, they'd lived and worked in Birmingham but returned to London the first time Val became ill and wanted to be near her mother-in-law. Elliot's wife and his mother had a special bond, apparently. Val never got on with her own mother. Val recovered, and a few years later, she became pregnant with Katey.

'So, was the shop supposed to be your wife's, then?' Marta asked.

'Well, the idea was that we would run it together. Val wanted something secure after giving up the orchestra. We were struggling to make a living. We had a mortgage and we had Katey to think of. My mum put up a lot of money for the shop, released capital on her house and downsized to make the dream a reality.'

'Well, she had faith in you both.'

'She had faith in Val.' He looked down. 'I was a working musician, but work was getting harder and harder to find. Val couldn't get into an orchestra in London. She was playing harp at wedding receptions, and I was teaching guitar. Scraping by. But it wasn't enough for Val.'

'But you were happy to be a poor musician?'

'I was being selfish. Irresponsible maybe. I love to perform, but it didn't pay the bills. And there were millions of those.'

It looked to Marta as if the effort of carrying a conversation was weighing Elliot down. She was asking too many questions. He could quite easily turn it around, put her under the spotlight. It was time to stop getting personal about Elliot's life so hers could stay hidden. Keeping her personal life so closed off from everyone was a form of torture. At times, she wished she could scream about it. It might even help Elliot open up if she were to. But she didn't want to shock him. It wasn't that she was a criminal or anything sinister, but she had hurt people, people she loved. She had hurt herself, too, hurt her heart. Some mornings, she would wake to a pounding in her chest; her heart was being struck like a gong, sending a shudder around her body with every strike. In her dreams, a small boy with eyes that looked familiar, with lips that were pink and pursed and waiting to cry, would always appear. That same small child had stepped out of her dreams and into her waking life. Followed her. She saw him standing next to her when she looked at her reflection in a shop window. He stood across the road from her bus stop, ignoring everything around him; he would just stare at her until her bus came. When it did and she'd climbed aboard, she'd look back across the road, but he had gone. One time, she thought he was chasing her. She saw him in a playground. She stood and watched him play until he saw her. Once he had, he ran to the gate, pushed it open and began chasing her. She'd turned and run as fast as she could because she was afraid of what he would ask her, afraid of what he would say to her if he were, in fact, real. Of course, he wasn't real. She just wished she could stop imagining him into her reality.

'Can I get you anything else?' she said as the last track of the album finished.

'No, I should go. Katey might be back.'

'I don't really know her, but is she all right about me being in the shop?'

'Why wouldn't she be?'

Marta shrugged. 'Oh, you know? Young girl who has lost her mother, she might resent seeing me in the shop when she was used to her mum being there.'

'No,' Elliot said and then paused a while. 'Not Katey. I don't think so.'

'But you don't know. I would like to get to know her, show her I come in peace.' Marta giggled.

'I think it might be good if you two talked. I'm not good at being a mother to her.' Then quickly, he added. 'I'm not looking for a mother for her.'

Marta giggled again. 'Don't worry, Elliot. I didn't ask you here to seduce you and hope you would marry me. I just wanted us to be friends. I don't have any, or not any that I've kept.'

'I'm worth keeping?'

By this time, they were both standing, both very tipsy and not in complete control of their words.

'Of course you are, Elliot,' Marta said. 'I would love to keep you.'

'That's nice.' Marta felt his hands slide up her arms, and they stood close, staring into each other's eyes. 'I like the idea of being kept.' And for the briefest of moments, their lips came together. A warm, soft touch of skin, and they stepped apart.

'I'm sorry,' Marta said. 'I don't know where that came from.'

'Me neither. I'm sorry. I'd better go.'

'You don't have to rush away. I promise I'm not a seductress.'

'No, no, it isn't that. It's just. I think I should go. When I drink, I'm bad company.'

He walked to the open living room door, then looked back for his jacket.

'Elliot, I'm a lesbian.'

He stared at her.

'Shit,' she said. 'I am a lesbian. I'm thirty-two years old. I've slept with three men and not one single woman, and I've never ever told anyone before. But I am a lesbian.' She began to laugh, the light, song-like laugh that rang out in the shop every day. She laughed at the expression on Elliot's face and the way he was rooted to the spot in the doorway as if she were watching him on a frozen computer screen. She laughed at how ridiculous she had been to have kept the truth inside now that she was away from Katowice. This was one of the secrets she no longer needed to keep.

'I'm not sure what I should say here,' Elliot finally said.

'You don't have to say anything. I am the one with things I should say, things I should have said. Before. When it mattered. Now it's too late.'

'Well, you'll always be a lesbian, so…'

'So I should just get on and be one, right?'

Elliot nodded. She'd made him uncomfortable, looking unsure about what to do with a host who was in fits of laughter and now had tears falling from her eyes.

'Do you really have to go?' Marta asked when the laughter had subsided. Finally seeing the absurdity of her reaction, she sniffed and walked towards Elliot. 'Yes, I'm a bit of a mess. I probably need therapy, but I don't want you to go because I made you feel awkward.'

He took both her hands. 'Actually, Marta, I've had a really good time. I've loved being here. You're great company, and I'm sorry I kissed you. Well, not sorry. I'm sure lots of people, women, want to kiss you. But I don't know how to be with people anymore. I just like you a lot, that's all. Is that okay?'

'It's wonderful, actually. I just like you a lot, too. I won't be weird anymore. I won't tell everyone who comes in the shop that I'm out. They wouldn't care.'

'I care. I'm glad it made you that happy to say it. You never know what opening up can do for you and where it can take you. That's something Val said to me all the time. I'm not like her. Open. She didn't try to make me be like her, but she had all the best advice.'

'You should take it. Be open.'

He looked down and released Marta's hands. 'I'll try. I'll see you on Tuesday, and thanks for having me. It's the first time I've accepted an invitation to anywhere since…'

'There you go. We are starting to be more open. For me, it feels great. Val knew what she was talking about.' She handed Elliot his jacket.

He left quietly, and Marta looked forward to Tuesday. In fact, she was looking forward to every new day. Maybe now, with one of her secrets in the open, she would be able to come to terms with the others.

10

Elliot

Their honeymoon was a weekend at a friend's cottage in Devon which was vacant for a few days. It was made from local stone. The wind blew loud and fast. The windows in the low-ceilinged lounge rattled and let in a tremendous draught. Elliot and Val knew how to get a fire going, and their friends had left enough wood and tinder. They laid out blankets on the floor in the living room and scarcely left the glowing hearth for the entire weekend.

Lying on their stomachs, blankets and throws covering their bare bodies, they toasted bread in front of the fire. They speared the near-stale slices with kitchen utensils, holding them up for an eternity before a tiny hint of brown appeared around the edges of each slice. There was no butter just some fruit preserves that they found on the kitchen table. In their haste to begin their honeymoon, they'd forgotten to shop for food. They'd stopped at a service station, but as Elliot was filling up the tank, Val nibbled his ear and ran her fingers over the tight curls in his hair. He'd cut his hair very short so the texture was different, more smooth than afro and more black. Caught up in their intimacy, at the petrol pump and at the service station counter, they inevitably forgot about food.

'I love your hair. Will our babies have this hair?' Val asked this question several times.

They got back into the car, and Elliot followed the slip road back to the motorway, traffic rushing past like a flame along a trail of gunpowder, no opportunity for him to pull out. He'd had to concentrate hard on the road with the feel of Val's hand squeezing the skin of his upper leg to find a gap in the traffic.

'I don't think we should have children,' Elliot answered.

'What? Never?' she'd asked, moving her hand away with a jerk.

He looked at her swiftly before checking his rear view mirror and moving to the outer lane.

'No, not never. Just not yet. We have a lot to achieve. Finding work, good jobs in music, is going to be tough. Neither of us are there yet.'

'You did want to marry me, though?'

'I don't understand the question.'

Elliot had wanted to marry Val the day he left her room at her shared house at university. The morning he walked home from there, it was still raining. The rain was light, like a fine film over his face. He'd looked up as he took a shortcut through the park. The rain fell into his eyes, and he'd been blinking so fast he almost walked into a tree. He knew he was falling in love, and for some unknown reason, the thought of marriage came into his head, as if he could see into the future, that marriage was inevitable between them, it wouldn't even need discussion. He hadn't even stopped to ask why the change of mind, considering how damaging his parents' marriage was to their lives. He knew by the time he'd arrived at his own student accommodation that he would never want to be without Val and that one day he would marry her.

The first slice of fireplace toast was a disaster: the bread bent and folded as Elliot tried to spread jam onto it with a spoon.

'I think that's mould,' he said. 'Do you want to eat it?'

'No,' she said. Instead, Val tossed the bread into the fire. Tiny sparks shot up, and the bread quickly crumpled into black ash. Val held Elliot's face close to hers and then pulled him onto her. The blanket slipped off the bottom half of their bodies as she ran a toe up the length of his leg and drew him even closer with the crook of her own. Earlier, before they'd managed to start the fire, they'd made love leaning over the back of the sofa. They hadn't minded the cold or that the wind from the ocean was rattling the hinges of the old windows. It was afternoon when they arrived, and now it was dark outside, but they had no concept of time. In fact, they had very little knowledge of their surroundings, exploring only the bathroom and kitchen, their bags still half packed as they scrabbled inside for the bare necessities: towels, toothpaste, condoms, a hairbrush that Val only used on the morning they were leaving.

On the drive back, Val said, 'I want a girl who looks like you and a boy who looks like me.'

'Shouldn't that be the other way around?'

'No. I know what I'm talking about. But I think we should have them sooner rather than later.'

'Why?' Elliot had asked. 'I'm in no rush to go anywhere.'

'Don't say that like we have all the time in the world.'

'But, we're only twenty-one. We do have time.'

Val had contemplated this on the drive home and had said nothing more about it to Elliot. At the time, he wondered why she was thinking about how much time they had together, though he didn't press her on it. Later, in years to come, the question of how much time they had left would come up again.

11

Charlie

Just one more minute, one more moment to stroke her smooth brown skin as she lay in bed, on her stomach, naked. Brenda was humming, her cheek propped up on her folded arms, her hair a mess. She was facing the door, and Charlie kept looking from her bare back to the door. His time was limited. He stroked her body with his fingers, from the deep dip at her waistline and up along the groove of her lower back. He felt her wriggle beneath his touch. She stopped humming and rested her head on the pillow as if she was about to sleep. Brenda did that sometimes, closed her eyes and didn't open them when she knew he had to go. Charlie would kiss her eyelids and tell her to dream something good about him. He'd say, Don't be angry, don't be upset, we'll be together soon. Her face never showed anger: she was beautiful, never giving him a hard time about having to go. She just preferred not to watch him.

As he traced the bony protrusions at her neck, Charlie sighed. 'I don't know when I can see you again.'

Brenda rolled over, pulled the sheet up to cover her body and waited for him to explain. She wasn't going to argue, she wasn't going to shout. At times, he wished she would. When Ana shouted, it made it easier for him to walk out, get away for hours. But Brenda never got mad.

'I know you want to tell me I'm a bastard,' he said. 'I know you want to tell me I should leave her, but I can't. It's not easy to do. This family, it's so big. I have so many obligations. So many people respect me, look up to me. I don't know how to leave them. Imagine the tears, the fights, you name it. I don't know how to do it.'

'I know it's hard. I know you had a life before you met me. It's just…'

'Just what?' he said. He shifted up the bed to lean on the headboard.

'You sure you want to hear this?' Brenda's large brown eyes followed his.

'I think you have the right to say anything you want, my love.'

'I wish you wouldn't call me love when you're about to leave. Say love when you get here. Say love when we're eating together, drinking, at a party. But don't build me up in one breath and knock me down with the next.'

He got up and reached for his underwear, dressing slowly, watching her elegant body roll over onto her side. She stared up at him. The covers had slipped from her upper body, and he eyed the large dark nipples that he'd kissed and heard the eruption of pleasure she got from it. He hadn't stopped there, he'd kissed the entirety of her body until she could do nothing more than pull him into her and clasp his waist with her long legs.

'What did you want to say to me? Before? The thing I don't want to hear,' he asked in a quiet voice.

'I wanted to say that I know leaving is hard. I know you have a lot of people in your life. They look up to you, yes. You are helping lots of people with money, advice, all kinds of things. But does any one of them just want to give you love and ask for nothing in return?'

He knotted his brow.

'It's a simple question, Charlie. I don't demand anything. I don't expect anything. I only want to love you, openly. No more secrets, no more lies. I would give up anything to be with you. If you can't do the same, then can you really and truly love me? Like you say?' Brenda sat up, now; holding the sheets up to her chest, she looked deep into his eyes and waited for him to say something.

Charlie was at a loss for words, for once. What she said made perfect sense, would make perfect sense to anyone who wasn't thirty years into a marriage with a business, two houses in London, two in Greece, three daughters and a wife. A wife he vowed to love and cherish all the days of their lives. The houses, the money, the business would be hard to give up, but the pull of blood: his daughters, his grandchildren and then his wife? They argued a lot, but he and his wife had been through so much. If he built up the courage to break her heart, and his children's hearts, how could he ever live with the guilt? It was very clear now that his relationship with Brenda was not a casual fling. He'd had one of those, a one-night stand, when Ana was away for months in Athens looking after her mother and Charlie and his brother got drunk one night and went to a Greek nightclub. The women, not all of them Greek, were young, beautiful, and he allowed himself a night of weakness. Not even a night, an hour, in his single brother's spare room. He had gone to confession, wouldn't leave the confessional until the priest practically had to throw him out. His penance hadn't been enough for what he'd done to Ana. Now this, this relationship with Brenda, it was nothing like that night. This was a woman he loved. A woman that made him realise that the love he once felt for his wife hadn't compared to his feelings for Brenda. How many times had he wished they'd met when he was a young man before commitment and guilt dictated what he must and mustn't do. He would have given up the church, the language, being Greek, just so he could have a life with Brenda. Even on first seeing her, nothing about Brenda spoke of one-night stands. He wanted nothing sordid with her, but he knew in the next breath that he could never have with her the kind of life that played out before his eyes as he watched her on stage. He'd tried to pull himself together, see Brenda for what she was: a beautiful woman with a beautiful voice whom every man in the room must think they're in love with. Love. He'd started thinking about love when he first saw her.

So many times, he'd thought about the chain of events that led him to that very night club on that very evening. It was a Thursday, Ana had booked an office party at the restaurant, a celebration of some financial milestone or other. The company had wanted a belly dancer, loud music and they insisted they smash plates. Charlie wanted none of it.

'We're not that kind of restaurant,' he'd raged. 'They can go to the Kalamaras Tavern if they want tacky. The food is rubbish, but these people are not coming here for food. They want to mock us.'

'They can do what they like as long as they pay. I'm arranging it, you just have to smile.'

'Like I always do these days. You want to do it all, Ana.'

'I do it better.'

'How can you be so arrogant? I built this place, I paid for it. Made it into a success. My brothers just stood around and twiddled their thumbs while I worked my fingers to the bone for this family. My name is on the deeds. I run this restaurant. I ran it when you were running around in bare feet with only two words of English in your whole vocabulary.'

'So, here we go again. When I came here, I learned everything from scratch. I saved this restaurant when there was a recession. I put The Lantern back on the map.'

'Why is everything a fight with you these days? Why do we have to compete with each other?'

'I don't have to compete? I know what I'm doing. If you don't like it, give yourself the night off and come back later to count all the money that goes into *your* business because *I* know how to be a business woman.'

He had looked over to his younger brother who was replenishing the bar. His brother had nodded to him, knowingly, and then whispered to him that he would take Charlie out for the night. Try something new. Let Ana and her party smash every plate in the place.

They'd laughed all the way to the night club in Soho. The sight of Brenda, the sound of her voice and he'd turned serious for the first time. He and his brother had drunk a lot of whiskey, told a lot of jokes and Charlie hadn't thought of Ana or the restaurant once. All he saw was Brenda.

'I'll do it,' Charlie said to Brenda after a long silence. 'No more secrets, no more lies. I will tell Ana everything.'

As the time went by, almost a year in fact, Ana would come to find out about Brenda, but it wasn't through Charlie. When the truth about his lover was discovered, lives would turn upside down, shame would be felt and Charlie would lose Brenda forever. He would not only lose love, he'd lose respect, and Brenda would disappear, carrying with her a love that Charlie would also lose.

The night time carers putting Charlie to bed had found him quiet and pensive. His eyes stared far into the distance, and no matter how hard they tried, they could not get him to engage. His limbs were heavy when they tried to wash and change him. He had started wearing incontinence pads, and he was reluctant to do any of his physiotherapy exercises. They'd seen this before in dementia cases. The client became listless. Their lucidity came less frequently, and more often than not, they stopped coming back to the present. The health problems would get worse at this point: a complete loss of appetite, a stroke perhaps or depression would take over and gradually time would start to run out. A nursing home: that was the next step, or hospital, if things started to shut down completely. Maybe lungs first, maybe the brain. They would have to report this to the family. The family would take ages to respond, but eventually a decision would be made. The carers would make the report, and soon the Manolis family would tell the care company manager what they wanted doing with Charlie.

12

Ione

Mum described Shepherd's Bush Market in such a way, I'd conjured up a magical place that was vibrant, full of life, filled with amazing people and stallholders who sold items you could never hope to find anywhere else. When I arrive, I don't recognise anything about the place from her description. She had talked about it with eyes that glittered, a smile on her face and a far-off look that told me she was actually there and could taste and feel it. She had said the market had the smell of a West Indian house that you walk past when a pot of food was cooking on the stove. You're not quite in the kitchen, though, so there are other smells, aromas and fragrances that interrupt the smell of cooking but somehow compliment it. The smells twisted and turned around each other, and when they hit your nose, you'd feel happy. A feeling of returning to the place you belonged and wondered why you'd been away for so long.

'So you felt like you belonged in Shepherd's Bush?' I'd asked her. We had been on our way to the supermarket, the enormous one in the centre of town. Our weekly ritual. When I was little, before shopping, she would take me to have cake or hot chocolate or ice cream, depending on the weather.

'Yes, it was my home,' she'd replied.

'So why couldn't we have just stayed?'

She had gone on to say, ignoring my question as if I hadn't even been walking beside her, that in the market there were the colours, too. They clashed and collided but they never made you dizzy. These were the colours of the fabric shops, the dresses that hung from plastic hangers on rails and rope above the clothes stalls. They were the colour of the faces of people walking by. Some busy, some slow and stopping regularly to look around. Sometimes, especially on a Saturday when everyone came, you might get jostled as people walked past, but they weren't unfriendly. You shouldn't be surprised if they didn't rub your arm and say something like, 'Sorry sis, I didn't see you there.' And you shouldn't be surprised, if from the time you entered the market, weaved and wriggled through every path and around every stall, to the time you were leaving, that at least five people called your name and asked after you. You needed time to walk through Shepherd's Bush Market. It was like a home away from home.

It's windy when I get to the market. I look at the scrunched-up newspaper being blown towards my feet. It was previously wrapped around something greasy. I watch it tumble carelessly on the wide path through the centre of the market and land as the breeze subsides. People step on it as if it's not there and walk past me as if I'm not there. I carry on walking as a breeze picks up, and the greasy paper glides past me, too. I don't see a single litter bin, all I see is litter. The smell, if I'm to describe it, is of old fat that has fried one too many chips. Something else has been through the same deep fat fryer. It has an unusual smell which could be animal or vegetable, nothing discernible.

No one seems friendly. In fact, everyone is ignoring me, eyes looking straight ahead or down to the concrete walkway. Mum had said stallholders called out, tried to entice you to their stalls, but all the ones I've seen have been rubbing their hands to ward off the cold or they're on their phones. The main colour I can see is black. Well, there's grey, too. It's weird, but no matter the colour of anyone's skin, they all look grey. Then I see someone familiar. The colours of her clothes remind me of the colours Mum used to wear: bright happy colours. It's the girl from Val's Music Shop. Marta. She hasn't seen me. Something that radiates from her makes me want to walk up to her and talk. I don't know if it's her bright clothes or the brightness in her eyes as she smiles, conversing with a stallholder and holding up a suede shoulder bag. I want her to see me because I'm sure she'll smile and wave me over, or at least wave to me. All of a sudden, I'm shy and have no idea how I can strike up a conversation with a person I hardly know. I'm sure she'll be friendly, but still I hope she will spot me first and come to me. She probably doesn't remember me. I was in the shop last week, and goodness knows how many customers they've had since then.

I'm a step away from Marta, and she turns around just as she waves goodbye to the man on the handbag stall.

'Hi,' I say, feeling my cheeks heat, finally building the nerve to make the first move.

'Oh, hello,' she says. 'I remember you. From the shop. Have you had any callers from your advertisement?'

I shake my head. 'Not a single one. But it might take time. There must be hundreds of piano teachers.'

'But not many who make their own adverts by hand with beautiful handwriting, instead of using the computer.'

'Maybe that's what I should have done. Maybe people might take me seriously.'

Marta laughs. 'You're a serious music teacher? I would have thought you'd be fun. You look it, anyway.' This time Marta blushes, and I don't feel like such an idiot. 'Have you bought anything?'

'I just came to look,' I say. 'Someone told me about the market. My mother, she grew up around here. I think I was expecting something…' I look around, aware that the stall-holder with the bags is looking straight at me and might hear the disappointment in my voice as I search for the right word.

‘Something *more*?’ Marta comes to the rescue. ‘Bush market is an acquired taste. It can be useful, though, the market. Sometimes. Sometimes you wonder why you bothered. I come because I think if anything does change, I don’t want to miss it.’

I smile at her and start to relax.

‘If you want a good market,’ Marta says, nodding her head in the direction I’ve just come from, ‘jump on the tube to Ladbroke Grove and go to Portobello Road Market. That’s the one I love.’

‘I’ve heard Camden Market is good, too. Never been to either, but I’m sure I will one day.’

‘You haven’t been here long, have you?’

‘A month. And all I’ve done is go to work and come back home again.’

‘And come to the music shop.’ She laughs in a high-pitched yet soft way. ‘Well, we should change that.’

‘Change what?’

‘Well, that you haven’t done anything. I’m always out and about.’

‘So you’ve lots of friends?’

‘Not really, but I like meeting new people.’ She eyes me for a second, looking as if she wants to ask a question but isn’t sure how I’ll take it. She takes a deep breath. ‘What do you think of Pilates?’

‘Pilates? Well, I’ve gone a few times. With my friend in Manchester. She’s always looking for excuses to get out of her house.’ This time I giggle, remembering how since my divorce, Jeannie has dragged me along to salsa classes, hot yoga classes, spin classes and pottery classes. She didn’t have a flair for any of those things and talked most of the way through every class. We were constantly being told to shush. Jeannie would leave exercise classes without a bead of sweat on her and complain about how hard she’d had to work. Then she would drag me out for a drink and sit and complain about her family.

‘Someone just handed me a flyer.’ Marta rummages in the cloth bag she has over her shoulder before pulling out a blue A5 flyer. It is creased, and she smooths it open to show me. On it is a picture of someone in a yoga position and the words, Come To Pilates written across the top. ‘It’s tonight.’

‘Is it close by?’I ask, reading some of the details, still unfamiliar with locations.

‘Yes, it is. So you’ll come?’ She looks at me with as much hope as a child asking for one more sugary biscuit.

‘I could give it a go.’ I take the flyer from her and see that the class is held in a church hall. I don’t know where anything is, but I’m sure I’ll find it. I know I like Marta, and I know staying indoors, on my own, with nothing to do but stare at the television or Mum’s urn, hearing her talk about her life here in Shepherd’s Bush is not all I should be spending my time doing. I need to get out. ‘I should take the address down. Maybe I could meet you there?’

‘You take this. I know exactly where it is. Seven o’clock. I can be there at ten to. What about you?’

‘I can do that. Thanks for asking me. I hope I’m not coming across as a charity case.’

‘Not at all. You’re doing me a favour. I was considering it, but I prefer to go with someone. Anyway, I have to get back to work. I’m on my lunch break. You having a day off work?’

‘I don’t work on Tuesdays.’

‘Sounds curious. You can tell me all about it when we meet later?’

‘Well, not during the class but maybe a coffee afterwards?’

‘Perfect. Better run. See you … Ione.’

‘You remembered. See you later.’

I smile, seeing the market in a slightly different way now that I potentially have a new friend. Jeannie would tell me not to allow Marta to become my best friend. She had clear dibs on that. Jeannie was the one who never gave up on me when I started to retreat into myself, becoming a shadow. A shadow that floated beside my body, watching how it shrank in size, slumped in demeanour, hung back and cowered like a frightened pup.

Someone slips a blue A5 flyer into my hand. It's a woman wearing long thin braids with red beads running the length of one of them. She's bony, tall and dressed in a black sweater dress with skinny jeans underneath. It's the same Pilates flyer I already have in my bag, but I fold it away and place it next to the creased one Marta gave me.

Today I might have made a friend. I decide to walk the length of the market, find a new route home. This is my home now, and my resolve to build a new life after David, though it has faltered lately, is returning. The bad memories must not shape my life, I must.

13

Marta

It was chilly when Marta arrived at the church for the Pilates class, just as it had been chilly on the day of her wedding. A beautiful bride at age twenty, long hair under a mesh veil, a face so pretty everyone in the family cried when they saw her in her dress. Marta shivered under the dress, her sister's dress that was intended for a summer wedding. Marta married in the autumn. Goosebumps covered her arms; her hands shook as they held the small posy of red roses and peonies. There was no honeymoon. Tomasz undressed her in the small flat he rented and made love to her every morning. They thought they could afford a place to buy with both of their salaries, but they'd have to save quickly before Marta fell pregnant.

Marta went along with all of Tomasz's plans. They made a lot of sense. She trusted him. She lay back on their bed with the metal frame and thin mattress. The bed creaked and groaned with their lovemaking. Marta moaned with pleasure each time. The more she seemed to enjoy it, the more Tomasz wanted to make love to her. She held him around his slim body and looked up to the ceiling wishing she could fall in love with him, but every day was proof that she could only love him as a friend, not as a partner. For Marta, there was no real partnership. She co-operated with everything Tomasz said; she smiled and she dressed in bright colours to create the illusion of a happy wife.

Marta wrote to her sister and told her she wasn't happy, and her sister tried to convince her of bringing Tomasz to London so they could start a life there and she would take care of Marta and see that she was happy. When Marta discovered she was pregnant, a year after she married, she wanted desperately to go to London, but not with Tomasz. She needed to escape the life he'd built for them, run away to London and hope that her sister would be true to her word. That she would take care of her, and that she would help her find happiness.

The flyer said that the Pilates class was in the hall to the side of the church: *Follow the hedge along the right-hand side of the church*. When she got there, she looked around for Ione, wondering if she would actually come. She might have changed her mind. She didn't know Marta, really, and she might have thought it odd that a near-enough stranger had asked her to come to a class that she herself had never attended. Marta was early. A good twenty minutes.

The hall was open, the lights were on but she waited outside for Ione. Gradually people began to arrive, all of them carrying a yoga mat. The flyer had said to bring your own mat but some would be provided. Marta didn't have a mat.

At last she saw the tall, slim Pilates teacher jumping out of an old Volkswagen Golf. She trotted down the path to the hall, her braids flapping on her back, and she was carrying a long sports bag with yoga mats poking out of the top.

'Hi,' the teacher called when she saw Marta hovering by the door. 'Come in! Welcome.'

'Thank you. I'm just waiting for a friend, but I might run up to the front of the church in case she's waiting there,' Marta said. As she turned to dart back up the path, she collided with a black woman about to come inside. 'I'm so sorry. I wasn't looking where I was going.'

'You're all right,' the woman said. She was wearing a black tracksuit. The bottoms were a skinny fit and the top with a zipped up front was also a close fit. Over it she wore a black padded gilet, and under her arm she carried a purple yoga mat. She put out her hand, close to touching Marta's shoulder. 'I'm a bit out of it myself. You not staying?' Her teeth were large and white; she had a slight overbite that she quickly covered by closing her full lips. She was waiting for Marta to answer, but when she didn't, or couldn't, she went on, 'It's good. The class. She's a good teacher. I know her. I mean, she's a friend of mine.'

'Oh. All right. But yes, I'm staying. I was just waiting for a friend to arrive.'

'Well, don't be shy. Come back before the start. I'm sure you'll like it.'

The black woman smiled, a warm smile that made her eyes squeeze to almost closed, and Marta stared at the smooth kohl line painted on her upper lids. She wore no other make up, and her skin blazed a golden brown, shiny patches on her nose and cheeks.

'Thank you,' Marta said.

Just then, she saw Ione. They waved to each other.

'Am I late?' Ione asked.

'We're just on time, I think.' She gestured for Ione to follow her in.

'I hope I can keep up,' Ione whispered as they walked to the front of the hall towards the Pilates teacher who had stripped down to a pair of high-waisted leggings, a long-sleeved t-shirt and bare feet.

'Me too.' Marta looked around the hall to see if she could see the woman she'd bumped into just before Ione arrived. She was at the front of the hall, rolling out her mat, oblivious to Marta who was now staring at her. Marta couldn't have stopped herself if she'd tried.

'It's seven pounds,' the Pilates teacher was saying to Ione. 'I never have much change so next time, try to bring the exact money.'

Ione was nodding, handing the teacher a ten pound note.

'Could I pay for a mat?' Marta asked as the teacher gave Ione her change.

'You can just borrow one of those. No charge.' The teacher hurried them to settle, accepting the exact money from Marta and nodding her head towards the pink mats leaning up against the wall beside her.

It had been hard for Marta to concentrate, turning her head towards the woman she'd spoken to at the door with every opportunity she could. She knew it was rude to stare like that, but she was fascinated by her. At the end of the class, after an hour and fifteen minutes of stretching and moving in ways that Marta had found particularly tiresome, she rolled up her mat.

'What did you think?' Ione asked her. 'I think she's really good.'

Marta nodded, her mat spiralling outwards instead of into a neat roll.

'I think you should try that again,' Ione said.

'What?' Marta looked down at the mess she was making of trying to roll up the mat. 'Oh yes. Stupid.' She shook the mat out and knelt down to try once more. She made a successful job of it, even though she had kept her eyes towards the front of the hall where the Pilates teacher was in a deep conversation with the woman with the warm smile. She wondered who they were to each other, keeping her eyes on them both to see if she could detect any telltale body language or chemistry between them. There was nothing perceptible, nothing to give away a relationship that went further than friendship between the two women.

'Are we going to get that coffee?' Ione asked.

'Oh yes, yes of course. I know a nice place near here.'

'You really know your way around.'

'Sort of, but I have been living here for a year. I need to return this.'

Marta walked to the front of the hall. The Pilates teacher was putting the used mats back in her bag while continuing to conduct a conversation with her friend. Marta overheard something about a dinner party.

'Um, thank you,' Marta said, standing beside the woman and sensing the smell of deodorant. It hadn't been a particularly strenuous class, but it did cause Marta's forehead to glow with tiny beads of perspiration. She was sure that had she paid closer attention or had tried a little harder, she would have sweated enough for the odour of her deodorant to take effect. Her head turned slightly towards the woman. She was looking straight at Marta.

'Well?' she asked Marta.

'I'm sorry, I didn't mean to interrupt,' Marta said, her cheeks turning pink.

'No,' said the woman. 'What did you think of Callie's class?'

'Way to put a person on the spot, Louise.' Callie shook her head and put the last mat into her bag. 'Don't listen to her. I hope I'll see you next week. Was it your first Pilates lesson?'

Marta nodded. 'I did enjoy it.'

'I'm glad,' Callie said and went to put on her jacket. 'Need to lock up.'

'Cool, Callie,' Louise said. 'I'll buzz you in the week.'

'Good,' said Callie, picking up her bag.

Marta stood awkwardly for a second, not sensing at all that Callie wanted to leave.

'See you next week, I hope,' Louise said to Marta and continued chatting to Callie. Marta turned to the door. She saw Ione standing there and realised she'd forgotten about her.

Ione was smiling.

'Is that a friend of yours?' she asked Marta.

'Who? Louise? Actually, no.' Marta said. She led Ione to a pub further on up the road. It was dark like a winter night, though London was clinging onto the last traces of autumn. The Plough wasn't busy. In fact, apart from two members of the bar staff, only three other people sat drinking in the main saloon.

'Do they do coffee?' Ione asked.

'They do, but how about a glass of wine?'

'I can handle a glass of wine. I'll get these. What'll you have?'

They found a seat on the sofas by the window. Ione began talking about something or other, but Marta realised, after a minute or so, she had no idea what was being said. Her mind had drifted to the black woman dressed all in black and who moved gracefully through the series of exercises. Marta had taken her eyes off her for as long as she could, but somehow she kept returning her gaze. She hoped she'd been subtle.

Marta remembered a time, several years ago, when she had noticed how much Tomasz from accountancy had stared at her. Of course, he hadn't been subtle at all. He'd smile at her every time they ran into each other. Marta felt sure he'd found excuses to visit her office floor just so he could see her. She had liked his smile, liked his face, too. She'd thought straight away that he was someone she could live with, make a life with.

She shook the memory of what she'd done to poor Tomasz from her mind and tried to focus on Ione. Her new friend had been talking about her school, the posh high school in Holland Park where she worked part-time and had managed to settle in very quickly.

'What instruments do you teach?' Marta asked, sipping wine from the glass she'd hardly touched.

'I don't. I'm there to teach history of music and theory.'

'Isn't that boring if all you want to do is play music?'

'Not really. I quite enjoy it. When I play music, my mind wanders too much and I let it go to places it shouldn't.'

Marta studied Ione's face, and for the first time, she noticed some marks at the base of her neck. They were silvery scars that Ione absently ran a finger or a thumb over as she spoke. Marta couldn't help wondering about the significance of those tiny scars.

'Did you come to London for the job?' Marta asked. Inwardly she shrank, knowing that the second she asked why anyone moved from where they had been living, the question could just as easily be turned to her.

'Not exactly,' Ione said, touching her neck again and looking out of the window very briefly. 'I just needed a change.'

'Oh,' Marta said, sipping some more wine. She wanted to change the touchy subject as quickly as she could.

'Okay,' Ione said, a sigh of resignation just audible. 'The truth is, it's not a big secret anyway, I had an abusive husband. We divorced and I had to get as far away from him as possible. Well, there are places further than London, I know, but I've always felt drawn to it. Shepherd's Bush, actually. My mother grew up not far from here, and she used to talk about her life in those days. So much so, it felt like I'd lived here myself. In many respects, it's like coming back home.'

'Is it what you hoped it would be?'

'I'm still finding my feet, but so far, so good. The job keeps me grounded, and once I have music students, it'll occupy my time and I won't keep looking back. I look back too much.'

'We can't help it,' Marta said. 'That's the way life is. Where we came from is significant.' She stopped suddenly. Leading the conversation to her past was not what she intended. 'I'm looking forward to Pilates next week.'

'That doesn't surprise me.' Ione smiled and looked directly at Marta.

'You enjoyed it, too?'

'That's not what I meant.' Ione shook her head. 'I'm sorry, it's none of my business.'

'What isn't? This sounds mysterious. What is none of your business?'

'That woman, Louise, the one you said wasn't your friend. Forgive me if I got this wrong, but I got the feeling that …

oh, nothing. My friend Jeannie says I read too much into things. I just thought there had been something between you. Some history.'

'Honestly, I only bumped into her at the door tonight.'

'I think she likes you.'

'What are you saying?'

'I think she might like women, particularly you.'

Marta smiled, broadly. She moved her long hair off her shoulder, the whole of her face reddening.

'So,' Ione said, 'you like her, too?'

Marta nodded.

'So I was right. That's what I meant when I said I'm not surprised you want to go back. It wasn't because you liked the workout—if anything, you were hardly moving.'

They both laughed.

'Was I that obvious?' Marta said.

'Well, you were to me. But don't worry, like I say, I think she likes you, too.'

Marta looked out of the window. The outside was like a photograph, so still. She wondered if time had stopped, and if it had, how amazing if Louise was in the photograph so that she could stare at her longer. If she were outside now, what would she say to her? Maybe she could be as unsubtle as Tomasz had been that day he met her before they entered the lift at the same time. They had travelled up and down seven floors while Tomasz mustered up the words to ask Marta out for a drink. She had been charmed by him. He wouldn't let her leave the lift, saying constantly, 'This won't take long, I just need to find the right words … I just need to tell you that …' The lift stopped at every floor, and each time, the door would open onto a dark corridor and there would be no one there. Tomasz would get sidetracked and have to start his speech again after the doors closed and the lift went to the next floor. Marta had even wondered if Tomasz had a stutter. He hadn't, of course, he had just been so taken with her, so attracted to this tall skinny girl with long hair, no make-up and dressed in a drab navy dress.

'You can just say it.' She had tried to encourage Tomasz. After all, she had only left her office to do some filing. They would be expecting her back. 'I won't eat you.'

'Neither will I,' he'd said. They had both laughed aloud. Both very nervous. They were so young. 'Would you like to come for a drink?'

Marta had nodded and left the lift at the wrong floor. She'd wanted to put Tomasz out of his misery. 'Meet me outside after work tomorrow. Okay?' she said before heading for the stairs. Tomasz was a young man her parents would find acceptable. She had been lucky to find him.

Someone walked past the pub window, and Marta became aware that Ione was reaching for her jacket.

'I think I should probably get going,' Ione said.

'Yes, sorry, I was miles away.'

They discovered that they were going most of the way together and walked to the top of the road. At the main road they parted ways. Marta, still thinking Louise, told herself that it couldn't be that easy, she couldn't have met someone she could spend time together with, romantically. Inside, she knew she had, but could she allow herself to let it happen? She had hurt a string of people, ones who'd loved her but that she had let down so badly and so cruelly, too. In the process of letting people down, Marta's heart had also been broken.

Her footsteps grew heavy, knowing she felt this attraction for Louise but wondering how could she love someone when she only had half a heart.

14

Louise

Louise let herself into Charlie's house and was surprised to see him in his chair by the window instead of in bed, a blanket over his knees. The television was on, but he wasn't watching it. She turned down the volume.

'It's me, Charlie.' She leaned down to his eye level, making sure he looked at her and not vaguely at the space between his eyes and hers.

'Is that you? Louise?' he said. His voice was croaky from lack of use. She knew the other carers came for as short a time as possible, fed Charlie, made sure he was comfortable and then left. She used to work as part of a pair but fell out with her partners who cut too many corners and had no business looking after other people's elders as far as she was concerned.

She had worked as a nurse for ten years. The hours had been long and hard, the shifts had been gruelling. The money was not nearly enough for the job she was doing, and she was always being overlooked for promotion, no matter how hard she worked. Leaving nursing and starting a degree in psychology had been one of the biggest decisions of her life. Her girlfriend, Danika, who'd said she'd support Louise, told her she should just go for it, a better and more fulfilling job awaited.

The plan was that Louise should work and study part-time. She could keep up the rent payments, but Danika would be paying the lion's share of bills. She'd assured Louise she had it covered. Danika told everyone she loved the idea that Louise was going back to study something she loved. She applauded her girlfriend for finally following a path that meant a degree and a serious profession to follow. Danika had done the university thing, was working in the city in a very well-paid job. She had wanted Louise to be as happy and as well paid, but it was money that drove the wedge between them. Or at least, Louise's lack of it. Study and shifts as a doctor's receptionist coupled with shifts as a carer were not only making Louise as tired as she was as a nurse but caused Danika to become more and more dissatisfied with their lives. Maintenance bills for the apartment by the river in Hammersmith were going up and, in Danika's opinion, they were still not making enough time to socialise with friends. Louise tried on numerous occasions to tell Danika that it would take time but things would get better. Danika ran out of patience and slept with a woman from her office after a party.

The last time Louise saw Danika was two years ago when she was collecting the last of her things from the swanky riverside apartment and moving into one room in a shared house in Shepherd's Bush. She promised herself every morning when she woke and had to wait for the bathroom to become free that it was only temporary. Psychology was her dream, and one day, she'd be in her ideal job. She might even end up in her own apartment by the river one day.

'Yes, Charlie it's me, Louise. How you feeling today? Did you eat all your lunch?'

She was going to be there for an hour today. Charlie's daughter had arranged more carers to start coming to the house for an hour in the morning and an hour in the afternoon, just to keep him company. These visits were in addition to the washing and mealtime visits. The care agency manager had approached the family about the possibility that Charlie could do with a little more stimulation, someone to talk to him or read to him as he seemed to be becoming morose at times and that wasn't good for his well-being. The daughters had discussed this, but none of them, between their work, the restaurant and their busy family schedules, had the time to sit with their father for a few hours just to talk.

Louise's manager had told her that Charlie's daughters hadn't had very much to say to their dad since their mother kicked him out of the house and demanded they get divorced. Twenty years ago.

'Are you warm enough, Charlie? I think your girls will have to get the heating switched on. Winter is back.' She rubbed her hands together and took out a copy of the Metro.

'Louise?'

'Yes, Charlie.'

'When you going to sing to me?'

'I've told you, Charlie. I'm not a singer. That was Brenda. She was the singer. Right?'

'Oh, that voice she had. Beautiful. Like you.'

Louise smiled and settled in the chair next to his. 'Should I read to you about what's going on in the world?'

'I saw her singing in that club. The um … the… Damn it. What was the name?' He didn't remember names of places. He could tell you the names of all of his daughters, but he couldn't identify which was which if they were all standing in front of him. He most certainly couldn't remember the last time he'd seen any of them.

'What did she sing?' Louise asked. She saw the frustration in his face when he wanted to remember but couldn't.

'Not in that club. At home. At her flat, she sang my song.'

'You have a song?'

'Our song.'

'What was it called? Do you remember?'

Charlie had a worried look on his face. He was trying to think of the name of the song, but it wasn't likely to come to him. Not these days. Not anymore.

‘It’s all right, Charlie. I’ll pretend I know. Or, I can put on the radio?’

Charlie started to hum. Even though his voice was low and scratchy, Louise recognised the song he was humming, instantly. She took out her phone and quickly found the YouTube app. She searched the song, a favourite of hers, too. *Midnight Train to Georgia* by Gladys Knight and the Pips.

‘Is this it?’ Louise held up the phone. She turned the screen so that the video would show in widescreen. She doubted very much Charlie could see it without his glasses, which she looked around for but saw that they weren’t close at hand. She was reluctant to stop the music or move away while Charlie was so engrossed in the song. He hardly ever engaged this well, and she didn’t want to break the spell.

Tears came to his eyes. ‘This one—they’ll play this one at my funeral.’

‘Really?’ said Louise. ‘Who told you that?’

‘Louise told me.’

‘No, I’m Louise, Charlie. And we’re not talking funerals now.’ She put the phone on her chair and started dancing as the song played on towards its finale. ‘Fancy a dance, Charlie?’

His eyes were closing. Louise continued to dance.

‘At my funeral, they’ll play this song,’ he whispered. Before the song finished, Charlie looked up and smiled. ‘The Soho Cellar. Big club in Soho. Important back in those days.’

‘Nice one, Charlie. You remembered the Soho Cellar.’

There was a knock at the door, and then the doorbell rang.

‘Are you expecting someone?’

Louise went to the front door and saw a young man, maybe in his late teens.

‘Yes?’ she said, holding the door open by a small gap.

‘It’s Nico. I’m Nico. Just come to visit my granddad.’

‘Really?’ Louise was taken aback. She had seen one of Charlie’s daughters but just the once. A skinny woman with a pinched face and long dark hair that was streaked with wisps of grey. Louise remembered how she spoke, in a short and clipped manner, about making sure to leave things as they were found. It had annoyed Louise who had been a carer long enough to know how to do her job. The daughter hadn't offered a hand to shake but had introduced herself as Athena Christou.

'No disrespect,' Louise told Nico, 'but could you tell me how I can be sure you're who you say you are? What's your mum's name? I could phone her.'

Nico put up his hands. 'No, I don't want her to know I'm here. My mum is Charlie's youngest daughter. Her name is Athena. I'm her son, Nico. My aunties are Theia Maria and Theia Crystal.'

Louise stepped back. She knew the names were accurate, she also saw a family resemblance in the boy, Nico.

'Sorry,' she said. 'You can't be too careful.'

'I know. Sorry. It's just that I don't know my granddad that well, and I thought I'd try to get to know him a bit. No one talks about him. Well, not to me, but my aunts and uncles talk about him when they think we're not listening.'

Louise was confused by this. She knew his daughters rarely visited, but she wondered what it was they had to say about this dear, sweet man in secret. It occurred to her then that all this talk of Brenda had something to do with it. Louise had no idea where she figured in Charlie's timeline, often wondering if Brenda was actually real.

She and Nico stood in the hallway. He towered over Louise. She noticed a rucksack for the first time, slung over his shoulder with graffiti written in felt pen all over it.

'It's a shame you don't know him that well. He's in the living room.'

'Thanks.'

Charlie barely looked up at his grandson. Louise stood in the doorway watching the interaction. Charlie was her responsibility, so she should keep an eye on Nico. Despite the age gap, the family resemblance was strong. Louise had seen pictures of Charlie as a young man, perhaps older than his grandson was now but just as tall and broad shouldered. Charlie's hair was thin and white, his scalp showed pink and frail with thin lines. Liver spots had sprung from his crown to his forehead. They covered his shaking hands where blue veins formed tracks that snaked around them. The pictures Louise remembered, in the drawer near his bedside, the ones Charlie had insisted she see on a regular basis, showed Charlie with thick dark hair and brown eyes that flashed life, a little mischief thrown in, perhaps. Nico could have been the young man in the old photographs. As they sat together, in silence, the younger man staring at his grandfather, the older man looking down to his blanket, Louise hoped Nico's family would allow him to keep visiting.

'He's not asleep,' Louise said from the door. 'You can talk to him. Can I get you a tea or anything, Nico?'

'Water. Please. If that's all right.'

'Sure. You just talk to Charlie. He might not look like he's listening, but I'm sure he hears a lot.'

She left them. Went to the kitchen. It was polished and clean but looked as if it wasn't lived in. As she found a tall glass, Louise heard footsteps and turned to see Nico at the door. His cheeks were red.

'I don't know what to say to him,' he said. 'Mum doesn't even have pictures. I overheard her talking to Theia Crystal about him, but I always thought he was dead. I told people only my Yiayia was alive. I never knew I had a Pappoús.'

'Well, he's very much alive.' She turned to fill the glass then left it by the sink. 'I wonder why they never talked about Charlie.'

'I think it was because they're all ashamed of him or he brought shame or something like that. I don't get it. I asked Mum. Kept asking her until she said where he lived but that he was being looked after and he'd lost his memory. She said he wouldn't know me because the last time he saw me was at my christening.'

'Wow.'

'I asked her for pictures of my christening, and I tried to look for him in them. I didn't know who I was looking for. He could have been any of them or not in the pictures at all.'

'I'm sure he must have been in at least one. Look, come back to the living room with me. I'll introduce you both.'

Louise led the way, constantly looking back over her shoulder at Nico, imagining she was taking a look into the past at a young and cogent version of Charlie. She smiled to herself, seeing images of Charlie at a club listening to his sweetheart, Brenda, singing to him. She pictured a small dark venue full of people, the music loud and that Brenda was as beautiful as Charlie said she was, that her voice was wonderful and that Charlie loved Brenda on first sight. She wondered where Brenda was now. She felt sure that Brenda had been the reason Charlie brought shame to the family. He was married, and they must have been lovers.

'Here we are,' she said as she pushed her face in front of Charlie's. She caught his attention, and he looked up at her, seemingly aware of her presence. 'Charlie, you have a visitor. Your grandson, Nico, is here to see you.'

'Um, hello. You don't know me but I'm Nico. I'm Athena's son.'

Charlie's eyes raised upwards to the tall young man standing to his side.

'Are you going to say hello?' Louise said. 'He's come especially to see you.' There was no response from Charlie. In fact, Charlie's eyes turned downwards, almost closing. 'Don't worry, he's probably tired. Just talk, say anything. I'm sure he'll be glad to hear a friendly voice.'

'Okay, I will.'

'I forgot your water.'

'It's okay. I'll just chat to Granddad. I need to get home soon.'

‘Fine.’

Louise left them alone again. She heard Nico talking to Charlie, telling him about school and that he was in his exam year. He told his granddad which A levels he’d be sitting in the summer and his plans to study music. He talked about the restaurant, and how he worked there some weekends. He said he liked it there.

Louise looked at the time. Her hour was almost up, and she wondered if it was okay to leave Nico. He was a relative, she was sure that wasn’t against the rules. Just then, Nico came out into the kitchen where she’d been sitting at the small dining table reading messages on her phone.

‘I think I’ll be off now,’ Nico said.

‘Did you get much out of him?’

Nico shrugged.

‘It’s like that sometimes,’ she said. ‘He was talking about Brenda. Was that his wife? Your grandmother?’

‘No, Gran, Yiayia, is called Anastasia. Ana.’

‘I see. And do you know anyone called Brenda? He’s talked about Brenda. Said she was a singer?’

Nico’s cheeks reddened again.

‘Have I said something I shouldn’t?’ Louise said. She inwardly chastised herself. It was foolish to bring up a memory of Charlie’s. She might have repeated something that Charlie didn’t want anyone in his family to know about. Patients with dementia don’t have filters and neither do they necessarily have memories that have any semblance to their history. Seeing how uncomfortable Nico looked confirmed her suspicions about who Brenda was to Charlie. She was the reason he lived almost in exile from his family.

‘Oh, just forget I said it,’ she said, walking Nico to the front door. She opened it, but Nico hovered by the mat.

‘I’m not sure, but I think Brenda was a mistress. You know? My granddad’s mistress. He didn’t stay living with Gran. Actually they divorced. The aunts talked about a black woman, a singer, I heard that name. Brenda. I guess that's the one.'

'Look, don't mention this to your mum. I mean, I really shouldn't have opened my mouth. You're just a boy. It's not our business. It's Charlie's.'

'No way am I going to say anything. Mum doesn't even want me here. They don't seem to like Granddad. I suppose because he had an affair or something.'

'That makes sense, I suppose.'

'I like him. Granddad. I think he's all right, and what if he's sorry about her?'

'He probably is. Especially if he missed out on watching you grow up.' She smiled at Nico. 'I hope you can come round again. But don't get yourself into trouble. I'm here every day at this time. I'm Louise, by the way.'

'Right. Thanks. See you soon, yeah?'

She waved and shut the door. It was all making a lot more sense to her now. Charlie was always saying Brenda and she were alike. He'd meant because of her colour. Brenda, a black woman. A singer. Off the top of her head, she didn't know a black female singer called Brenda anything. She could have been a soul singer if she sang Gladys Knight songs. Or gospel? She wondered what the Soho Cellar was like and if it still existed.

'Charlie!' she said animatedly. 'Let's have your song on again. I have to dance, though. Don't try to stop me.'

Louise danced and sang in the living room. Charlie, looking on, grew tired. A slow-moving tear, one that gathered for a few moments at the corner of Charlie's misty eye, rolled down his face. Louise wiped it away, but she realised she'd lost him to his retrospective world again. She hoped he was with Brenda, hearing her voice, feeling happy. Smiling the way he had when she'd first appeared for her shift that afternoon.

15

Ione

It's as if I'm not here. Watching Marta and Louise as they get to know each other. It's cute really, but I wish they'd just let me leave. I know it's polite of them to tell me to stay and finish my drink, but I feel as if I'm in the way of something. Something big and important. Could they be falling in love? Am I a witness? It's a good feeling to have, though it makes me feel homesick. Or something like that. Like I want to get back to something as pure as what these two women are sharing right now. But how can I be homesick for something I've never had? Not anything real and certainly not a love that was ever worth keeping. In my reflection in the pub window, I notice the ridiculous grin on my face. I can't help it, I'm being influenced by the feelings Marta and Louise are generating. Warmth, lost emotions being found and of possibilities. I look around the pub and wonder if anyone else can feel it, too.

The pub is as quiet as it was when Marta and I popped in here last week after our first Pilates class. The class tonight was just as good. I could relax more, stop being so self-conscious. What did it matter if people looked at me? During the class, I can't touch my scar. I do try not to. I've been trying to occupy my hands as much as possible so that I don't. It's part of the new me that I hope will emerge from this new phase in my life. I'm always finding something to do with my hands whether I'm at the flat alone or when I'm at work. I play my piano, re-organise the music equipment in the storeroom at school. Something. Anything. I know it will take a while to get back to being me. The real me. Not this washed-out version, still frightened by her own shadow. Jeannie says she has already noticed the change since the move. I do feel it, though I have the occasional wobble, but I am feeling stronger.

'Another?' Marta says.

'Not for me.' I drain the last of an overly sweet wine. I chose the house red and have to remember not to have it again next time. If there is a next time. Maybe Marta and Louise won't invite me.

'Come on,' Louise says.

I like her. She's funny and she seems to match Marta. I can't ruin what is, for all intents and purposes, their first date. 'No, really. I'll see you guys next week.' I touch my scar. I pick up my jacket. I put it on and go to leave. Marta hugs me.

'Thank you,' she says. I look at her quizzically and then she winks. I understand what she's saying. At the end of the class, when Louise was talking to the teacher again, I persuaded Marta to stay behind and try to get a conversation going with Louise. She insisted she couldn't be so bold. I told her that it was better to see if Louise was interested in her. If not, we could move onto another Pilates class where maybe there'd be lesbians who were twice as good looking. She'd laughed in that high and delicate way, and Louise had looked around. Louise approached her, a conversation began and I was dragged along to The Plough with them.

On the walk home, I suddenly realise I'm not coming out onto the road I thought I would. I left the pub in a hurry and tried a different way of getting to the main road, believing I was taking a short-cut. But this road is long, dark and unfamiliar. So, now, I'm inwardly chastising myself for trying to be so damned smart. I'd waved to Marta and Louise and was immediately distracted by my plans for the following day: the preparation for lessons, the call I owe Jeannie. Now I'm on a quiet street and probably heading in the completely wrong direction. I could get out my phone and try to navigate my way home, but I can't see the name of the road.

Ahead, I see a left turn which, if I'm lucky, will lead to the main road. So I continue on, pulling the collar of my jacket tighter around me and looking back over my shoulder. I'm not making a sound in my trainers, and the street is eerily quiet and menacingly long. To my right, a low wall with tall railings surrounds a park, on my left, two-storey houses with not many of their windows lit. Just before the left turn, across the road, I see that iron gates form a break in the railings. Though locked now, I can see more of the park. For some reason, I'm compelled to cross the road to get a better view. Through the centre of the park is a long avenue that leads all the way to another locked gate on the other side of the park. Chance must have brought me here. Clasping the cold metal gate, I peer into the park from Mum's story. The place she used to meet Charlie and they'd pass love letters to each other. I can't believe I'm here. A picture of them meeting, on a bright day, not daring to look at each other, comes to mind. I'm reminded of the time Mum was dying and the many times I wished I'd known how to get hold of Charlie. Not just because I wanted to know my father but because I thought Mum would have liked to have seen him one last time. He could have been a comfort.

Mum told me that, one day, she and Charlie stopped right in the middle. They forgot themselves for one moment. They stood in the pathway and stared into each other's eyes. Mum said Charlie was smiling, smiling so that everyone could see he was happy.

'My Brenda,' he had said. 'I miss the way you sing to me.'

'If I sang to you now, what would you like me to sing?'

'You know the song. The greatest love song of them all.'

'I could sing it, but it's not so great.'

'Why?'

'Because the girl in the song is giving up everything so she can follow the boy. He's giving up nothing.'

'Yes, but the words are still perfect.'

'How can that be?'

He was still smiling, broadly. He stepped in closer as if he was going to pick her up in his strong arms, wrap them around her body and swing her the way he did when there were no prying eyes. She moved back a step.

'Well?' she asked. 'How can it be perfect?'

'I would give up everything to follow you. I know that now. You asked me once before, and I said it was impossible. But I know now, just seeing how you're looking at me today, that if you ever leave, I will drop everything. My family, my life, everything and I will follow you. So it's our perfect song, Brenda.'

Mum looked quickly round the park that day. She was unsure. Was it that easy for Charlie to change his mind about leaving his family? Would he really drop everything to follow her? The truth was, she didn't want him to follow her anywhere. This was her home, right here. She wanted them both to stay and to be together. When she saw Charlie looking furtive and moving slowly away from her, she realised it was all talk. He had a lot at stake. If she left, he would never follow, she knew that to be true. Mum had to be the one to end their affair. But not yet. She loved him too much. More than he could ever love her, she thought, but one day it would all come to an end.

They passed each other on the path, their homes in different directions, and Charlie would go back to his large house. Back to his family.

The image of them that day fades back to the dark night and the silhouette of trees around the lawns. I think I see a dark figure sitting up from a bench and begin to move towards me. I step away from the gate and rush back across the road.

I walk as fast as I can to the main road, heart pounding a rapid beat in my chest. My throat is dry. I'm cold, yet perspiring. When I see my flat, it is with relief. I lean my back against the closed door, close my eyes and breathe deeply until my heartbeat returns to normal.

16

Marta

Louise left early the next morning. She had coursework notes to write up and a client to see in the afternoon. Marta sat up in bed, hugging her knees to her chest and watching as Louise dressed. After Ione decided to leave The Plough, she and Louise had talked a lot about Louise's studies and her job as a carer.

'I couldn't do it,' Marta had said. 'I can't imagine myself looking after an old person who wasn't my relative.'

'Neither could I at one time, but after years of nursing, seeing people at their very worst, having to patch people up, watch them crumble, in pain, see them at their most vulnerable, you can pretty much do anything.'

'But old people can be so miserable.'

'I know, but I think they've earned the right. We complain about aches, pains, sickness, injustices, bad relationships, bad hair days…' Here, they'd both laughed. 'Imagine a lifetime of all of that and more. Then imagine having to cope with the knowledge that there's only one way this can go. Your life is at an end, you've been through so much, and even if you wanted to keep going, you couldn't. You're too weak, you're too frail, your memory is shot. Or you've been struck by some illness that makes your life even tougher or unbearable. I'd be miserable. I'd be pissed off, angry as hell. They can't do for themselves, they don't have choices.'

'It's true.' Marta had quickly become wistful. 'I know what it's like not to have choices. Or to think you don't.'

She'd stared out of the window. It was a clear night, no one passed by, there were only occasional cars along the street. Solitary drivers in a hurry to get somewhere.

'What is it?' Louise had put her hand on Marta's and squeezed. 'When did it happen?'

Marta snapped her head round to look at Louise. 'When did what happen?'

'You said you know what it's like not to have choices. I wondered what that meant.'

'It's nothing.' Marta had shaken her head. Louise's hand remaining on hers. She stroked Louise's long fingers with her thumb. 'I was young and stupid. I actually did have choices, I just didn't know it at the time. I was too young and probably too afraid and…' She moved her hand to her wine glass.

'It's all right,' Louise had said. 'You don't owe me anything, Marta. We just met. I like you, and I don't want to get all heavy on you. I don't want to get serious at all. No pressure, no promises.' She'd raised both palms up. 'Okay? We'll keep it casual. I'm not into heavy relationships.'

Marta had looked at Louise, closely. She wore no make-up. Her lips, a purple brown around the outer edges, were pink in the centre. They were smiley lips. Her skin was the colour of autumn. There were slight blemishes on her cheeks and one tiny pimple on her brow. Most striking were her eyes, Martha had thought. They were so alive: the whites conspicuously bold, her irises a rich mahogany.

'Should we go?' Louise had said.

'Do you want to go out somewhere?'

'I just meant go home.' Louise smiled.

'Oh, I don't live far, actually.'

'Is that an invitation?'

'No… I just—'

'It's okay, I was only joking. I should just get going.'

'But, I would like it if you came round. It's just that…' Marta had looked furtively around, but they were the only customers in the saloon bar. ‘I want to invite you. It’s just that I never…’

‘Wait.’ Louise sat back in her chair. ‘You’ve never been with a woman, have you?’

Marta shook her head. ‘I’m sorry.’

‘What are you sorry for?’ They’d become quiet again until Louise said. ‘If you’re not far and I’m invited, let’s go to your place. If that’s your choice, it’s mine, too.’

They’d joked and laughed on the way to the house, Marta’s hands shaking as she unlocked the front door. She’d felt weakness in her legs as she’d climbed the stairs.

Louise had held her cheeks between her hands very gently, and they’d kissed for the first time.

‘Do you want to take this to the bedroom?’ Louise had asked.

There was the scent of vanilla essence from the candle that always burned at night in Marta’s bedroom. She blew it out just before sleeping. The candle had once been tall and stood in a brass holder next to a ceramic bedside lamp whose bulb had blown and not been replaced. It was already burned to almost nothing when Marta had struck the match in the dim bedroom, lit only by the street lights spilling in from the window. Lying on the bed together they’d undressed, stopping to kiss, to explore skin, limbs and hair with soft strokes and slow caresses. Marta had allowed Louise to lead the way and found herself lost in feelings of emotion and an overwhelming passion she had never experienced before. Her instinct had been to cry, but instead she’d laughed, a tiny tear slipping from her closed eyes.

‘Was that all right?’ Louise had asked. Marta had only nodded and then held Louise tighter. They’d fallen asleep in each other’s arms, the candle still burning.

Marta had awoken first the next morning. Her arm was around Louise whose short coarse hair was tickling her chin.

Not long after Louise left, Marta got ready and left for work. There were traces of Louise everywhere in the flat, the lingering smell of her deodorant, the oils in her hair and the toothpaste kiss she'd left on Marta's lips.

Marta smiled all day at the music shop, sitting at the stool by the window reliving the night before. She barely noticed Elliot leaving to deliver a guitar he'd repaired.

'So you're okay to lock up?' he asked. 'Marta?'

'Oh yes, yes of course I am. Where are you going?'

'I just said, I'm dropping this off in person.' With a sigh, he held up a guitar case.

'You don't do deliveries.'

'Marta, I just said, it's on my way to look at some equipment I need.'

'Of course, yes. Sorry, I'm miles away.'

'Right. See you tomorrow. And you're locking up, yeah?'

'Yes. See you, Elliot.'

She noted the look of worry on Elliot's face, drew in a quick sniff of air to come back to her senses and vowed to herself to lock up properly come closing time and set the alarm.

After school, Katey walked into the shop. Marta waved to her and called out, 'Hi,' though Katey was already making her way straight to the back room.

'He's out,' Marta said just as Katey got to the back door.

Katey leaned back into the shop, balancing on one foot. 'Has he gone home already?'

'No, he went to deliver a guitar.'

Katey shrugged, headed back to the door then stopped. She walked over to the counter, dropped her school bag on the floor and began fiddling with the flyers on the counter. The pile of glossy A5 sheets advertised everything from music equipment to Elliot's repair services and local gigs and events. Marta spent a lot of time during the day arranging and re-arranging them. Whenever someone came in, they'd invariably move them, take them or drop them back so that they were a mess.

‘How was your day?’ Marta asked after watching how precisely Katey replaced each flyer.

‘Not bad. Actually, it was quite good.’

Marta noted the shift in Katey’s demeanour. She had walked in with her usual attitude: a mix between not wanting to be approached yet quietly leaving a slight opening for uncomplicated exchanges. Marta noticed that the opening was much wider; if she chose to enter, Katey would most certainly let her in.

‘That’s good,’ Marta said.

‘Yeah. So, Marta?’ Katey finally stopped running a finger over the flyers.

‘Yes?’

‘What is it with you and Dad? Are you two seeing each other or something?’

Marta’s sing-song laugh filled the shop. She shook her head. ‘Not at all. I wouldn’t.’

‘Wouldn’t what?’ Katey looked serious. ‘He’s all right looking and he’s single.’

‘Yes, I know he’s single, but he’s not really my type,’ said Marta.

‘What’s your type then?’

‘I don’t know. Are you being protective of your dad? It’s really sweet but you can relax. He and I are just friends.’

‘That’s good.’

‘You don’t want him to see anyone?’

‘No, I do. What I mean is I’m glad you’re his friend at least. He doesn’t have any.’

‘Not one single friend?’

‘He ditched everyone after Mum. He went, I don’t know, weird and reclusive. Doesn’t talk to anyone. Just plays music and gets on my case.’

‘I get it. You want him to have a girlfriend or some friends so he can leave you alone.’

‘Exactly. I mean, Dad is cool and everything, but all he does is sit and worry. He never says anything to me unless it's to tell me I can't do things because he's worried something will happen to me.'

Marta looked out of the window. Even knowing Elliot wouldn't be back, the last thing she wanted was to have him walk in and find them discussing him. 'I can understand a parent worrying about their child.'

'You have children?'

Marta shook her head. 'I think you're lucky to have someone as caring as him.'

'What about you? Do you have anyone?'

Marta smiled. 'I met someone just a week ago.'

'Nice.' Katey walked around to Marta's side of the counter. 'You know you're blushing like anything. They must be pretty special.'

Marta remembered that Louise had said she didn't want anything heavy and neither had they exchanged telephone numbers. She wondered how special it could be when the next time they would see each other was at the Pilates class next Tuesday. Louise hadn't even said, I'll see you there.

'And you?' Marta switched the focus. 'Anyone in your life?'

Here, Katey put her head down. She began running her finger along the edge of the glass counter, leaning one elbow on the glass and looking in at the guitar string packets.

'It's okay,' Marta said. 'You don't have to tell me.'

'Well, I did ask you so it's only fair. There is a boy I like. At school. But he's right quiet, and I don't know if he even likes me.'

'And he doesn't have a girlfriend?' Marta turned fully on the stool to face Katey. She couldn't believe how different Katey was being. Open and friendly. Maybe she wasn't a sullen teenager after all.

'I don't think so,' Katey said. 'Someone would know if he had a girlfriend or not. One of my friends would have found out and told me.'

'So they all know you like him?'

‘Only three of them know. My best friends. But they won’t say anything.’

‘Well, don’t you think somebody should? If you like him and he doesn’t know then you’ll never know if he likes you. You could, maybe, just tell him?’

Katey shifted weight, stood up straight. ‘Ah no, that’s mad. I can’t just come out with it. What if he hates me and turns me down? In front of everyone. You don’t know what it’s like in that school. Everyone will be talking about it. I’d literally be mortified. I’d have to kill myself.’

They both laughed.

‘Well, don’t kill yourself over him.’ Marta stood and stretched, realising she’d been sitting on the stool for over an hour, thinking back on her night with Louise before Katey came to the shop. She’d contemplated calling her new friend, Ione, to talk to her about it. ‘It’s not easy being young. So many things to think about. So much happens, and you’re never sure how to handle it.’

‘So did you have it hard when you were young?’

Marta turned to look at the counter and then fussed over the position of the stool. She didn’t want to give anything away in her face. Her face had an awful habit of speaking volumes, and her younger days were not something she could talk about. Especially not with Katey who was too young to understand. Not wanting to belittle her problems with boys, Marta suspected that Katey would not have and may never have to face some of the decisions she’d had to make. A life of regrets was something she hoped Katey would be spared.

‘I grew up differently,’ Marta said, moving the viola hanging in the window so that it swayed uncertainly from side to side. She held it still and turned to face Katey. ‘I had very strict, religious parents. I couldn’t do anything, and I wasn’t allowed to put a foot wrong.’

‘They didn’t lock you up or anything mad like that?’

'No, but I might as well have been locked up. The only opinion that counted was my father's, and my mum walked around all day, when we were little, telling us not to bother him. He didn't play with us. They had two children, both girls, and I don't think my father ever understood us. He just wanted us to read a lot, pray a lot and get married. That's all we needed to do in our lives so he could be happy.'

'Is that why you came to England?'

'In a way, yes. But it's complicated. I just think that even if your dad is a worrier, at least he worries and he cares about your happiness. He lets you be your own person. You might not think it, Katey, but compared to lots of girls, you're very lucky.'

'I'm not sure I'd call myself lucky.'

Marta slapped her hand to her mouth. 'Oh God, Katey, I'm sorry. I wasn't thinking. I almost forgot about…'

'It's okay. And it's okay to talk about Mum. I wish Dad would sometimes. Or just talk to me. We only seem to argue and upset each other.'

'It must be hard for both of you. But I'm sure he tries his best. At least he must understand you better than my parents understood us.'

'Hmm, you'd think. I mean, Dad's not a religious nut. No offence. But he didn't know what to do with me after Mum died. Do you think it would've been better if I was a boy?'

'I doubt it would make a difference to Elliot. The only thing I can see is that he loves you a lot. He might not show it but I think he wants you to be happy. You're happy, right?'

'I suppose? I mean, I miss my mum and all that but I keep telling Dad life goes on, right?'

'You're very well adjusted for your age. Maybe talking to this boy at school might be easier than you think. That's if you think he's worth it.'

'What would I even say? We don't do any lessons together. He's arty and I'm a maths nerd.'

‘I was a maths nerd. So that’s a good start.’ They both laughed. ‘Can’t you do something arty and get his attention that way?’

‘He likes music. He plays guitar, like Dad.’

‘Why don’t you learn guitar. Your dad could teach you, or you could ask this boy to teach you.’ Marta nudged Katey’s arm. ‘Does he know your father has a music shop? Maybe you could talk about that.’

‘No way. Then he’ll think I’m trying to sell him a guitar. Plus, I don’t want Dad meeting him here and giving him grief.’

‘I know!’ Marta skipped over to Ione’s postcard pinned to the noticeboard. ‘I know this lady. She teaches piano. If you learn something musical, then maybe you’ll find a way to get into his circle.’

‘Dad’s always going on about me learning an instrument. And this guy is in a band at school. I could find a reason to hang out with some of them. My friend, Parminder, does clarinet and she talks to him. Or maybe I could just get in with Parm a bit more and she could introduce me.’

‘Or…’ Marta said, coming back to the counter with Ione’s card. ‘Kill two birds with one stone. Is that what they say? If you learn an instrument, you make your dad happy and give yourself something to talk about with Music Boy.’

‘Music Boy.’ Katey rolled her eyes. She reached for the card. ‘Cute,’ she said, getting out her phone and noting down Ione’s number. ‘And she’s safe, this Ione?’

‘Safe? You mean nice?’

‘Yes.’

‘Extremely safe.’

17

Elliot

'You know I can teach you piano, right?'

'Yeah, but isn't that like teaching someone you know how to drive a car? You both get angry and have a massive blow up?'

'Not necessarily. Anyway. You're probably right. Maybe you should ask someone else.'

'I know. I've already called her, and she sounds really nice. Ione.'

'So you booked a lesson and everything?'

'I already said I had.'

'But when is it?'

'Tuesday after school, and I can get off the bus early and walk. It's dead easy, and I can either come to the shop to do my homework or come straight home. You cool with that?'

'Maybe I should come and check her out and see where she lives and everything.'

'No, Dad. I'll be fine. I'll text you when I get to her door. I'll do that thing where she opens the door, I take her picture and tell her I'm sending it to at least fifty people who know my location and my Dad is chief of police.'

'I think that's only on American cop shows, Katey. But yes, text me, and text me when you're on your way home.'

Katey saluted as if she was in the Royal Marines, picked up her laptop and left the kitchen.

Elliot was cooking. Something quick because he was late back from dropping off a guitar repair at a recording studio of a friend. He'd lingered at the studio, chatting to his old friend, Sylvester, whom he'd known from his days as a performer. Sylvester had called him out of the blue about the work he'd needed on his guitar. They'd talked about the old days, mostly about Val and what a talented musician she was. Elliot had always wondered how far Val's career could have taken her had she not been diagnosed with cancer that first time.

To say that time in their lives was difficult was an understatement. Being back in London was like starting all over again. Radiotherapy went well, Val was given a clean bill of health, but there was no orchestra work for her in London. Elliot wondered if the decision to leave Birmingham after her diagnosis had been a rash one. But Val had insisted she wanted to be near Elliot's mother, Corinthia. He couldn't understand how his wife managed to stay so positive and upbeat in those years of constant struggle to survive, not only the cancer but to keep a roof over their heads. He was always worried and wondering how long it would be before the house was repossessed.

When Katey was born, Elliot had a fierce love for that small bundle cradled on her mother's chest. Within seconds of her life, Elliot felt his love for Val grow tenfold. She had done that, she had delivered this joy into their lives. After the hours of intense pain she'd gone through that day, the cries of desperation and the look in her eyes when she thought she couldn't go on, Elliot had marvelled at Val's strength, how she'd finally delivered this beautiful, healthy, baby girl.

'All women can do this,' Val had said to Elliot. 'I'm not superwoman or anything. I'm just me.'

To Elliot, Val had always been more than that.

Then, one day, Val was gone, and every morning, Elliot woke up and looked at the empty space beside him on the bed. The only time they had slept apart was when Val was in hospital. When she had Katey, the first time she had cancer and then again when it came back. He couldn't accept that the last place Val slept was the place she had suffered, finally closing her eyes until the pain could release its claim on her body. How he'd wished he could have fought with that cancer. A physical battle for which he could summon the fortitude that Val had for bearing pain. Given the chance, he knew he'd win.

Every morning in the first year of Val's death, Elliot cried. He wept quietly in his room so that Katey wouldn't hear him. Just looking at his daughter made him want to weep, for her, for him, for them both. Any conversation about Val could cause him to cry aloud, so he'd avoid talking about Val to Katey until, little by little, he was scarcely talking to her at all. He wept on the inside when, in trying to be strong for Katey, he would sit on the side of her bed as she cried herself to sleep every night. He handed her tissues, he brought her water, rubbed her back, held her, he told her she didn't have to go to school if she didn't want to. But he never opened up to her, never knew what to say. Always too afraid to show weakness. He had to be strong.

In the second year, he stopped instinctively reaching across the bed, hoping to find Val there. A warm, soft shape beside him. Her wayward curls having unleashed themselves from the binds of her silk headscarf, looping and waving around her pillow like a wild flame. Talking to Katey was still hard. Meeting her eyes, almond brown and alive, exactly like Val's, and the memories of the three of them together would overwhelm him so much he would often just leave the room. He could tell his daughter was pulling away, but he was doing the pushing, refusing to talk about Val, something he still found unbearable, even after two years. The tears were always on the brink of spilling, and the need to wail until his lungs exploded was very much still there.

Katey grew into an amazing young woman, despite him, he always thought. Was it his wife's strength that forged this girl? She coped so much better than he had, and in the third year of Val's death, he had to learn to be more like Katey. She was on top of her studies with predictions of all A grades in her A levels. She had friends. She had a full and captivating smile that he only saw if he looked at her Instagram pictures. There she was, smiling, grasping life with both hands just the way Val always did. He was failing Katey, he knew that. He was failing Val, not adhering to one of her dying requests: *Be there for our daughter, she'll need you.*

Katey was already doing things for herself, booking the piano lessons without consulting him, arranging homework evenings and evenings out with her friends. She cooked occasionally, never had to be told to clean up after herself. She asked nothing of him.

His daughter had become a fully functioning person, on her own. It was only in recent months that Elliot gathered the ability to start functioning as a whole person. He'd vowed not to carry on the way he had. The need to cry or to be angry was no longer there. He could taste, feel and think for a whole day at a time without wallowing in a sad, lonely or bitter thought. He knew he was healing, knew he was coping now and, though it felt like a betrayal to Val's memory, he knew that his complete recovery was what would serve him and Katey the best. This one act of Katey's, to book a piano lesson of her own accord, sparked something in Elliot, and he felt awake and ready to claim his place in the real world. It was a world without Val, and he had come to accept that.

Only recently he'd admitted to himself that he found Marta attractive. He'd wanted to kiss her that night and went away acknowledging that he could make room in his life for a lover. It had been a while since he'd fantasised about making love with Val. He wondered if it was possible, after having loved Val so completely, whether he could fall in love again. To love and to have it reciprocated. It happened to other people.

'Katey wants me to find a girlfriend. It's been over three years. I get the feeling she was wondering what I was waiting for.'

'So she's given you permission, then?'

'I suppose, but how am I supposed to meet anyone? At my age, how do you do it?'

'Dating apps?'

'No way. I'm not getting into that.'

'Well, don't be surprised if Katey isn't setting it up for you. My kids got my ex on Tinder.'

'Shit, really? I thought that was for people who just want to get laid.' Elliot had tried not to laugh aloud.

'It *is*! Man, I was vex when she told me she was seeing someone. A younger bloke and all. Big muscles, big car and probably a big piece. She looks well happy.'

Elliot looked down, didn't want his friend to see him smile.

All the way home, he'd reflected on the idea of meeting someone, how hard it would be and how, as Katey had intimated, it was time. When he'd kissed Marta, the touch of a woman's lips on his, other than Val's, was not unthinkable, not any more.

Upstairs, Katey's music shot up in volume. Her timing was such that she wouldn't hear him call up the stairs when dinner was ready: he'd have to go upstairs, knock on her door and then wait until she'd acknowledged him above the music.

He made a stew of minced lamb, courgettes, onion and carrots. He poured it onto jacket potatoes and headed up the stairs.

He knocked on Katey's bedroom door.

'Katey?'

She pulled the door open almost immediately, flashed him a smile that shone through her almond brown eyes.

'Yep?'

'Katey … Katey, I…' He reached out, put his arms around her and fiercely hugged his daughter. He held her head against his chest, lowered his chin towards her thick hair and cried. He cried so that his body shook, he cried until he was unable to breathe.

Katey clung tight to her father and said, ‘It’s all right, Dad. We’re going to be all right. I understand.’

‘I’m sorry,’ he said when the tears finally subsided.

‘What for? I’m not.’

‘I want to be here for you,’ he said with a sniff.

‘You are, Dad. It’s all right. Really.’

He softly released Katey, wiped his nose with the back of his hand, then used a sleeve to dry his eyes.‘We’re okay, aren’t we?’ he asked, his voice shaking. ‘Me and you?’

‘You don’t even have to ask. We miss her. We always will, but it’s you and me now, Dad.’ Her lips trembled, but she pinched them closed.

‘I just want you to be happy. I don’t mean to get on your case and stuff. I think we just need to be happy, right? For a change. I’ll do my best.’

‘I know. Like I say, it’s all good. Don’t worry so much.’

‘So, okay,’ he said. ‘Turn off the music. Dinner’s ready. And it’s probably cold.’

‘I don’t mind. Just give me a sec and I’ll be down.’

A wide smile danced on his face as he walked back down the stairs to the kitchen. He hadn’t smiled so brightly in a long while. Katey made him smile. Whatever happened next, he had to stop missing out on these moments. It was time for him to start living again.

18

Louise

Her bag was buzzing as she got off the bus. Louise had caught an early lecture and was on her way home to grab some lunch before her shift at Charlie's house. She was tired, working flat out to complete an assignment and not coming up for air. The course work was more intense than she'd expected, and trying to research the case file she was working on was also very stressful. Louise's financial situation and the mountains of study made her stressed and short-tempered. She tutted and rolled her eyes when she got jostled in the tube station. Her shoulders seemed always to be drawn up to her ears. Even when she was supposed to be relaxing, she sensed it happening, the feeling of hunching forward, shoulders up and stiff. Sometimes she'd observe it, shrug and try to relax her body, breathing mindfully to calm her nervous system. It was no good, of course, it would only start again. It was the same when Louise worked as a nurse. Years of long hours on the wards doing back-breaking work that became less and less like a vocation and more soul destroying every day. Louise wondered about how unbearable she must have been when she lived with Danika. She hadn't meant to be so intense and uptight: work had made her that way. She took what she did seriously. At times, she wondered why it was so hard for Danika to understand the way she dealt with stress. Louise was trying to lighten up; Danika could have had more patience. She'd been patient with Danika who had not been out to her parents for the whole of their relationship. Once she'd broken up with Louise, Danika posted about her struggle with sexuality on Facebook, along with a picture of her with her new girlfriend, a Latin American beauty with fierce blue eyes. The two of them looked so happy. Louise had unfriended her ex immediately. Stupid to think they could stay friends. Stupid to keep letting the way Danika treated her affect her even now.

Finally, Louise stopped to pull her phone from her bag when it started buzzing for a second time. The caller was Cathie, the manager at the carer's agency.

'Thank goodness you picked up, Louise. I'm desperate.'

'What's up?' Louise was a few streets from home, her stomach was growling and she was in no mood for an emergency situation.

'You're going to see Mr Manolis today, aren't you?'

Louise stopped abruptly. 'Has something happened to Charlie?'

'No, he's fine, as far as I'm aware. I just don't have enough carers on today, and I wondered if you could stay on longer for him. Do dinner and then someone will be along to help you get him ready for bed? Once that's done, you can go.'

'Oh.' Her sigh was one of relief mixed with frustration. Relief that Charlie was okay but she was frustrated because she had Pilates tonight. It was the one time in the week that she allowed herself to stop thinking about work, about living in a poky room and constantly playing catch-up with the long reading list for her course.

'Please Lou. I'm desperate. I mean, I'd go myself, but my son is ill and I've got to go and pick him up from school.'

'Am I the first one you called?'

'No. I know you're strict about the shifts. The problem is all the carers with kids are off. Back to school bugs and stuff. Every year it's the same. I'm so, so sorry to ask.'

‘Okay, I’ll do it.’ Maybe she’d get to the Pilates class before it finished. She’d slot in the back of the hall and try not to disturb anyone. ‘And don’t call me Lou. I hate that.’

‘I’m so sorry, but thank you. Thank you so much, Louise.’

‘Yeah, whatever.’ Louise hung up. She was close to home. She slowed down and remembered she should have stopped for milk. A sandwich and some black coffee, that’s all she’d have before heading over to Charlie’s. Maybe he would sleep and she could catch-up on some reading.

When Louise arrived at Charlie’s house, she wondered if his grandson, Nico, would pay a visit. He’d dropped by often since his first visit and had brought his guitar because Louise had told him Charlie loved music. They had witnessed the huge grins that grew on Charlie’s face when Nico played. Louise had tried to get Charlie to clap. She held his hands, pulled them together but he allowed them to drop to his lap.

‘I know he likes singers,’ Louise said on one of Nico’s visits. ‘Don’t happen to sing as well, do you?’

‘No, no, no, no.’ Nico had blushed furiously.

‘I know he likes that song, *Midnight Train to Georgia*. It’s by Gladys Knight, but you probably haven’t heard of her.’

He’d shaken his head, creasing his lips into a shape that said, ‘Beats me.’

‘Anyway, Charlie says they’ll play it at his funeral. I assumed he meant one of his daughters would arrange it for the ceremony?’

Nico shrugged. ‘First I’ve heard of it. I doubt they’d go to the trouble if it’s for Granddad. No one seems to care, really.’

Charlie hadn’t been very responsive during Louise’s visit, but she settled down in the chair beside his bed in the downstairs bedroom so she could read to him. Just then, Nico came to the door.

‘Hey dude,’ she said as she let him in. ‘I see you brought the guitar.’

‘Yes, and I learned that song, *Midnight Train*. It’s sick, actually. A simple one but some nice chords.’ Louise led him into the bedroom where Charlie sat looking wistful. ‘I learned it off YouTube.’

‘Charlie?’ Louise leaned over his bed. ‘Nico’s here. He’s got a surprise for you. Go ahead and play. I’ll go and do some reading of my own for a bit before I do his dinner. That okay?’

Nico nodded and Louise went to the living room to pull some books out of her bag. She had only just found the chapter of the book she wanted when Nico rushed in, flushed, a look of panic on his face.

‘I don’t know what’s wrong. I was just tuning up and—’

Louise jumped to her feet. ‘Show me.’

Nico ran behind her along the hall. ‘Next thing I knew, he was slumped over, and I don’t think he’s breathing.’

‘Charlie? Charlie? If you can hear me, squeeze my hand. Charlie?’ Louise felt for a pulse. There was one, faint but present. ‘Nico, call an ambulance. I think your granddad has had a stroke and we need to get him to the hospital. Quick! Now!’

‘Y-yes.’ Nico dialled on his mobile. He gave details to the ambulance crew, Louise prompting him, all the time trying to rouse Charlie.

‘Tell them he’s unresponsive,’ Louise told Nico.

‘They’re on their way, they said.’

‘Okay, good. We need to call your family next. Can you call your mum?’

Nico nodded and dialled her number. ‘Voicemail.’

‘Call your aunties. All of them are down as emergency contacts.’

‘Okay.’ He looked at the list of contacts before dialling. ‘Mum is going to kill me. I’m not supposed to be here.’

‘It’s okay, Nico. You could always go. I can stay with Charlie until the ambulance comes.’

'You kidding? I'm not going anywhere. Besides, once I tell one aunty, it's as good as calling Mum direct. Hello? Theia Crystal…' he continued the call in the hallway.

Louise had several duties to perform in these circumstances. One of them included handing over her client's care to the ambulance staff but, as she held Charlie's hand, felt it limp and frail in her own, she knew she would not leave his side. She looked up to see Nico returning to the room.

'No one can come,' he said shaking his head. 'I said I'm going to the hospital with him, and I have to call them later to let them know if he has to stay in.'

Louise rolled her eyes, catching herself immediately for reacting emotionally in front of Nico.

'I know,' Nico said. 'It's lame of them, but at least I'll be there.'

'I'm coming, too, Nico. They'll probably take him to my old hospital. I know most of the A and E staff. They're good, so don't worry.'

'I'm okay. They're here.'

'Okay, get the door and I'll grab some stuff for Charlie.'

Louise looked around frantically for a suitcase. In the bottom of the wardrobe upstairs, she found a holdall. She quickly packed a clean pair of pyjamas, a dressing gown, some underwear, slippers and toiletries. After she gave details to the ambulance team, they hurriedly placed Charlie on a stretcher, covered him in a pale blue blanket and headed for the front door.

'We're both coming,' she told the staff. 'He's family and I'm his carer.'

In the back of the ambulance, Louise looked at the way Charlie's face sagged to one side, how the arm that had feebly fallen to his side had been held fast by a belt around his middle. She knew what this could mean. Paralysis. Loss of speech. Maybe worse, depending on how massive the bleed had been. She found her lips moving, saying a silent prayer for Charlie. Let the stroke be a mild one, let him come through this, let us dance to *Midnight Train to Georgia* tomorrow afternoon. Inside, she knew that any form of stroke for someone in Charlie's condition could have serious knock-on effects to his health. If he wasn't suffering enough, he'd be up against it after this.

She tried to hide the worry on her face, fixing a soft smile on her lips when she noticed Nico glancing at her from time to time. She winked at him.

'Here we are.' The female EMT attending to Charlie readied him as the driver pulled open the door. The sky, having swallowed up the remaining beams of autumn light, was a dull grey, and it had become cold. Louise realised she'd left her bag and her jacket behind in her rush to help Charlie.

'Stick with me, Nico,' she said. 'We need to stay out of their way, but we'll follow them. Don't worry. Your granddad is in the right place now.'

19

Marta

What was the right word to describe how she was feeling? Anxious. Nervous. Excited. Worried. Perhaps a combination of all those things. The joy Marta had felt after waking to the sound of Louise breathing; feeling the warm breaths on her naked torso was disarming. It was as if a new world had opened up to her. The possibility of a future that could somehow erase the past was in sight. Of course not every aspect of her past needed to be eliminated, only the ones that caused her sleepless nights. The ones that crept into her day when she was least expecting it, reminding her that she'd done something wrong, that she'd broken someone's heart, that she'd lied and thought only of herself.

On those days, she dressed her brightest, smiled her widest and was the most kind she could be to anyone she encountered.

Marta considered her current circumstances: she had settled into her new flat, found a job with people she liked, she'd made a friend in Ione and she'd met Louise. Maybe that was the universe's way of telling her that she could stop trying so hard, that she was forgiven everything. The time to fall in love and live the life she dreamed of was within reach. If she had been forgiven, then she would no longer have to see herself as a terrible human being. There would be no need to bring up the past and what she'd done. Neither Elliot nor Ione had to know. If she was forgiven, she could move on with her life and they would only have to know about the

Marta they knew now, not the former Marta. She allowed herself to imagine that she could have a future with Louise.

How wonderful to be able to move on, for no one to find out she was a fraud. A person who smiled on the outside, was kind, generous but who covered up the fact that really she was not such a nice person after all.

She shook the negative feelings away long enough to make a deal with herself. Tonight would be a test. A sign that her sins could be forgiven. If Louise was at the class, Marta would know that she did deserve happiness. No more pretending to be the happy, smiling, flamboyant version of herself. She did use to smile, once. She had been a good person, once. Years ago when she was an innocent girl, she was good, did her best to please.

A buzz from her phone disturbed her imaginings. Her first thought was that Louise was calling, but they had not exchanged numbers. It was a text from Ione.

Running late but I will be there. I x

Marta had bought a yoga mat. A present to herself from the sports shop near Shepherd's Bush Station. Louise had not been the only draw to the Pilates class. Marta did enjoy it. It was a safe space in which to lose herself. Yes, there was physical effort involved but she felt a sense of belonging among the group, mostly women, a camaraderie she had never had before.

That evening as she left for the class with her new mat, a bitter wind whipped at her face. A wintry sort of wind. Next would come the long dark nights, the chilly mornings, condensation on the windows. Then Christmas, bringing memories of Poland and family, making the nights longer still, the freezing mornings darker.

She was the first to arrive for the class. She held up her mat to the teacher, Callie. 'Look, I'm investing in my new healthy future.'

'Good for you.' Callie was busy setting the volume on the PA system for an atmospheric piece of music playing on her phone. There was the sound of rain in the track. Marta lay down on her mat, listening to her breathing and to the raindrops, keeping one eye on the door as she looked out for Ione and Louise.

The class began five minutes late. Ione arrived, but there was no Louise. About twenty minutes into the class, the door opened. Someone was unbuttoning a coat with slow fingers, drawing breaths that were loud and panting as if they'd had to run all the way to the class. Marta heard how the person took off their shoes, tiptoed to a space at the back of the hall and began to roll out their mat. Callie continued to instruct, but the person's mat hit the floor with a thud, most likely having slipped from their hands. Marta's heart rate went up. She had her eyes closed and was imagining Louise's smile of white teeth and soft lips, her closely cut afro hair that she twisted into little bumps all over her head. The first time she'd seen Louise, there were tiny beads woven into her hair. Marta remembered the scent of oils in Louise's hair and the cocoa butter on her skin. She inhaled it now, smiling as she did and remembering her first night with a female lover. How different it had been. How unlike the men she'd slept with. Her husband, Tomasz, had been a gentle lover, one she trusted with her body while her mind was elsewhere. Tomasz never made her body rise to his touch or come to life with his kisses, not the way Louise had.

She grew impatient for the class to end. She could no longer wait to find out if Louise had yearned for her for an entire week. Had Louise seen her face every time she blinked, every time she sighed and closed her eyes? All week, every time Marta caught her reflection, she found she was smiling.

At the end of the class, Marta opened her eyes and sat up. She spotted Ione a few mats away from her. They waved to each other. Slowly, Marta, her cheeks warm, looked to the back of the hall. She did a double take. There was no Louise.

The person who came in late was still lying on her back, arms at her sides, feet splayed. Where was Louise?

Marta had her sign. She was not deserving of any real happiness. Louise would not have missed the class. It wasn't by accident they'd not exchanged numbers. Louise shied away from the idea of a call. Marta remembered that now. Louise had gone on about being busy, and it was a hasty exit she'd made the following morning. It was clear. She had not been forgiven her past. And why should she?

For weeks, Marta had taken money from her and Tomasz's joint account. She'd stolen the money they were saving to buy a flat of their own. She did it systematically. She smiled at him every day, made love to him at night, ate all her meals with him and slept on the bed with the concealed envelope of cash between the mattress and the bed frame. The time for her escape came after she'd been in contact with her sister who said yes to Marta coming to London for a visit. Marta had begged her sister not to say anything to their parents. Asked her to swear on their mother's life. She'd convinced her sister, Agnieszka, that Tomasz was bad, that they were having problems and that she needed breathing space.

At the airport, she'd carried a small suitcase. She'd packed it when Tomasz went to work, telling him she was too sick to go in and was taking the day off. It was easy to feign sickness: her eyes were puffy from lack of sleep and her face was pale. He didn't know Marta was six weeks pregnant and neither did her sister.

Marta arrived in London and, for two months, said nothing about her marriage to her sister. Never spoke about anything and forced her sister to lie about her whereabouts when their mother called in anguish after Tomasz reported her gone. Marta's brother-in-law was furious with his wife for lying, and all they did was argue. Eventually, Agnieszka was forced to tell her mother and Tomasz about Marta. But by then, Marta had run away again. This time she told no one, and no one knew about the baby she carried or where in the world she could be. She had left Katowice, and then her sister's house, without a trace.

'You all right?' Ione asked as she knelt beside Marta, her mat already rolled up. 'Are you still spaced out from the relaxation?'

'Probably.' She smiled at Ione, hoping she looked genuine enough. 'Did you enjoy it?'

Ione nodded. 'I did. And guess what?'

'What?' Marta tried to broaden her smile.

'I had my first piano lesson. A school girl, but she called and pushed the time a bit later for some reason so that's why I was running late.'

Marta got up, still looking around the hall. It was thinning out now. There was a chance that somehow she had missed Louise, but that would mean she'd rushed off and not wanted to talk to her.

'Your first piano lesson,' said Marta, turning to her friend with a smile. 'That's amazing. How did it go?'

'Well. It's actually nice teaching complete beginners. Are we going for a drink?' Ione looked around.

'She's not here,' Marta told her.

'Oh,' said Ione. 'I am sorry. Did you hear from her in the week?'

Marta shook her head. 'It's all right. That's just how it is. Let's get that drink. Look, I bought myself a new mat.'

'Nice.'

They left for The Plough. They chatted all night. There were a few more people in the bar than usual, making the place more animated, but Marta's mind had wandered far into the distance. She chastised herself for having been so hopeful. She tried all she could to stay focused, to be a good friend to Ione, but all she could think about was losing everything in her life, including Louise.

20

Charlie

Charlie woke up in a strange bed in a room he didn't recognise. The window was open. White net curtains blew inwards like fine mesh wings that settled when the wind died down. The smell of the ocean floated in from outside, as did the cry of gulls. They soared high above the building he was in and then off into the distance. It was slightly chilly in the room though the sun's rays pierced the white clouds. The clouds moved across the sky at speed. He saw them race away every time the net curtains swooped open.

Charlie tried to roll over, but one side of his body wasn't co-operating. It felt dull, almost lost to him. He rubbed his shoulder and tried to massage life into a limb that lay idly at his side.

He heard music playing. He couldn't tell if it was coming from outside or from another room. Looking around, he knew he wasn't in his bedroom at home. The white walls looked severe, clinical almost. On the wall opposite him was a large unframed photograph. It was a picture of the sea. A black and white still in which the sea was rough, and he wondered if this was the beach he could hear in the distance, the place the gulls were flying to. In those first seconds of wakefulness, he couldn't understand why there were gulls flying over his house or remember when he and his family had moved to the coast.

'Good morning, sleepyhead.' At last, something familiar. A female voice. 'Finally decided to join us?'

'Brenda.'

'Yes, baby, it's me. Boy, you really went for the whiskey in a hard way last night. I had to carry you up here.'

'Where's here?'

'Damn it, Charlie. Were you really that drunk? Maybe you still are. I bet if they tested your blood, it would be one hundred proof. Yep, there'll be whiskey in those veins and lots of it.'

She sat beside him on the bed. The white towelling bathrobe she was wearing gaped, and he caught a glimpse of her naked body. Charlie's arm was laid out beside him, and she playfully slapped the veins on the inside of his arm. He felt her hand. His arm had come back to life.

'Are you going to get up today?' Brenda asked. 'It's not raining, so we can walk along the promenade. Would you like that?'

Charlie nodded.

'Then, good. Get up. I'm not carrying you around all day if you're still drunk. You promised me a nice meal, but you got drunk at the pub, and all I had was a bag of crisps. Can you tell I'm dying of starvation? And don't tell me you're too hungover to eat breakfast because I need to eat.'

Brenda stood. She hovered over Charlie and kissed his lips.

'Oh my God. You smell like the whole damned distillery.'

As she tried to walk away, Charlie pulled her back by her wrist. 'Wait. I'm sorry, Bren. Give me two minutes and I'll buy you breakfast.'

'Damned right you will.'

She pulled away, wrapped the bathrobe more tightly around her and disappeared through the door from which she'd emerged.

Charlie heard her singing. It was the music he'd heard on waking. Brenda's voice was like an orchestra.

The evening before, he'd held her hands across the small table in a pub near the sea. They drank champagne from a wine glass. It was tart and bodiless. Charlie sent it back and asked for their finest whiskey.

'I really think they're having a laugh with that so-called champagne,' he'd said to Brenda. They'd had reservations for a Greek restaurant Charlie knew. When Brenda was dressed in her tight red dress, her hair smoothed straight and her lipstick just so, they'd left the expensive hotel, deciding on a quick drink before the meal. They were supposed to eat with his brother but, of course, they never made it to the restaurant. His brother, Costas, would have dined with his lady friend, Victoria. They were both staying in the same hotel as Charlie and Brenda, two floors down.

Costas had arranged this little trip. It was the only holiday Charlie and Brenda would ever have together. Charlie's wife, Ana, shooed him and Costas away when Costas described the amateur golf tournament in Kent that they were supposedly going to. Instead, Costas had left his wife at home alone, picked up his mistress, Victoria, and his younger brother and Brenda and driven them all to Brighton.

One night away, that was all it would be. Charlie said that while they were away, she could have anything she wanted.

'Anything?' she asked, moving coyly towards him across her Formica dining table.

'Yes. You name it.'

'In that case I name Charlie. Kàralos Manolis. I name you.' She touched her fingertip to his chin.

He had looked down at the table, blinking fiercely to abate the tears that fell so freely whenever the mention of their staying together forever came up.

Brenda laughed, merrily.

'Don't start worrying yourself into an early grave,' she said. 'I can wait. I know it'll happen one day. I believe in you, Charlie, and I know it isn't easy. But you know, your children are all grown up now.'

'They're still my children. They love me and they look up to me.'

'Lucky you.'

He stood abruptly. 'Brenda, don't do that. You know I love you. You know I want to be with you. But there are problems, financial, at the restaurant. I know we look like we're doing well but… I know you don't want to hear this, but I have to leave Ana with something.'

'But you're lying to her, Charlie. Are you lying to me, too? You said you would follow me anywhere I went. What if I left right now? Would you try to find me?'

'Don't leave me, Brenda.' He sat back down and took her slender hands in his. 'I love you so much. I have to do this right for everyone. Sometimes I feel like I'm drowning, losing my way. I thought the weekend would make you happy. We can do what you said. Hold hands in the street and not be afraid. You said that, right?'

She nodded.

'I promise you, Brenda, this trip to Brighton is the best I can do for now. We'll hold hands and walk in the street.'

'Like proper sweethearts.'

'Like proper sweethearts. Until one day, it will be true.'

'But for now, I have to pretend.'

He touched her cheek. 'Promise me you won't go anywhere. Promise you believe I will leave her. Just give me a little more time.'

Brenda nodded and then Charlie had to leave. Go back to the restaurant, back to his wife.

'Mr Manolis. Mr Manolis? Are you still sleeping?'

He tried to blink his eyes open, but they were heavy. He tried to smile at the voice above him, but he couldn't control his face.

'How was his night?' another voice asked.

'Good. It wasn't a severe stroke. With a little rehab, he'll be back home very soon. The paralysis is practically gone. He gripped my hand, and he did open his eyes earlier. We just have to get him to eat. We don't really want him on a drip. Would you like to feed him his lunch?'

'No, I have to get back to the family business. It won't run itself. Besides, my son, Nico, will be here after school. He represents the family. You update him, and he'll tell me what's going on with Dad.'

Charlie heard the sound of heels along the floor. They disappeared very quickly, and the sounds of the hospital ward filtered through to him. But the dream about a beautiful black woman holding his hand on a beach did not come back to him. Perhaps, on occasion, it might return, if Charlie was lucky.

21

Ione

Just saying it out loud to Jeannie made me feel like such an idiot. It's obviously hard for her to believe me, especially when I don't have any real evidence or any proof that I'm seeing anything at all. It's half term and Jeannie has come to London for the day. I'd asked if she was bringing the twins —I haven't seen my godchildren in a while—but she insisted we had a girls-only day. Oliver took a few days off work and planned to take the twins to the cinema and to have pizza. It seems like an eternity since I last saw Jeannie, but it's only been months, less than two actually. Not enough time for me to have completely lost my mind, but she's looking at me as if I have.

When she arrived that morning at my door from Manchester on the first train to Euston, I was so happy to see her. I'd had a bad night, my eyes had circles under them and my skin was blotchy. I had woken up every hour on the hour, believing I'd heard a noise in the garden or that someone was trying the front door. In the week before, I was convinced I'd caught glimpses of David. He'd be there, maybe close to the school gate, or he'd dart out of sight if I looked in his direction after spotting him out of the corner of my eye. Twice I thought I sensed him in the street, and when I looked back, I thought I saw a figure, a man built and dressed like my ex-husband, scuttling into a shop.

Her face darkens as she listens, and I wish I'd kept my mouth shut. The counsellor told me that recovery was not instantaneous and that only time will see me fully healed. Even when I might be at my best, doubt and insecurity would creep in. This is just the kind of negative talk I need to avoid, but being able to get it off my chest helps. I know these images of David are only in my imagination and Jeannie does her best to put my mind at ease.

'I'm not saying I don't believe you, Ione,' Jeannie says. 'But if you think about it, David isn't the type to stand on ceremony. If he was down here, looking for you, when he found you, he'd come up to you. Say something. He wouldn't skulk around in doorways and what have you. He'd be on your case, and you'd be straight on to the police.'

'What could they do?'

'You could get a restraining order. But look, hon, it won't come to that. He's not here. I can usually smell a rat, and I can't smell David, so you'll be fine.'

'I'm being silly, right?'

'Not silly, just letting your imagination get the better of you. Now, come on. You were going to show me around the delights of Shepherd's Bush.'

'It's not exactly delightful, but it is interesting. There's a nice-looking Caribbean restaurant I've been dying to try. I can buy you lunch.'

It's Monday, I'm hoping the restaurant is actually open. Our walk takes us past Val's Music Shop which is closed.

'Look,' I say to Jeannie, 'this is where I advertised my piano lessons and met Marta. This is where she works.'

Jeannie stops and she looks up at the sign. Inside, the lights are out, but there is a bright light coming from the back. My card is still there, in pride of place. I've had a few callers, but so far I've only got a school girl called Katey signed up for lessons.

'Who is that tall drink of water?' Jeannie says lasciviously.

'Where?' I look across the road to see if I can see who Jeannie is looking at. She was always pointing men out to me, always trying to fix me up with some guy or other.

'No not there, in here. Look. He's looking right at you.'

I stare into the music shop window, my hands above my eyes so that I can focus, and I see a tall black man staring straight out at me. He's closing the glass panel of the counter cabinet, a packet of guitar strings in his hand. I jerk away from the window, embarrassed, but Jeannie is signalling to him. The man looks confused but comes to the locked door.

'What time do you open?' Jeannie shouts through the window of the door. I shrink behind her. I know exactly what she's doing, and I can read as plainly as she can that the shop is closed on Mondays.

After a few farcical exchanges, Jeannie manages to get the poor man to unlock the door, which also means having to turn off the alarm before he can open it.

'Sorry, I was trying to say that we're not open again until tomorrow,' he says. He looks from Jeannie to me, apologetically.

'Oh,' Jeannie says as if she has only just taken command of the English language and had no idea how to read up until then. She points at the blatant sign. 'Got it. It's just that we saw you in there, and my friend is a musician and wanted to find out about tuning her piano.'

He looks at me, just briefly, before speaking, and I want the earth to swallow me whole. I will kill Jeannie, and I'll make her pay for lunch.

'I'm sorry, I don't actually tune pianos. More of a specialist in guitars but hold on…' He holds up a finger, disappears into the unlit premises and comes back with a flyer. On it in bold letters are three words: Professional Piano Tuning. Underneath a picture of a piano. He hands it to me, but our eyes don't meet.

'Thank you.' My voice is quiet. I stand awkwardly for a second, trying to edge Jeannie away, but she is stock still, grinning at this poor man and leaving him lost for words. 'I'll give them a call,' I say and look at Jeannie.

'And you'd recommend them?' Jeannie says in a loud and, for some reason, suddenly brash Manchester accent. She's stalling for time, and if I could drag her away without making more of a fool of myself, I would.

'I don't actually know them,' he says. 'But I know they're local. So, good luck.'

'Thanks.' Finally I can push Jeannie away. Even she doesn't have a come back for a statement that is very final. In fact, the shop owner is pushing the door closed. He smiles but I can see he's bemused.

As we walk away and get closer to the restaurant, I slap Jeannie's arm.

'What?' There is laughter in her voice. She doesn't regret barging in on the shop owner for one second. Jeannie never changes.

'You know what,' I say. 'You embarrassed the life out of that guy.'

'And you?' She laughs, playfully, but I shake my head.

'Yes, I was embarrassed,' I say. 'You have to stop doing things like that.'

'What?'

'Trying to sort my love life out.'

We reach the restaurant. The food smells divine from the outside. We're quickly seated.

'If you tried to sort your love life out yourself,' Jeannie says as she scans the menu on the table, 'then it would save me the trouble.' Jeannie's bull-in-a-china-shop approach has caused problems for me in the past.

Jeannie had been pushing for an invitation to my house for dinner, but David kept cancelling the arrangements. Once, he'd called from work saying he had to work late and made me postpone our dinner with Jeannie and Oliver on the actual day. I could have gone ahead without him, but the repercussions for disobeying him were unfathomable. Another time, David pretended to be sick and stood over me while I called Jeannie, an hour before they were due to arrive, to tell them that he was unwell, throwing up, had a high temperature. The next day at school, Jeannie barely looked at me. The evening I finally arranged a dinner that David didn't cancel, Jeannie came to understand why I'd cancelled on all the other occasions.

Jeannie chatted throughout the evening, Oliver looked embarrassed and David barely engaged with our guests. I'd sat, poker straight, in a dress that David had picked out. It was old and uncomfortable, and I looked as if I was going for an interview rather than having a casual evening in with friends. The dress had long sleeves: it covered up a bruise I had above my wrist. The ever-astute Jeannie spotted the purple-blue mark when I went to collect the plates after eating. She followed me out to the kitchen, carrying an empty serving dish.

'How'd you get that thing?' She leaned against the dishwasher, watching me in the same hawkish way David watched when I carried out any task: cooking, dressing, even the way I showered. He had to find fault in something. He had to find a way to tear me down, strip back any layers of self-confidence I had left and burn them to cinders along with my dignity.

'What thing?' I softened my voice to cue Jeannie to follow suit. She didn't. In a loud voice, she asked again.

'That thing, there. On your wrist. Looks like a blooming bruise or something.'

I immediately yanked at my sleeve, dragging it to my wrist as far as the fabric would give.

'It's a bruise,' I said softly. 'I just. I just hurt myself. Can you help me with the dessert?'

'Course I can, love, but first, you have to promise me something.'

I looked intently at her, then at the kitchen door, which she'd left wide open. I could hear Oliver telling David something about the children. He was laughing loudly; I prayed to God that David couldn't hear us in the kitchen.

'I don't know what you want from me,' I said, hurriedly taking a banoffee pie out of the fridge. 'Not sure I can promise anything.'

Jeannie walked straight up to me, pulled me to face her. 'If I ask you a question, will you promise to answer truthfully?'

I shrugged but nodded anyway, trying to underplay her intensity.

'If you're in trouble here, if you're ever in danger in this house, will you make sure you call me? I'll be here, with Oliver, and I'll get you out. Do you get me?'

I nodded. 'If it happens, then I will.'

'You will what?' David was at the kitchen door swinging an empty bottle of wine. He held it at the neck and swung it by his thigh, looking directly at Jeannie. 'What you girls plotting?'

'Nothing, David.' Jeannie picked up the pie and walked it into the living room. 'You coming?' This was directed at me.

'I-I'll get the bowls,' I said.

David barely moved to allow her space to leave the kitchen. With trembling hands, I sought out the pudding bowls. They clattered onto the counter top as I looked for a serving spoon. I pulled out a spatula, the first thing my nervous hand could find.

'What the hell are you doing with that?' He came to my side.

'My mistake. I need this.' I pulled a serving spoon off the hook.

'Enjoying yourself, love?' David was loud, the worse for drink. I left the kitchen quickly, calling back to him to bring another bottle of wine with him on his way back.

At the end of the evening, after Jeannie and Oliver left—something I foresaw happening because after two and a half years of marriage, I could read the signs—David grabbed for me. He squeezed my upper arms, pinching the skin so that it burned. I did all I could not to react, not to say a word because the wrong syllable made my punishment more severe, more drawn out.

'Don't ever embarrass me like that again.' His spit rested on my upper lip. Eyes bulging, the whites red with alcohol, he pushed me away. Hard. My back hit the table in the hallway. It rattled and I heard something topple over. 'You think I don't know when I should bring out wine for our guests? Am I some kind of imbecile? Is that how you see me?'

'No, of course not, David.'

Sometimes, if I said his name when he was angry, David's temper could rise to an immeasurable height. On those occasions, I didn't know if he would leave me alive or dead. That night, David would have killed me. As each blow and kick sent me stumbling and crawling from one room to another, I managed to pick up my mobile. David saw too much red to notice. He was unstoppable. When I finally managed to lock myself into the downstairs bathroom, I called Jeannie. She was there, followed by a police car, as quickly as she could.

The police took David away. It wasn't the first time. Neighbours had heard my screams, my pleads for David to stop, my begging him not to kill me. He'd been arrested before, but he was always released without charge.

I remember how I cried into Jeannie's shoulder while a police officer questioned me.

'For Christ's sake,' Jeannie bellowed. 'Won't you just let her have a good cry?'

Divorce proceedings followed. Jeannie wouldn't hear of me giving him another chance. Jeannie had made it her life's goal to ensure my future happiness. She never left my side while papers were signed, when estate agents priced up the house. She was there, every day, online with me trying to find a new job. I had a lot to be thankful for, but Jeannie wouldn't or couldn't understand that I'd rather not have a man in my life. Not for as long as I could help it. Probably never at all.

'Jeannie,' I say now. 'If I ask you a question, do you promise to answer truthfully?'

'Here we go,' she says. 'Of course I bloody don't. The truth isn't always easy. But the truth is, you need a man and you shouldn't deny yourself.'

'Truthfully, all I want is lunch and for you to back off. Can you promise me that?'

She raises her hands. 'Okay, I've backed off,' she says. 'But I can't promise I won't try again. Ione, you deserve to know what a good relationship feels like. Now, what you eating?'

I shake my head. Jeannie is stubborn. I can only thank goodness that she isn't living around the corner from me as I'm sure she'd drag the guy from the music shop to my door and command him to ask me out. At least while she's in Manchester, I'm safe from the matchmaking.

I think about the music shop. That strange vibe I got from it the time I first dropped in, a feeling that something was drawing me in, it was there again today. I won't breathe a word of this to Jeannie.

22

Ione

'Whatever you do, make sure you live your best life.'

One of the many things Mum said to me in those last days was just that. I think about those days. I never left Mum's side. She never ate. Nothing passed her lips for a week, and all I had were cups of tea. I had no appetite. How could I? Mum would say to me, 'Ione, my darling, did you eat something today?' And I always said, 'Yes, Mum. Of course. You know me.' But that was just it. She did know me; she knew I was lying.

I remember her lying in bed. The bedspread with the red and yellow roses. The pillows propped her up, but she still looked like a pencilled drawing against them. There was nothing of her. Her eye sockets were hollow, her ebony coloured eyes watered down and misty. Her cheeks protruded. Her skin soft as silk, delicate as puffs of dandelion seeds floating in the air. The woman who'd raised me on her own, had held my hands and danced me around in the kitchen while a chocolate cake baked in the oven, who'd picked me up from school with a smile and sang to me all the way home, was saying her goodbyes.

I remember how angry I was. Not only at Mum because she was leaving me but because I'd wanted so much for her. The only thing going round in my mind as I held her hand, staying awake until my eyes watered and my shoulders ached, was the injustice of it all.

Here was a warm, vibrant and loving woman who only ever had me as company in her life, and I didn't feel as if I'd been enough. She devoted her time and gave all of her love to me. I had so wanted Mum to meet a good man, to fall in love and be happy. I felt like a traitor for going off to university when I did. Mum spent all those nights alone. When she was younger, that had never been the case. She was the life of the party, free-spirited, she loved company and knew how to enjoy life to the fullest. I worried about her more than I thought of myself.

Mum laughed at me. Told me I was nothing but an old lady, fussing and carrying on. She was just fine. She never tried to find another love after Charlie, and I never thought that was fair. He had his family, and Mum only had me. The hardest story she ever had to tell me about those times was of the time just before she left London. Ran all the way to Manchester and never looked back.

They came, all of them, the wife and the three daughters, banging on her door until she had to let them in. She had been ironing a dress for the evening and left the hot iron on the collar before she went to the door. They were making such a noise on the outside landing, Mum was ashamed and didn't want the neighbours to hear what they were saying. They called her whore, they called her slut, bitch and *aràpis*. Years before, Mum once uttered that word under her breath before she fell asleep. Though she'd insisted she never knew a word of Greek, I'd remembered the word and repeated it until she'd said, 'Stop! You don't know what you're saying, and I don't want to hear that word.' Then she admitted that she and Charlie were together in the park once, and a Greek man had said it loud enough for them both to hear. Charlie told her it was the most derogative term anyone could call a black person and that he had never, and would never, use it. He'd slap the face of any person in his family that dared to use it, too.

Charlie's wife spat the word at her, like she was spraying venom when she and her daughters turned up at Mum's door. Mum had opened the door to four women. Two rather portly, two thin and stern, all raven-haired and dressed in expensive clothes.

'You think you can come into my family and try to break it up? You are nothing but a cheap whore. I know what you do. You dance in nightclubs, you swear and you smoke. You have all kinds of men in your house. Don't think because you wrap your legs around my husband that he will ever love you. I will personally make sure you lose this flat and that job you have in the dry-cleaners. I know these people, and they'll help me get rid of you.' And there was that word, used not once but twice. It pained Mum to tell me the truth about that day, but I'd pressed and pressed. I wanted to know what could be so awful she could give up the life she loved and run away. It was the part of her story I only ever asked about once. Once was enough, and I never asked about anything concerning my father again. I never pressed for anymore details no matter how many times I'd wondered if I could find him. Meet him. After hearing that, I'd been afraid of coming into contact with his daughters. They were my half-sisters, but I knew they'd never accept me.

Tears had inevitably fallen from Mum's eyes as she recounted the story. Her voice never broke, and she didn't try to dry her face. I did that for her. I took a tissue from its box and dabbed at her cheeks. I took another and another as I checked the flow of salty tears always ready to fall. We held hands. I told Mum I was sorry.

Mum said, 'I had the love of my life with me when I left. You were nothing but a tiny dot in my tummy, a secret I could never tell. But you were all mine. No one could take you from me, and no one could wreck your life so completely as that family tried to do to me.'

'And you never looked back? Charlie never knew about me?'

'Never, and that's just the way I wanted it. I only wanted you, my sweet Ione. That's all. Just you.'

Looking out onto a rainy Tuesday afternoon, I wonder if I've done right by Mum. I didn't live my best life while married to David, but I came to London for a second chance. I shouldn't spend it worrying if the shadows I see are David following me. It couldn't be him. I know this.

My phone rings and it's Marta. She's calling from the shop. I haven't told her I was there and had met who I assume was her boss. I probably never would, either—too embarrassing; she'd only laugh.

'How are you?' I ask.

'A bit confused, actually.'

'Is this about Louise? Are you wondering if you should come to Pilates tonight?'

'You're going, right?'

'Yes, I am. Please tell me you'll come.'

'I want to, but what if she's there?' Marta sounds anxious.

'Well, if she's there, then maybe she'll explain why she was a no-show last week.'

'She doesn't have to. She has a right not to show up.'

'True, but I'm sure there was a good reason.'

'I just keep thinking…'

'Tell me.'

'Well, why couldn't we have each other's numbers? Why did she make sure it never happened? Was she just testing me? Using me?'

'I don't think so. I saw you two together. It's like you were a long-term couple already. You looked made for each other. Didn't you get a good vibe?'

'I thought so.'

'Don't overthink it,' I say. It's the type of thing Jeannie would say to me. 'So, you are coming tonight. You'll turn up with your yoga mat, smile and enjoy it. You'll see, there'll be a perfectly good explanation for her not showing up. And when you hear it, you'll kick yourself for stressing so much.'

'And what if she pretends I'm not there?'

'So what? There are plenty more lesbian fish in the sea.'

'Okay, thank you. I'll see you later, all right?'

'You will. Oh, my student is here now. She's just outside on her phone.'

'Oh, I forgot to tell you, the girl you're teaching is my boss's daughter, Katey.'

'Oh, right. I see.'

'Enjoy your lesson. See you later.'

23

Ione

Katey taps on the door. I let her in and see the resemblance between her and her father straight away. The biggest difference is their eyes. I do remember his eyes.

'So, you came back for more,' I say, smiling. I lead her to the living room where my black upright Steinway leans against the wall next to the patio doors. 'I didn't scare you off.'

'No,' Katey says as she peels off an oversized donkey jacket. 'It's funny, but my Mum and Dad are both musicians, and I was never interested in playing. Mum used to sit me on her knee and pluck at her harp strings. I wasn't big enough to play it, I just used to bash on the woodwork. When I was big enough, it didn't interest me. Dad tried me on piano and guitar but … nah. Just wasn't for me then.'

'So why now? What makes you want to learn piano?'

I see her cheeks grow rosy. She smiles and hesitates before answering.

'You really want to know?' she asks.

'I really want to know.'

'It was for a boy.' Her hands come to her brow. 'I know, embarrassing, right? I realise I can't become a musician overnight, so I wouldn't have anything musical to say to this boy, not yet anyway. I mean, he's way past learning the scale of C major.'

'Just keep practising. You'll get there.'

'I have been. At home. On Mum's piano. Dad says I have a good feel.'

'You have.'

'The funny thing is, though. I got talking to that boy anyway. I pass him all the time, and for the first time, we just got talking. Like, out of nowhere. He's really nice. I mean, his guitar playing is amazing and he plays piano. He showed me in the practice room.'

'Well, let's see how well you remember C major, shall we?'

'Okay.'

I take Katey through a few exercises, and she says she wants to learn the song *Midnight Train to Georgia*.

'That's an old-fashioned one for you,' I say. I'm watching her fingers across the keys. Long and elegant. Perfect for piano or the harp if her mum still wants to teach her.

'This boy at school, Nico,' she says. 'He was playing it. Says it's an old favourite of his grandfather. But it's pretty cool. I saw it on YouTube.'

'Well, I know I've got the music for that. It's one of the first songs my mum sang to me.' I did have lots of sheet music. Mainly lead sheets that Mum stocked up from the songs she used to sing. 'Actually,' I say, 'my music for that song is probably old and tatty by now.'

'I can get it. From my Dad's shop. He's got a music shop, and there are stacks of sheet music books. Old and new stuff. It's probably in one of the soul music compilations. I'll find it.'

'Great.'

I notice how fast time passes. An hour doesn't seem long enough for Katey, either, and she reluctantly stands to leave. She stretches as she looks around my living room, her eyes landing on the box with Mum's ashes in.

'Who's that?' she asks.

'That? Oh, those are Mum's ashes.' I look at the box, wondering now if it was a mistake to keep them in the living room if I'm going to have students. Maybe everyone feels like David, like they're being haunted. Jeannie was here just yesterday, and she made no comment about it at all.

'We scattered Mum's ashes,' she says very simply, walking to the box.

'Did you?' I don't know what else to say. It wasn't implied in the way Katey spoke about her mother that she might have passed away.

'Her name was Val, and she once played in an orchestra. I heard some recordings.'

My heart softens that bit more for Katey. I know how she feels. I know how much she must miss her and how sad her mum would have been to leave Katey. Her father's face comes to mind I'm immediately struck by guilt because I had felt an attraction to him. I hadn't stopped to wonder if he was with anyone.

Katey turns to me after she pulls her gaze from the urn.

'I'm not being funny, but how long have you had your mum's ashes and how long are you keeping them for?' she says.

'Well, Mum died several years ago. I thought I'd scatter them or bury them in Shepherd's Bush, where she grew up.'

'Didn't you grow up here?'

'No, I grew up in Manchester.'

'Thought so.'

'The accent?'

'Yeah, I like it, though.' She reaches for her jacket and puts it on, slowly. 'We had a burial plot for Mum. It's somewhere we can go and visit. Me and Dad. In case you're wondering, it's coming up for four years. I'm all right talking about it. About Mum. Dad, not so much.'

'Everyone is different. I can talk about Mum.' I'm looking at her urn now. 'I never stop thinking about her.'

'Me neither.'

We get to the door and Katey opens it.

'I can do more practice as it's half-term.'

'It's half-term for me, too. I teach at Cardinal Vaughan in Holland Park.'

'A friend of mine went there. Posh, right? The teachers wear gowns like university professors?'

'That's right. But I never had a single lecturer at uni who wore a gown.' I grin.

'Okay, thanks, Ione. I'll see you next week.'

'Bye.'

I hear my phone. It's a text message from Jeannie:

Already wish I was back in London. These guys are driving me mad. Who invented half-term anyway. Love you x.

I have a week to myself and nothing to fill it with. I go back to the piano and start trying to work out how to play Katey's song without the music. I used to know it by heart. Mum sang it a lot. Note by note, I find my way around it and I can hear Mum singing. I play until dusk falls, until I hear the person from the upstairs flat return from work, until sprinkles of rain patter at my window. And when my fingers and hands ache and I no longer conjure up my Mum's voice in the room and feel her standing next to me, I get ready to leave for the Pilates class.

24

Marta

Marta was nervous about the class, jittery and shaky, like Katey talking about the boy called Nico she had finally spoken to and who seemed to like her. To be that young and innocent again, Marta would have given anything. Ione had told her there was a good reason why Louise hadn't shown up last week. Marta was so hopeful she would see her again, but just an hour before the Pilates class, she had allowed herself to sink into a dark place in her mind. She hadn't mentioned the sign to Ione, but she knew that yet again Louise would not be at the class. She didn't deserve this happiness. Abandoning her husband and family was not the only thing she was being punished for. There was the little boy.

Marta had gone to the clinic determined to cut all ties from Katowice and her old life. It meant the baby had to go. She couldn't keep a baby. She was jobless and in temporary accommodation. Marta was desperate. She remembered the look on the doctor's face when, at eighteen weeks, Marta had said she was definitely sure she wanted an abortion. The appointment was arranged, the time and the date set and Marta had someone from the shelter coming to meet her afterwards as required for such an advanced stage termination. Then she felt the kick like a little ripple of movement, and she knew it was hopeless. She had to see the pregnancy through to the end.

The boy would be ten years old. Marta would be haunted by him for years to come, and if he ever found her, she would have no answer for him when he asked, 'Why did you leave me?'

Ione greeted Marta with a hug.

'You made it.'

'Sure,' Marta said, but her eyes were scanning the hall. There was no sign of Louise.

At the end of the class, Ione tapped her arm. She smiled at Marta, and Marta beamed a magnificent smile back at her.

'You don't have to pretend for me,' Ione said. 'I can completely understand how you feel.'

'Can you?'

Ione nodded, yes.

'In that case, can you explain it to me?'

'Oh, Marta.'

By now, they had become friendly with a few of the other participants of the Pilates class, and as Marta and Ione rolled up their mats, a couple of women drew them into a conversation.

Only partly listening to the idea of trying out a Saturday class, Ione nudged Marta who followed Ione's gaze. Hovering at the back of the hall, she spotted Louise. Overcome by seeing her so unexpectedly and seeing a large grin on Louise's face, Marta left the group of women and headed straight to her. Something like the flutter of a tiny bird's wings took over the mechanism of her heart. Not the valves opening and closing allowing blood to pump through, not the beat, beat, beat of the muscle itself. She felt as if she'd floated out of her body. Somewhere close to the ornate ceiling of the hall, Marta watched herself moving towards Louise. From up there, her heartbeat was working hard. It pulsated and boomed loudly enough for her to look down at the rest of the dispersing crowd to see if anyone else had noticed. Ione was still chatting, the teacher was demonstrating a move to a student.

Not knowing how she came to arrive there, Marta found herself in front of Louise. 'Marta, how are you?'

Marta could see the apology written on Louise's face. 'I'm very well. How are you? Are you all right?' Marta softly replied.

'I am. I didn't want another week to pass and for you to wonder why I wasn't here. I wanted to be here.' Louise waved to Callie, the Pilates teacher. Marta looked around for Ione. She was still talking, one eye on the two women, one on Marta.

'I'll get my mat,' Marta said. 'The three of us could go to The Plough?'

'I'll wait outside,' Louise said.

Marta rushed towards Ione who handed her the yoga mat.

'I'll see you next week,' Ione said. 'Or maybe you can call me?'

'You're not coming?' asked Marta.

'Of course not. I think you've got things to discuss.'

Marta kissed her friend's cheek, brushed her arm and ran to the dark lane outside the church hall where Louise was blowing warm air into cupped hands.

'When winter hits, it's like, Bam!' Louise said.

'Well, this isn't really cold for me. I'm Polish, remember?'

'I do. I remember everything we talked about, and I missed you.'

They walked towards The Plough, but Marta had a thought. 'How about we buy some wine and take it back to my place? Is that okay? I mean, if you'd like.'

'I would. But you'll have to put your heating on this time. I'm not Polish, and I feel the cold.'

'Absolutely.'

They stopped at an off-licence. They bought two bottles of Valpolicella and arrived at Marta's with a large bag of chips into the bargain. Marta said she had nothing in the house to eat, and Louise said she deserved something greasy and fattening after the week she'd had. It wasn't until they were sipping wine after the last of the chips had gone, sitting on the soft sofa, colourful cushions supporting and surrounding them that Louise began to tell Marta why she hadn't shown up the week before. Marta was playing the same John Coltrane CD she played when Elliot had come for dinner. Louise said she didn't mind a bit of jazz now and again.

'I've got really close to one of my clients. Charlie, his name is. An old guy with dementia. He's not with it a lot of the time. Drops in and out of a world of his memories, and when he's in the present, if he comes back, he always looks as if he wants to go to wherever it is his mind takes him.'

'I think that's sad.'

'It is. It's sad to watch your loved ones go through that.'

'So his family must really feel the loss. Is he married? Children?'

'He's got three grown-up girls, a few grandkids. Don't know how many. I've only met one daughter and her son. His wife is alive, but they're divorced.'

'Oh, so he lives alone?'

'Completely. And I mean completely. They hardly come to visit.'

'Well, that's even more sad.'

'I know. Well, last week, I was there, and Charlie had a stroke.'

'Oh no.'

'I know. But he's back home now. I was just with him. That's why I was late. I got a late shift. My manager knows I don't like to do extra shifts, course work and everything, but she was short of carers and she knows how I feel about Charlie.'

'I see. You take your job seriously. I admire that.'

'Well, he's the one I feel the most for. Last week, I went with him to hospital. His grandson was there, but none of his children showed up for him. Can you believe they were all too busy?'

'Really?'

‘Yes.’ Louise edged forward in her seat and placed her empty wine glass down. She went to the CD player to find a new album to play. John Coltrane’s album had ended, and the room was suddenly too quiet. ‘I mean, who does that?’ Louise had her back to Marta as she read the CD cases. ‘I find it completely irresponsible, cold and heartless to just blank out a part of your life. But particularly blood. Family, to me, is important, and I really don’t have time for heartless people.’

Louise was forthright in her opinion, slapping CD cases back into place as if she were delivering a speech on the evils of not observing the importance of family. ‘I’m so annoyed at them. Who can just turn their back on family like that?’

Marta felt the tears rising to the surface the moment Louise mentioned cold hearts and leaving family behind. Blanking them out as if they never existed. It was all too much for her. She had tried to keep smiling, tried to be a person who could be loved and trusted.

‘Marta?’ Louise finally turned to face her, not having had any response to her tirade.

After a little while, Marta’s voice came quietly. ‘I did that.’ She sniffed, placing her wine glass down and walking to the window. There, she held her upper arms, tight, so she couldn’t escape Louise and not tell her the truth. ‘I turned my back on my family, Louise. I’m that heartless.’

Louise rose to join her. ‘What are you saying?’ she asked. ‘You have an elderly parent you left behind in Poland?’

Marta turned to face her. ‘I left everything in Poland. Louise, I was married. I married a young man when I was just twenty. He was in love with me, and I broke his heart.’

‘So, you didn’t know you were gay?’

‘I knew. I just deceived him. I didn’t want to. I wanted to be a good wife, but I couldn’t keep it up anymore. He wanted us to have children together, a big family with lots of them running around. I thought I could do it, but I felt trapped. I couldn't go on living a lie.'

'But it was better that you did, wasn't it? At least you didn't string him along forever. You know people do that. Can't face up to their sexuality. Try to fit a lifestyle. Then they break their partner's heart by leaving later in life. You know? Wasted years and everything? At least you didn't do that.'

Louise tried to hold on to Marta, but she pulled away. She sat on the sofa, folded double, hands still clinging to her upper arms as if she'd shatter or fall if she didn't hold on.

'I made him fall in love with me,' Marta went on. 'I made him marry me, and then I ran away. It must have destroyed him.'

'So you divorced?'

Marta shook her head. 'I could imagine the shame for my father and my mother. They must have disowned me long ago. When I got on that plane, I knew I wouldn't go back. How could I have left my husband like that? My family?'

At first lost for words, Louise sat next to Marta. 'I dated someone for years who didn't come out to their family,' Louise said. 'I know how hard it was for her. It's not easy for everyone. I was lucky, having the family I had. I'm sure you could call your family, now that you're older, tell them. No matter how they react, you really should. Marta, it's one secret you thought you couldn't say, but now…'

Marta shook her head and looked down. Unravelling her body and clutching her knees. 'It's not just one secret. I came to London, and I made my sister lie for me so my family wouldn't know where I was. And then, all of them, my parents, my sister, my poor husband … I didn't tell any of them I was pregnant when I left Poland.'

'Jesus.'

'I know. If this is all too much, you can just leave now. You must think I have no heart at all. I have no family values.'

'Families can be complicated, I know that. But it doesn't have to be. Just tell the truth about the abortion. They'll be upset, but they're your blood after all.'

Marta looked down at her hands, saw they were shaking, felt her body turn cold. 'I didn't want my sister to know.' She spoke as if she were in a trance. 'She'd tell them, you see? So I just left, in the night, like a thief.'

'Don't say that. You were desperate. Having an abortion isn't an easy decision. And you were on your own.'

'But that was my choice. I chose to be alone over being with my family and telling them the truth. I just ran away, and no one, not any of them, knows where I am now. They don't know if I'm alive or dead, Louise.'

'I'm so sorry.'

'Don't be sorry. Not for me. I didn't have an abortion. I had the child. A little boy, and I miss him more than anything in this world. I gave him up for adoption. I held him for one hour before they took him away. They said I could change my mind, but I didn't. I had a choice, and I chose to leave my son to a stranger. To a children's home. To anywhere. I have no idea where.'

Marta looked at Louise, but she had her eyes on the coffee table. They were quiet a long time until Louise spoke.

'But you can trace him.'

'Maybe I could but I won't, and I don't deserve him. What would I say to him? I'm sorry. I wanted a new life away from everything, and that meant you? He was an innocent child, and now he haunts me. I see him everywhere. He reminds me I'm not a good person. He reminds me that I am a liar. I break hearts and I destroy.' She got up abruptly and faced the window again. 'And I don't deserve you either, Louise. I don't deserve to be happy with you. I thought you didn't want me and you didn't want to see me again. It's what I deserve.'

'Look.' Louise stood behind Marta who had not turned to face her and had been crying a steady stream of tears for every lie, every broken heart and every time she ran away from people who loved her. From family. 'I don't know what to say to you, Marta.'

'It's okay. It's impossible.'

'It's not an impossible situation. Everything you've told me is in the past. But you don't have to leave it there. You can write to your husband, to your sister. Hell, even your folks in Poland. You can make amends. There's time. You have time.'

'I've been away for over ten years, Louise.'

'It's still not too late.' Louise heaved a sigh. Like she was tired and had just climbed to the top of a mountain. 'You know the difference between you and Charlie's family?'

Marta shook her head, drying her tears with her sleeve and still not turning to face Louise.

'The difference is,' Louise went on, 'they can never make amends with their father. All they ever did was punish him. Now he isn't in his right mind, and even if they wanted to make amends, he wouldn't understand. He wouldn't know what they were telling him. As for Charlie, it's too late to beg their forgiveness. I don't suppose they'd want his apology anyway. They are broken and they always will be. You. All you have to do is pick up a phone, or a pen or send a carrier pigeon. Anything to tell them, Hey guys, I'm here! I'm alive.'

Marta turned now. She smiled though her face was racked in pain. Every one of the last ten years weighed down on her, and she felt completely hopeless. 'I don't know,' she said. 'I really don't.'

Louise said nothing. She was tired. Marta could see that.

'Maybe you should go,' Marta said.

'Maybe I should. It's late. I didn't think it'd get so heavy.'

'And you don't want heavy.'

'No, you know I don't. I've had heavy. I'm already carrying a lot.'

'I understand.'

‘So, I’ll go.’

Marta nodded. The greys and the blues surrounded her instantly. There was no more colour, she’d rubbed it all away. The vibrant, the bright colours, they had all faded with every word of her confession. Louise walked to the door, she turned and showed Marta a thin smile, one that almost reached her eyes but not quite. She left without another word.

The front door downstairs clicked closed, and Marta struggled to hear Louise’s footsteps on the pavement outside.

‘Please. I don’t want you to go. I really don’t want you to go.’ Marta whispered into the quiet of her living room. She thought she heard Louise say, ‘That’s okay, then. I’ll stay.’ But when she looked around the room, she was all by herself.

25

Elliot

Music reached Elliot's ears just before he stirred from a ragged sleep. He hadn't shaken off the dreamlike state he was in before one note and then another filtered into the field of tall grass where a woman stood and waved to him. A faint light hit his eyes before they were fully open. Slowly, he rose from the warm bed, the sheets and blankets circling his torso like vines, and he wondered if he'd been rolling in the tall grass of his dream. Rubbing his eyes, he yawned.

It was cold in the room. The heating hadn't kicked in. Katey had already been demanding he extend the timer on the boiler so it came on early and stayed on until after midnight. Being chilly indoors made her grumpy. He imagined her snuggled deep under her purple duvet, only her curls showing above the top. She wouldn't move, and she wouldn't be up for a few more hours. Maybe he'd surprise her and turn the heating on now. Make a large breakfast as he sometimes did on a Sunday. Although, when Katey normally got up, it was time for brunch.

Dragging himself from the bed, Elliot pulled open the curtains. The window panes were speckled with condensation, obscuring the view. He rubbed at the water droplets with his fingers, smearing the condensation clouds so there was a small gap to look through. He rubbed his damp fingers on his jogging bottoms. Outside, a faint sun suffused the grey sky. He yawned and fogged up the window again.

The musical notes he thought he'd heard on waking started again. He listened and envisaged Val at the piano the day she played Chopin in a tight T-shirt, her skin stretched around the eight-month-old baby she carried inside her. She told Elliot she could feel a kick.

'She likes music!' Val said. 'Do you think she'll be a famous pianist?'

'That would be something.'

He smiled at the memory and padded downstairs in bare feet, listening to the stop, start, stop, start of Katey practising a major scale on the piano. She'd stop if the pattern was wrong then she'd tut and try again.

'Hey Katey,' he said in a soft voice so as not to startle her. She jumped anyway.

'I didn't hear you come down,' she said.

'Don't stop playing. You're up early.'

Katey started another scale. D major this time.

'I was restless. Sorry. Did I wake you?'

'No, that's fine. Couldn't sleep?'

'I had a good, long sleep. I was listening to music in bed, and I just thought that if I want to be good at piano, I need to practise more. Ione could tell I was rusty on Tuesday. But she didn't say anything.'

Elliot sat on the chair alongside the piano. 'So you're serious about piano?' he said, looking impressed.

'Yeah. Why not? I have to keep up the tradition.' She grinned at Elliot.

'You go for it. I can help you whenever you need.'

'I know.'

Elliot got up. 'I'm making breakfast, then. It isn't too early for you, is it?'

'Actually, I'm starving.'

Elliot went to the kitchen and turned on the light. He heard Katey call to him.

'Dad, can you make your pancakes?'

‘Sure,’ he called back. He smiled to himself, switched on the radio and set about making the super thick pancakes he and Katey always loved.

In a little while, Katey came to the kitchen, bundled in one of her mother’s thick sweaters, woolly socks and carrying some sheet music. She sat at the kitchen table. ‘Do you think I could ever learn to play this stuff?’ She waved the sheets at Elliot.

‘Of course. But you know it’s going to take you a while. Your mum started playing at about six or seven. She had years of training. That’s why she was so good.’

‘She *was* good, wasn’t she?’

‘One of the best.’

‘Did I cut her career short?’

‘In what way?’

‘Being born, of course.’

‘I think having you was her career to be honest. I think she wanted you before she met me.’

‘That doesn’t make sense.’

‘It was one of the first things we talked about. Mum wanted a baby girl. She had your name picked out. It’s like she knew you’d come one day. I said you can’t call her Katey if the name doesn’t suit her. The strange thing was, you looked like a Katey when you were born.’

‘All babies look the same. Red and scrunched up.’

‘You were scrunched up, you screamed the hospital down, too. But you were most definitely a Katey. Mum looked at me as if to say, *See I told you.* She knew everything.’

‘Did she know she’d die?’

Elliot had been making batter, whipping the fork to get lots of air into the mixture. The secret to his special pancakes. He looked like a professional chef the way the fork circled the batter, whirring like a mini tornado in the bowl, and not one drop splashed over the side. He lay the fork down.

‘You know what? I think she did know. Even after she recovered the first time, I think she knew it would come back and I think she knew when. I think she prepared. She tried to prepare me, but I didn't want to know.'

'I was reading about people knowing when they'll die. They might not know how but they know the age they'll be. Creepy, right?'

'In a way. But, you shouldn't be reading that kind of thing.'

'I don't anymore. I used to, at first. Now I don't.'

Elliot took up the fork again. Usually, by now, he would have changed the subject, finding it hard to talk about Val with Katey because the atmosphere would grow still, his words would become stilted and he wouldn't be able to look his daughter in the eye. He'd bury himself in a book, turn on some music or find he had some errand to run rather than say more than two words about his dead wife. Today there was a shift. He wanted to talk about Val, wanted Katey to ask more questions. He'd find the answers. Talking about Val had stopped feeling painful. He wanted to talk about her with pride and with love: these were the feelings she always evoked in him when they were together.

He admired how hard she'd worked to get a First in music, her resilience finding an orchestra after years of rejection. She'd take any job in music she could until she'd achieved her goal of landing a place in an orchestra, and she'd surpassed her expectations by finding one of the most prestigious ones in the UK. Katey was right, though. Her conception had forced the early close to a brilliant career. Once you left a good orchestra for any length of time, there were always hundreds of musicians waiting to fill your shoes. Val hadn't lost her spirit. She hadn't lost her zest for music, she just needed to find a way to make it pay in another way. And so the idea of a music shop was born. Val was undeterred by Elliot's scepticism. Though he'd grieved a long time for her, Val had in fact prepared him for a life without her. He was making a success of the music shop, working hard to establish his hold on the market for guitar repairs.

He smiled to himself. He celebrated once again, though silently, his wife's vision and her tenacity. 'Right,' he said to Katey. 'Time to get the pan on. You should pay attention. Learn how to do these yourself. Before we know it, you'll be away at university and you won't have me on hand to make them for you.'

'Trying to get rid of me already?'

'If you stayed here forever and never left, I'd be happy, but I know that won't happen. You're all grown up now.'

'Old enough for you not to freak out about me having a boyfriend?'

He swung around.

'A what now?' he spluttered.

'Dad, it's calm. I like this boy from school. We get on, and he kind of asked me out.'

'Only kind of?'

'Well, properly. So if you're not going to hold me to that staying here and never leaving, we might go out for a pizza or something at the weekend.'

Elliot turned back to the hot pan on the cooker and poured a thick layer of batter into it. The idea was to get it to heat up until it was just so. With such thick batter, if the pan was too hot, it wouldn't cook inside, not hot enough and you'd end up with a mushy chunk of batter that was only fit for the bin. He focused, not only on breakfast but on what was happening. Katey was changing faster than he'd thought. He acknowledged that time was moving on; he was moving with it. Katey's words: *It's calm.* And he was. He was calm. He was himself again.

He turned to Katey as the seductive smell of hot batter filled the kitchen. 'You know I have to meet him first, right?'

She threw her arms around him. 'I wasn't expecting anything less, Dad.'

26

Louise

She didn't lie to Marta. She definitely didn't want anything heavy. Heavy relationships had never worked out for her. After Danika, the last thing she needed was to fall in love when her priority was achieving a good degree, finding a good job and getting out of the shared house on Goldhawk Road. That meant working hard and keeping her sanity when she could just about cover the bills. At twenty-nine, she already felt behind when she looked at where her friends were in their lives. Good jobs, some married, some already had children. Her friends questioned her choices, often looked down their noses at her situation; some blatantly pitied her.

Having sacrificed everything, she couldn't get derailed with something as complicated as love. She couldn't allow herself to fall in love with a woman whose whole life was one of regrets, tangled emotions and deceit. That was just asking for trouble. It was enough. What she had to deal with was enough. There was no room for more. No room for Marta.

In the late morning, Louise made her way to Charlie's house. She tapped in the code on the keypad to let herself in and was surprised to hear female voices, raised and urgent, in the living room. Rushing through the hall, heart pounding, she wondered if something was wrong with Charlie.

Charlie wasn't in the room. Instead, there were three middle-aged women, all with a familial look, talking loudly and not noticing Louise at all. She recognised Athena Christou, Nico's mum, so presumably, these were the other two sisters. Sitting in the chair where Charlie would normally sit was an elderly woman wearing a headscarf and coat, presumably their mother, Charlie's ex-wife.

'Oh, it's Louise, isn't it?' Athena Christou turned to her, suddenly.

'Yes.' She looked at each woman then turned her head towards the downstairs bedroom. 'Is Charlie all right?'

'He's not here,' one of the sisters said. She looked slightly older than Athena. 'He's back in the hospital.'

'Oh no.' Louise felt her chest constrict. She thought back to the evening before. She'd left Charlie in pretty good spirits. He'd refused most of his food, but she'd made him comfortable. It had been obvious to Louise that Charlie had no idea who she was and regarded her as his paramour rather than his Louise, his favourite carer. Convinced she was Brenda, he kept saying the name over and over, and Louise didn't try to correct him. She thought that if Charlie believed she was Brenda then he'd at least eat. That hadn't, of course, been the case, but at least he was happy. At the time, Louise wondered why he hadn't chosen Brenda and left his family. Looking at them now, with their stern faces, their air of superiority, the unfriendly way they ignored her and spoke in Greek, she couldn't understand what had stopped him.

'Should I just go, then?' Louise said after having tried, several times, to cut into the conversation. They were not only loud, they all spoke over each other.

'What?' snapped Athena.

'Should I go?' Louise repeated.

'No wait,' said Athena. 'How long is your shift?'

'Two hours.'

'Perfect. We're going to cancel with the agency so you won't be coming back. But for today,' she looked around at her sisters, 'could you pack up all his things?'

The women all nodded in agreement. They must have been debating which one of them the task should fall to.

'So what's actually happening with Charlie, then?' Louise dared to ask.

'Last night, his temperature dropped, his breathing was slow and they called the ambulance again.'

'Oh my God.' Louise tried to remain calm.

'It's just that the doctors said to expect a negative outcome, so it doesn't look as if he'll be returning home.' Athena looked down at her designer footwear.

'Aren't you going to wait before packing away his stuff?' Louise asked. 'You never know with these things. He might pull through.'

'It's sorted,' said one of the sisters. 'The doctor was very final about it.'

'Besides,' said Athena, 'we're selling the house and Dad will go into a home if and when they discharge him. He'll need twenty-four-hour care. That's it.'

'So you want everything packed up?' Louise looked slowly around the room. 'You don't mean the furniture?'

'No, just strip the beds. Empty the wardrobe, cupboards, drawers, under the bed. All the personal effects you can put into suitcases and bags. I've got some boxes in the car. I'll leave them with you.'

'Kitchen stuff, bathroom?' Louise asked.

'Everything like that.' Athena walked past her. 'I'll get the boxes in.'

'We'll go,' one of the sisters said. She and the third sister went to help their mother out of the armchair. Louise noticed she hadn't said a word, just nodded occasionally and blinked her eyes in agreement with anything her daughters said.

They left Louise in the living room. At last, she felt she could breathe and think with all the noise, perfume and confusion gone from Charlie's house. Louise shivered at the oppressive atmosphere his family had created. Still, now that they were gone, it didn't seem right to be the one to pack away all of Charlie's things: she felt like an intruder. This was a job for the family. She marvelled at their callousness, wondering how it could be so easy for them. Her heart was breaking, and she was left with a job she did not want to do.

Athena came back with a stack of boxes. Louise rushed to help her, but Athena dropped them on the floor in the corridor at Louise's feet.

'I'll leave you to it,' Athena said.

'I have a feeling it'll take more than two hours.'

'We'll pay you.' Athena turned and left.

The arrogance, Louise thought: money wasn't the issue. If Charlie asked her to pack all his worldly goods away, she would have been happy to do it in her own time for no money. As it was, she had no choice but to get on with it.

Louise decided to start upstairs and work her way back down. She would do the best she could, be as careful as she could with Charlie's things and hoped this would satisfy the sisters.

She collected the boxes from the hallway. With two boxes, she made her way awkwardly up the stairs to the room in which Charlie's wardrobe stood. This room had once been his bedroom but was more of a storage room now. The whole of the top floor—two rooms and a small bathroom—was neglected now save for popping up for fresh linen, clothes and basins of water for bathing Charlie.

Louise sighed, dropping the boxes to the floor by the wardrobe and looking around for a place to start. In this room, apart from the wardrobe, was an old dressing table, a shelving unit and a bedside table. Charlie's dining table and chairs from downstairs were stacked against the wall and covered in old sheets to keep off the dust. His old bed was still there, unused, now that he had a motorised bed in the back room. The covers were outdated. Louise pulled at them, tugging them off the bed and sniffing them to see if they should be washed and dried before being folded away. They had been cleaned, she could tell, but there was a musty sort of smell about them, the smell of clothes that had been folded away for a long time, unworn and never coming into contact with fresh air. She opened the window. Would she need to take down the curtains? Possibly. But she'd leave those until last.

She folded away the bedlinen into an old suitcase from the seventies, which reminded Louise of one her mother once owned. The cream bedspread, the flat sheet, pillowcases and the thick brown blanket. Next came the fitted sheet on the mattress. Louise loosened the elastic edges away from the mattress and pulled it together so she could fold it up and squeeze it into the suitcase with the rest of the bedding. The mattress lifted, just slightly, and Louise caught sight of some old papers. Thinking they must have slipped down there by mistake, Louise reached under for them and found two white envelopes. Neither was sealed, and written on the front of each one was the name, Brenda Mason. Letters for Brenda, she thought, her heart racing with excitement. Charlie wrote to his Brenda, but he never posted them.

She waved the letters in front of her face, fanning herself because just ten minutes of folding and packing had made her warm. She looked around wondering where she'd put Charlie's paperwork and decided to put the letters onto the old dressing table for the time being. She continued packing, folding and sorting in this room before moving to the second room and then the bathroom. All the suitcases and large bags she could find were filled and so was one of the boxes. Louise picked up the remaining box, swept Charlie's letters to Brenda into it and carried it down.

She had been working diligently for about three-quarters of an hour and stopped for a cup of tea and to eat her sandwich. She would have eaten after giving Charlie lunch. Her mind had been on him all afternoon, wondering if he was back on the same ward, how he was doing and how long he had left to live. She would go to see him soon.

Louise's mind then went to the two letters to Brenda Mason she'd put into the cardboard box earlier. She fished them out. Taking them to the kitchen, she finished her last sip of tea and left the envelopes on the table before carrying on with the packing.

27

Ione

Marta is in pain, and I don't know how to help her. My go-to person when I have any problem is Jeannie. I wonder if I can deliver the pearls of wisdom Jeannie can—wisdom she imparts, whether I've asked for it or not, but somehow gets to the root of everything. Marta called this evening and asked if she could see me. I'd seen her just last night at Pilates when she left with Louise. She was flushed and happy then. She hadn't even buttoned up her jacket on a night when I couldn't wait to get home and get warm. My bed had called to me last night, that or to sit with a thick cardigan in front of a television drama, hands around a mug of hot chocolate. I'd thought about Marta when I got home, happy that she'd found someone special and that something wonderful might happen between them both. Marta deserved that. I know she'd been in London for many years, but, apart from me, I don't think she had any other friends.

Her shoulders slump as we sit around my kitchen table. There's thick granary bread in the toaster: Marta didn't have dinner and this is all she wants. As I brew a pot of lemon and ginger tea, I see her fidget with the salt and pepper grinders on the table.

'Here,' I say, placing down the teapot next to two mugs. 'I'm sorry I don't have any wine.'

'No, that's fine. It's probably best if I keep a clear head. I need to make a few decisions.'

'Is that what you wanted to talk about? The decisions?'

‘I think I do. The truth is, I don’t know what I’m really doing. I think one thing, and then I change my mind almost immediately, to the point where I think I’m losing it completely.’

The toast pops up. I place the two slices on a side plate in front of Marta and set olive spread and jam on the table, too.

I know this has something to do with Louise. Not much else could have happened in twenty-four hours to cause such a turnaround in Marta’s behaviour.

I sit, patiently, watching Marta spread jam. She makes slow and deliberate strokes of blackcurrant jam onto the toast, layering it deeply, not allowing any to slide down the sides, working with the accuracy of an artist. She replaces the knife, balancing it on the open jam jar and just sits and ponders it for a while, a masterpiece of hot bread and preserves that are to be looked upon rather than eaten, it would seem. That’s all we do, we stare at the toast and neither of us says a word.

In a few moments, when I’ve sipped some tea, burned my tongue and chastised myself for not knowing what to say to her, Marta looks up at me.

‘Oh my God, I’m sorry,’ she says.

‘What for?’

‘For coming here, interrupting your evening and bringing you down. I moped around the shop all day and asked my boss if I could go home early. He said yes, and all I’ve done is wander around like a lost soul. I feel broken.’

I reach my hand across the table. I know I haven’t known Marta long and maybe I’m not being British enough, keeping my reserve, but it feels like the thing to do. She looks at me and smiles.

‘I think I have blown it with Louise,’ she says.

‘Surely not. Did you fall out last night?’

‘You could say that.’

‘What was it about, if you don’t mind me asking?’

Marta hesitates. She looks at me closely, and she's wondering about how much she wants to divulge. 'It's just that I had things from my past that I felt I had to bring up with Louise. You know, lay my cards on the table and everything. Being upfront? Is that what you say?'

I nod.

'It turns out, being upfront was a bit too heavy for Louise. My past and her future don't match, and therefore she left me.'

'Oh Marta, I'm so sorry. I thought it was something like that. I didn't want it to be. I thought you two might have had something.'

'I don't think so. We're in different places.'

'It happens, you know? But, hey, better it happens early than to go on for ages, years even, only to break up because you were just too different. Or you wanted different things.'

'That's very true.'

'Something did come out of this, though, if you think about it.'

'What do you mean?' Marta picks up her tea and a slice of toast. She's poised to listen to my pearls of wisdom.

'Well, before Louise, you were still in a bit of a nowhere land in terms of your sexuality. Remember? That's what you told me. Now, at least, you know what you want. You know where you'll be happiest.'

'So I just move on?'

'Marta, unless you can call her, convince her that the two of you are right together, then you don't really have a choice. People will be who they are. She might change in time; you two might end up on the right page one day, but maybe the timing isn't right just now.'

She puts down the toast. Her eyes were watering over as I spoke. A flash of memory of Mum telling me these exact same words comes to me. Just a memory of Mum lying on my bed while I cried my heart out over a boy from university who dumped me after a year. And then the memory is gone and Marta's tear slides down her face like a train pulling out of the station, slow at first then picking up speed. Her tear drips off her chin and onto the table. I watch it land, and I watch Marta wipe it away with the sleeve of her sweater.

'Shall I get you a tissue?' I ask, not quite out of my chair.

'Actually, I have one.' Marta digs into her large shoulder bag and pulls out a tissue.

'Eat something, Marta, it'll make you feel better.'

'Comfort eating?'

'That's not a crime. It's better than comfort drinking or comfort cocaine snorting.'

'Are you sure?'

'Well, my mum's remedy for a broken heart is to sing and dance.'

'I don't sing and I can't dance,' Marta says and smiles, self-consciously. 'Well, I can but I wouldn't want any witnesses. You were lucky to have such a fun mum.'

Marta knew my mum had passed away. It came up in one of our conversations, as did the fact that I was married and divorced. Marta never pressed me on any of these points. She listened a lot and didn't say much about her background. She told me details of Katowice, where she was born and raised, about her job in an accounting department, about the day her sister got married and how she and Marta cried when her sister left to live in London with her new husband.

'She was a fun mum,' I say. 'She was always smiling. She did sing a lot. She used to be a singer, you know?'

'Really?'

I nod. 'She sang the blues. Etta James, Ida Cox. She knew all the oldies. Then she'd always sing *Midnight Train to Georgia*, which isn't blues at all. But she still sang it with so much emotion.'

'It must have meant something to her.'

'I guess. But there are lots of things I'm sure she never told me. One of them being, where I could find my father.'

'You never knew him?'

I shake my head at this, knowing that, apart from Jeannie, I've never spoken to anyone about my parents. How they met and fell in love. That I was the result of an illicit love affair. I could tell Marta now, tell her everything if it wasn't such a sad story. Sadder because it isn't a story—it was real life. Neither Mum nor I were lucky in love, and to tell Marta this right now will drive her into a more miserable frame of mind than when she arrived. Instead, I take her hand and drag her into the living room.

'Grab your tea and toast,' I say, not really giving her enough time to do either. She giggles and allows herself to be whisked along the corridor to the living room where I'd been listening to an up-tempo album on my music player. 'We're dancing. I don't care how you dance because I'm going to have my eyes closed.'

I turn the music up loud and start to move. My eyes are closed, but I'm aware of Marta dancing in front of me. I hear her glass bangles clink and jingle as they shift up and down her arm. She's more animated: I can tell because of the rustle of her loose Batik print skirt and her necklace as the beads roll together. She begins to laugh in a high-pitched, merry chirp.

'It's okay,' she says. 'You can open your eyes. I'm not doing any worse than you.'

'Really?' I say. I open my eyes and am amazed at how rhythmic and elegant Marta is. 'Well, I was only holding back because I didn't want to show you up. Watch this.' My body is more fluid, my arms move further from my body; hips, legs, feet, inventive and free.

We dance until we're hot, tired and feverish with laughter. I throw myself onto a chair, and Marta flops onto the sofa.

'Thank you,' she says, breathlessly.

'What for?'

‘For the therapy. I know what to do now when I’m feeling down. I think it might be better than drink, or food or cocaine.’

‘You’ve got Mum to thank for this.’

‘You miss her?’ she asks, and I answer yes straight away, eyes becoming watery.

‘I miss mine, too,’ Marta says. ‘I miss a lot of people.’

I turn off the music as I listen to the list of people Marta misses, and I listen to the story about the son she gave up. I think she will become more sad, but talking seems to improve her mood. It makes her determined to do something about these people from her past. She says she will reach out to them. Not the boy. She says he will be better off not knowing her. And she will also reach out to Louise. Maybe theirs will be a love story with a happy ending. Who knows? I just know that Marta is smiling and I didn’t fail her as a friend.

28

Louise

She sat in the kitchen, the two envelopes addressed to Brenda Mason between her fingers. She tapped them onto the surface of the table with a repeated rhythm. They were unsealed, but she wouldn't allow herself to read the letters inside. Louise didn't want to invade Charlie's privacy. But, at the same time, she knew the letters should not fall into the hands of Charlie's wife or daughters. They were his to do with as he pleased. She wished she could take them to him and ask him what she should do, but Louise knew from his manner since being released from the hospital after the stroke, that Charlie was a lot less lucid. Now that he'd been hospitalised again, the doctors expecting a negative outcome, she doubted he'd know her, and he'd probably have no recollection of ever writing them. She had tried hard to make Charlie remember her. His Louise. She played music to him. His song. At one time, she even pretended to be Brenda. Now, she had the property of Brenda Mason in her hands and wished she could be her, for five minutes at least. Just so she could read those damned letters.

Too preoccupied with what was in the letters and what to do about them, Louise had sat for a long time in the kitchen. Long after she'd finished packing Charlie's life away in old suitcases, battered holdalls and the used storage boxes. The thought of Charlie being close to the end of his life had a deep effect on her. Charlie wasn't family, but she regarded him as a good friend. She'd grown close to him, even though she came to understand that he had let his family down—Brenda, too, by the looks of things. She was convinced that Charlie and Brenda hadn't meant to hurt anybody by falling in love.

Slumped at the table now, Louise looked out of the small kitchen window at the overcast afternoon. She really should get home before it rained, but she hadn't decided what to do. She could give the letters to Nico, but she had no idea how and if she'd see him again. Besides, she didn't know what was in the letters and if a seventeen year old boy was the right person to take possession of them.

She wondered if she could find Brenda and deliver the letters herself. It seemed fanciful. Charlie had sent Louise looking for pictures of Brenda once before. She'd searched everywhere but to no avail. Once, when she'd thought about trying an online search to find a blues singer called Brenda, she'd abandoned the idea because she didn't have a last name. Now she had. Maybe searching Brenda Mason might reveal where she could find her.

Louise took out her laptop, went to her search engine and entered the name, Brenda Mason, and then the words 'black female blues singer' and 'blues clubs West End'. An exhaustive list, pages long, appeared. Brenda Mason was a common name, and a catalogue of female singers, not necessarily black with the first name Brenda or the last name Mason, came up. It was ridiculous. She scrolled the pages looking for the remote possibility that she'd find the right Brenda, but there was no clue. Not a single one.

The rain started. Large splashes hit the kitchen window. Her heart began to race because she knew what she needed to do. She had to read the letters. People very often put addresses on the tops of letters. If Charlie had done, then the mystery would be solved. All she'd need to do was put a stamp on the envelope. She didn't even have to read the whole letter. Maybe she'd send a covering note, telling Brenda that Charlie still talks about her, is probably still in love with her. She'd tell Brenda she needed to hurry because there might not be much time to see him again. She didn't have to go into too much detail, but she could leave her telephone number in case Brenda wanted to contact her about Charlie.

Slowly, she pulled out one letter. It was folded in such a way that the top of the letter couldn't be seen; she'd have to pull it out further, unfold it. In doing so, she saw the words, *Love* and *Why*. She quickly folded it away because there wasn't an address. She doubted there'd be one on the second letter, but she owed it to Charlie and Brenda to look anyway. Again, no address and again, Louise saw words and phrases she couldn't help but see. *I love you, I'll wait for you.*

At that moment, there was a tap on the front door. Louise almost leapt from her seat. She hurriedly returned the letters to the envelopes and shoved them both into her bag before going to the door.

It was Nico and with him was a young girl with sandy-coloured skin and two thick corn rows on either side of her head. They both smiled at Louise, but she'd been so startled by the knock on the door that her smile wasn't ready and she worried she looked guilty.

'Nico?' she said, at last, holding the door open just enough for her face to peep through. 'Did you want something?'

'I wanted to see Granddad.' He made to come in, his arm around the young girl. She looked at Louise, a slight frown appearing on her brow.

Louise shook her head and stood back from the door, opening it wider. 'He's not here, babes. Didn't they tell you?'

'Tell me what?'

'He was taken into hospital again.'

Nico and the girl looked at each other.

'Did you want to come in anyway?' Louise said. 'Your mum asked me to pack up his things.'

'What, everything? What's going on?'

Louise looked at her feet. Just as she shouldn't have hold of the letters, telling Nico about his grandfather's condition wasn't her responsibility.

'Is it bad?' he asked. The girl in his arm looked up at Nico.

'I think you should talk to your mum. She was here earlier with your aunts and maybe your Gran?'

'*Yiayia* was here? She never leaves the house.' He took a few steps back. 'It is bad. You can tell me, Louise.'

'No. You should go home or find your mum. Tell her you were here, and she'll tell you.'

'Okay.' He turned away slowly. The girl followed suit. Nico looked back over his shoulder. 'Thanks, yeah?'

Louise shook her head. 'It's nothing.' She watched them walk away. The rain was picking up and a draft was blowing through the corridor. 'Nico,' she called just as he was closing the gate. He looked back. 'Um … look after yourself, yeah?'

'I will.'

Louise called the care agency. Made sure they were aware that she'd done everything the family had asked of her and to say she was leaving Mr Manolis' house. Her manager thanked Louise and told her she'll have another client added to her rota to replace Charlie. Absently, Louise thanked her manager, gathered her belongings and left the house.

29

Charlie

By now, of course, there was no turning back. Charlie had made up his mind; he was going to tell his wife that the marriage was over, that he was leaving. He would leave the business to her and the girls, and he would go. He could leave quickly after breaking the news to the entire family. He decided on this little detail because he knew his wife would twist the story, make him into a monster, someone who had never deserved her and didn't deserve to have such beautiful daughters. At least if he spoke to his brothers, to Ana's family, to his own daughters and even the family in Greece, he could keep a modicum of integrity. He could let them all know that this was the hardest decision of his life and that, no matter what, he'd always be there for his children. He loved them with all his heart, but they were all adults and he couldn't spend the next half of his life in a loveless marriage. He wouldn't blame Ana. She was an amazing woman, a good mother and an excellent business partner. It was not her fault that he had fallen out of love.

Charlie was at the restaurant when he'd come to the decision. He was due to manage the evening shift. It was Ana's night off. He would come home and tell her, and the next morning, he would go to Brenda, tell her he wanted to be with her. He was in good humour, even though his heart beat like thunder and he knew that, after tonight, there was no turning back. Everything he'd worked for would no longer be a part of his life. After tonight, there would just be him and Brenda. They would no longer have to hide.

As he straightened cutlery, fixed centre pieces, moved the chairs so that they were all an equal distance from the table, he thought of what his life with Brenda would be. On his face, he wore a wide smile. He didn't notice how the waiters eyed him curiously as they lit candles and neatened the menus by the front door. Charlie smiled because he would be with Brenda, but inside, his heart was breaking at the thought of never coming back to The Lantern again. Tonight was his goodbye. He'd miss the smells from the kitchen, chatting to customers, the bustle of a weekend night, the laid-back Sunday afternoons when people stayed for hours eating *meze* by the platter. He'd even miss the late nights, the trips in heavy traffic to wholesalers, the bills, the tardy staff, the staff who stole from him. Everything. He was saying goodbye with a smile on his face. Of course, it would be a different story when it came to saying goodbye to his wife, Ana, and his daughters, Crystal, Maria and Athena. Crystal was pregnant, and he hoped he would see the child when he or she was born. He hoped they'd find it in their hearts to forgive him.

Charlie left the head waiter to lock up that night. He wanted to make sure Ana was still awake when he arrived home. It was time to tell his wife that it was over and that this was goodbye. He let himself into the house, surprised that the lights were all out. Ana must already be in bed. It would be hard to wake her, especially for the purpose of breaking up their marriage. He turned on the hall light, and when he did the same in the living room, he sensed a strangeness about it. Was the house already not his home? Before even packing a case? It struck him then that there was no evidence of his wife having been home for the evening. No side plates on the table by the sofa, her favourite seat for watching television. She always snacked while viewing, and it was always Charlie who took out the plate. In the kitchen, the sink, table and counter tops looked exactly as they had when he'd left for work that afternoon. The kitchen smelled fresh, no sign that an evening meal had been cooked. Not even a tea cup was left turned down on the sink tidy. Where was Ana?

Upstairs, there was no light under the bathroom door and their bedroom door was ajar. It was dark inside the room and he sensed its emptiness, but still he entered. He clicked on the light switch and looked all around as if Ana was playing a game of hide and seek with him. The bedroom smelled of Ana's perfume, Ana's cosmetics, her hairspray, but there was no Ana. Not in bed asleep, not on the chair by the window doing embroidery. Not anywhere. The last thing he did was check the other two bedrooms. They were cool with an odour of furniture polish. No one had been in them for a long time.

He ran down the stairs and looked out of the window. Ana didn't drive. She hadn't learned how. So looking for a car that didn't exist was ridiculous, but he did it all the same. His first thought was that Ana knew he was planning to leave. She always said she could read him like a book. Had she known his own mind? Even before he did? Armed with that knowledge, had she decided to be the one to leave or had she disappeared at this very moment just so he couldn't tell her, so that he couldn't utter the words, 'I'm leaving you.'

He picked up the phone and called Crystal, his eldest daughter. 'It's Dad. I'm sorry it's late, but is your mother with you?'

'No.' She hung up without a goodbye before Charlie could ask if she'd heard from Ana.

When he called Maria, the first thing she said was, 'Dad, I was asleep, it's late.'

'I know it's late, but I'm worried about your mum. I thought she was spending her night off at home, and she's not here.'

'Oh,' said Maria. She sounded as cool as Crystal had. 'She's not here.' She, too, hung up without a goodbye.

Of course, at this point, Charlie had no idea that his daughters were angry at him. Not their loving Papa, the one they cuddled when they were younger and hugged whenever they saw him. He called his youngest daughter next.

'Thank goodness you're up, Athena,' he breathed down the phone. 'I feel I'm going crazy here.'

'What is it, Dad?'

'Have I called at a bad time? You don't sound happy to hear from your old Papa.'

'Well, maybe that's because I'm not.'

'What's the matter, my darling?'

'You know, Dad. You know what you did. To Mum. To all of us. To our family.'

He lowered his shoulders, the skin on his face prickled, his body turned cold. His daughter's words needed no clarification. Ana knew. They all knew. 'Put your mother on the phone.'

'Forget it, Dad. She doesn't want to speak to you. In fact, she's finally gone to bed. She was exhausted from crying. I hope you're happy now.'

'I'm not happy. How could I be happy? You all hate me. Look, I'm coming over. I need to talk to her.'

'To say what? That you have a black whore for a girlfriend?'

'Don't say that, Athena.'

'You think we don't know who she is? We saw her. We were there today, and we told her what for. She knows she won't be getting a piece of the restaurant, so she won't want to know you now.'

'You don't know what you're talking about. What do you mean you told her what for? How did you even know where to find her?'

'Come off it, Dad. Uncle Stavrakis has a big mouth, and under pressure, he'll tell you anything.'

'Damn it, Athena. You had no right to do this.'

'Of course we did. It's our family we're talking about. You think we're going to allow that black tart to ruin us?'

'Don't called her that.' Charlie's voice was loud. The loudest it had ever been when talking to the girls. But his anger was hot. A rage had risen with every bitter word his daughter spat at him. He wanted to slam down the phone and drive straight over there, take her over his knee for once in her life. He'd spoiled them all. Given in to their every whim, and they'd often spoken to him with disrespect. He'd laughed it off, but this time it was different. 'She has more dignity than you will ever have. She loves me. She respects me. She's not like you.'

'I'm glad I'm not like her. And you should be glad you didn't raise a whore.'

His daughter slammed down the phone. He held the receiver, squeezing it in his hand until his knuckles turned white. Until it burned to squeeze any tighter. If he could snap the phone in two, he would. Instead, he grabbed for his keys, left the house, not entirely sure he'd heard the door close shut but jumped into his car without looking back. He drove with the rage still coursing through him. It blinded him, made him speed through a red light. It deafened him to the angry toots from drivers, the man who yelled when Charlie's speeding caused him to lose control of his bike and hit a parked car. He didn't see or hear the siren when a police car followed him along the Uxbridge Road, bearing down on him, headlights flashing. Swerving fast, he cut around a corner and parked with a screech outside the flat above the dry-cleaners where Brenda lived.

30

Marta

Marta will never see her son again. She'll spend a lifetime wondering about him, hoping that he has a good life, that he will be happy and that he will fall in love one day and find reciprocity for that love. That he will be a good man. At times, she will think about trying to contact him, and at times, she'll wonder if he'll ever try to find her. All her life, she'll see his face. One day, though, Marta will have a baby girl. This is a distant time in her life, one she isn't thinking about or dreaming of. All she does think about is her ability to make amends with the people she has lost and the collateral damage of realising too late that sexuality shouldn't hinder one's life but be accepted as part of it. Marta is still learning about who she is. The thing she is sure about is that she wants to see her sister again and she wants, more than anything, to see Louise, too.

With her friend, Ione, she had danced her sadness to the back of her mind, and by the morning, despite a turbulent sleep, she'd woken up with a sense of vitality and starting anew.

She called her sister, Agnieszka, when she got home from work in the afternoon. It had been so long since she'd spoken to her, Marta had no idea whether the number she had for her was still in use or where she would be at that moment. Would she be at work? Driving home from the supermarket? After ten years of not being in contact, her sister might have gone back to Poland for all she knew.

When the call was picked up, all Marta could hear were screams and shouts. They were loud and angry. They came from young voices. Her sister's children? Was she an aunt?

'Hello?' Her sister's voice was hurried and agitated. 'Hold on, let me go into the kitchen.' The young voices died down, and Marta heard a door slam. 'I'm sorry. Who is this?'

'It's … it's …'

'Who did you want to speak to?'

'Agnieszka.'

'Yes, that's me. Who are you? And I don't want to buy a thing before you go on.'

'No, Agnieszka … I-I'm not selling anything.'

Marta listened to her sister's sharp intake of breath on the end of the line before seconds of silence ensued. Then, finally, 'Marta? Is that you?'

Marta heard tears on her sister's voice. She had to blink her own away. 'It is Marta. It's me, Agnieszka. How-how are you?'

'How *am* I? I'm happy to hear your voice. To hear my sister after all this time. Marta, where are you? Are you in trouble? Are you all right? Are you in London? When can I see you?'

Marta giggled. 'You never did have any patience. How can I answer if you don't let me?'

'I'm sorry. Speak to me. Tell me everything. Starting from where did you go and why.'

'Oh my God. I don't even know where to be begin. I was just afraid you would hang up the phone and you wouldn't talk to me.'

'You are joking. I have been waiting for this day. I knew you would call me. I knew it. Where are you?'

'I'm living in Shepherd's Bush. I'm all right. I have a job and I'm okay.'

'Marta. How can you be so close and not come to see me? Or let me know you're all right? Look, is it okay to meet you?'

‘Now?’

‘Yes. I am more than happy to leave these animals in my house to kill each other. I’ve tried to calm them down, they just get more and more angry with each other.’

‘Your children?’

‘Yes, I have a girl and boy. Seven and nine. They’re not always this bad, but it’s like a war zone today. Their father is home any minute. They can feed themselves, kill themselves, lock themselves in their room. I don’t care. What’s your address?’

Marta’s heart swelled to the point of erupting from her body. The feeling of being cocooned inside a fake Marta, a Marta dressed in multicolours, laughter on the tip of her lips, brimming with cheer had ceased. The real Marta, the one she hid from her family, the one she hid from almost everyone she’d met in London these past ten years was about to emerge. The only people who had come close to knowing who she really was included Ione, Elliot, Katey and Louise. It was their friendship, kindness and time that coaxed her most of the way out of her hollow shell. Now the broken connection to her family would begin to fuse, the binds to blood re-established, as soon as her sister, Agnieszka, walked through her door.

Now that Marta had reached out to family, she had nothing to lose by doing the same with Louise. If she were to send a text message, the worst Louise could do would be to ignore it, block her number. Marta knew it was important for her to try, though. This whole experience of denying people from her life, not telling the truth and hiding her identity, had stifled the person within and she was choking on her mistakes. She couldn’t ignore the tug at her heart to reach out to Louise.

She sent a text message. It was long and rambling, childish in places, she thought, but she gave herself no room to manoeuvre out of the only thing she could do now. Agnieszka was on her way. Marta clicked Send, and within seconds, Louise replied.

31

Louise

Louise had never been to the coffee shop on Shepherd's Bush Green before that afternoon: it was a new place. She sat looking at the fast-paced view outside the glass-fronted shop. Cars raced carelessly around the green, narrowly avoiding collisions as the drivers negotiated double- and single-decker buses. Pedestrians of all walks of life passed the coffee shop. From the woman who spent half her day shouting at traffic to the young man in a trendy suit, carrying a briefcase and a Starbucks cup. He walked straight past the shouting woman, probably on his way to the station.

Louise was meeting Marta. She didn't think she'd see Marta so soon. If at all. Since their evening at Marta's flat, she had begun to consider their relationship as over, resigned to her 'no more drama' decision. The truth was, Louise missed Marta the second she closed the door to her flat but she was too tired and confused to go back and tell her so. Marta poured her heart out about her family, but Louise realised she'd never done the same with anyone about how Danika had broken hers. Somewhere along the line, her broken heart had stopped feeling so broken, but she still thought about Danika and so her heart might not be healed. All she knew to do was protect it. Vow that she would not get so close to anyone that they could hurt her again. She thought she could find happiness at arms length and, up until the time she'd met Marta, she'd been happy to conduct every relationship since Danika from the safety of distance. Marta had changed that. Before Louise realised, the distance had become hard to maintain. Her arms had closed around Marta and her resolve had begun to falter. This colourful and funny person with an enticing accent and a depth she longed to explore was getting close. Louise had been shocked to hear that Marta could give up her own child. To allow someone like that to get too close was a dangerous and foolish notion. Louise was afraid. Afraid she'd find herself spiralling out of control, unable to focus on her future aims, afraid of falling in love with Marta.

The night she left Marta's flat, she took the long walk to the bus stop, waited in the cold for the 237, but by the time she returned to her house with the ancient smells of pasta sauce, curry and stir-fry ingrained in the wallpaper, she knew she had fallen in love with Marta. The next day when she'd had to clear Charlie's things away, she'd thought of Marta. As she held the two letters that Charlie had written to Brenda Mason, she thought of Marta. And, two days later, when she was alone in her room and she heard the buzz of a text coming through on her phone, she had hoped it was Marta. It was.

She saw Marta approaching the coffee shop door, her dark hair bouncing against the back of the heavy, deep red jacket she usually wore to Pilates. Her cheeks were flushed from walking. Marta pulled open the heavy glass door, paused to look around and quickly spotted Louise at her small table by the window. She smiled at Louise who waved back.

'Can I get you another of those?' Marta asked, looking down at the half-empty cup of black coffee.

'Er, yes, please. Thank you.'

Marta went to the counter. The queue was mercifully short so it wasn't long before she was back at the table.

'Here you are.' Marta took off her jacket. She was wearing a fluffy purple jumper and a long blue skirt. She put the jacket on the back of her chair and placed her large bag at her feet. 'Thank you for agreeing to meet. I've only got an hour, though.'

'That's okay, like I said, I've got to see my tutor later so I need to go about the same time as you.' Louise absently checked her phone, hoping it didn't seem to Marta as if she was anxious to leave.

'Usually, I eat my lunch at the shop,' Marta said. 'But Elliot often insists I take the actual hour away from the shop for well-being reasons. So cute, but I love being in the shop.'

'You said he was nice.'

'The best.' She poured a packet of sugar into her cup of tea and stirred without looking up.

'You wanted to meet me,' Louise said.

'Yes, and thank you for coming. I suggested the daytime because I didn't want it to seem like a date or anything.'

'Right.'

'Because, you know? You don't want anything heavy.'

Louise nodded, blew into her coffee mug and took a sip.

'So, I know I said some things that didn't sit well with you,' Marta went on, 'but, it's just that … well … I just didn't want to have blown it completely. I mean, I really like you, Louise, and even if you only want me for a friend, then, I can be fine with that.'

'You can be? Meaning it will take you some time to be fine with it? Like, if I said, be my friend, you'd have to learn how to do that?'

Marta shook her head in confusion. 'You sound angry with me,' she said. 'I just meant that I know I have baggage. A lot, right? But I'm not a bad person. I thought that, if you wanted to, we could be friends.'

'Instead of…?'

'You know.' Marta gave a short laugh and blushed.

'Well,' Louise began but stopped. She looked out of the window for a moment to summon the right words. She saw the woman who shouted at traffic and thought for one moment she might walk straight out into the road and confront one of the vehicles she seemed to be so angry with.

Marta looked at Louise and waited patiently for her gaze to return to the small table.

'I'm sorry,' Louise said. 'I've been distracted for days. I was at my client's house.'

'Charlie? The one with the awful family?'

She looked at Marta, wondering if she'd see a hint of sarcasm in her face but only saw complete interest and concern.

'That's right. Charlie went back into hospital. The night we saw each other last. He took a turn for the worst, and now it isn't looking good. The doctors, apparently, told the family not to expect a positive outcome. They say that when they think a patient will die. I'd like to go and see him.'

'Did you want me to come with you?'

'No, it's okay, I can go myself. It's just that the family asked me to pack up his things and I found a couple of unsealed letters that he'd written to someone. His mistress, actually. The reason his wife and daughters hate him so much is because of his affair. I took the letters home because I didn't want the family to have them. I know it was wrong, but if you knew the situation…'

Marta quickly shook her head. 'I would have done the same thing.'

'Well, my mind is on that and not on this.' She pointed a finger across the space between herself and Marta. Then she sat quietly. She took a deep breath before she spoke again. 'Look, I'm sorry for being so quiet. It's difficult for me. You asked if I wanted to be your friend.'

'Yes.' Marta sat forward in her seat.

'The thing is, though I tried to resist it, I actually want more than that. I want us to carry on as if this was the day after that first night.'

A smile broke out on Marta's face. She blushed crimson. Tears welled in her eyes, and she bit her bottom lip to stop herself talking. She waited for Louise to continue.

‘I’m sorry, Marta. I was an idiot.’

‘No, not at all. I totally get it. I know what it’s like to be worried about relationships, how they are going, how they are perceived. How to keep my sanity and trying not to hurt another living soul. I would never hurt you, Louise. I just wanted you to know who I really was.’

‘I know, and I get that. Trouble is, I wasn’t being honest about how I really feel. I like you a lot. I want to be with you. Yes, I’m afraid about where this will lead us, but I didn’t want you to think I was judging you. I’m not like that. I was scared. I didn’t want to be with a person who might leave me so easily.’

‘The way I left my baby?’

Louise reached for her hands across the table. ‘Life gives us hard choices to make. I was unfair, thinking only of myself. No mother gives up a child for selfish reasons. Mothers love their babies and they want the best for them. You wanted the best for yours, and it was a hard decision you had to make. I know that. I don’t judge you for it. In fact, I admire you. You’re a brave woman.’

Now the tears came. Down they fell along Marta’s cheeks and onto the table. Louise was aware of everyone’s eyes on them, boring into her back, necks craning from across the aisle. Despite this, she reached over and wiped Marta’s cheeks. Dabbing at each tear with her napkin until Marta smiled back at her.

‘I actually reached out to my sister,’ Marta said. She sniffed. ‘Ten years and it was as if it had only been ten minutes. She came straight over. We talked for hours. Her husband kept texting to see when she was coming home.’

‘That’s amazing. You’re making amends.’

‘Well, with my sister, anyway. I’ll have to work up to contacting my parents. Tomasz. Apparently he remarried. It’s legal after so many years of separation, I believe. I just can’t get the image of him waiting for me out of my head. My sister said he waited for years. My heart broke for him all over again. He was such a sweet man, and I feel like a murderer or something.' Marta gave a light laugh.

'Hardly. Look, that's in the past. You have to move on. You'll speak to him or not. You'll know what to do.'

After a few moments, Marta said, 'And you? What will you do with the letters?'

'The letters? Jesus, I really don't—'

There was a loud crash from outside. Everyone in the coffee shop rose and angled their bodies to the window. Outside, a bus stood stationary in the street. In fact, all traffic and the sound of the street had stopped. People were gathering in the road, and Louise's heart began to thump in her chest. She reached across and pulled Marta's hand so that she was facing her again.

'I need you to help me think it through. The letters. But it's time for you to go back to work.'

'Of course.' Marta nodded. 'We both need to go. I wonder if we'll get out of here. I wonder what happened.'

Louise suspected she knew. The woman who had been shouting must have confronted a driver. Maybe even the bus. People were gathering close to the spot where she'd been standing. Louise pulled on her padded jacket and grabbed her bag.

'Come on. Let's go.'

32

Marta

Outside, everyone pushed and shoved. They craned their necks towards the unfolding scene, the cause of the halted traffic. Marta was momentarily lightheaded. Louise had held her hand on the way out of the coffee shop. She did not want to release it and lose the pulsating rhythm that filled her body. She looked intently into Louise's eyes.

'Marta! What are you doing? Let go of my hand—I have to go and see what happened.'

Marta watched Louise shouldering her way through the throng of people then quickly losing sight as bodies closed around her. Louise had disappeared, so Marta elbowed her way into the crowd, surprised at how easy it was to move people aside. Perhaps they thought Marta was the much-needed help they'd all been expecting. Had anyone called for help, yet? They all held up their phones and were recording the events.

At the centre of the mayhem, Marta saw Louise on her knees giving mouth-to-mouth resuscitation to a woman lying very still on the ground. Louise had covered the woman with her padded jacket. In the distance, above the murmurs, she heard an ambulance. Seconds later, a member of the ambulance crew and a police officer pushed and shoved their way through the crowd, begging the people to, 'Move aside!'

As Louise rose slowly from the ground, she mouthed something to the emergency crew. Spotting Marta, she gestured for her to follow her away from the people still milling very close by.

'Will she be all right?' Marta asked Louise.

Louise nodded. 'Let's just get away from this.'

Another police car arrived. Officers directed the traffic, making way for the ambulance to leave the scene and head for the hospital. The woman who had been shouting at the traffic was being dragged to one side by a constable. She kept on exclaiming, 'I see it all! It's a madness, me tell ya. It's a madness!'

Louise had a hand on Marta's arm as they walked away. 'She died,' Louise whispered.

Marta stopped. 'Oh my God. No.'

'She was more or less gone when I got there. I tried to save her. I think she said something, but I couldn't hear her. Her dying words and I couldn't make them out.'

'Should you say something to someone?'

'What can I say? I didn't see anything. Everything happened so—'

'Excuse me, miss.' Marta and Louise turned around to see a member of the police force towering above them, holding Louise's bloody jacket. He held it out. 'I believe this is yours. We also need a statement from you.'

'Of course,' Louise said. 'Give me a second to say goodbye to my friend.'

'I'm not leaving you,' said Marta.

'You need to get back to work. I'll see you later. I need to talk to you about the letters. After what just happened, I know I must read them. If I can find Brenda Mason before Charlie goes, it could be a good thing. Right?'

'Of course.' Marta nodded several times to drive home her concern and reassurances. Louise gently kissed her cheek and walked off a little way with the police officer who had a notebook in hand.

Shepherd's Bush Green returned, almost immediately, back to its usual busy speed, but Marta's legs were heavy as she walked back to Val's Music Shop. She had a lot to reflect on after that unusual hour: Louise's face, the light brush of her lips, holding hands across the table, the blood on Louise's jacket and a person had just died. How fleeting life can be, she thought. Such little time we have, we shouldn't waste it. It was no wonder Louise wanted to find Brenda Mason. That name seemed to have a meaning to Marta, but she didn't know why. Entering the music shop, she paid no attention to the flyers and notices that flapped upwards from the draught when she opened the door. One notice hadn't been unsettled. It was handwritten on a postcard: an advert for a piano teacher called Ione Mason.

33

Charlie

They didn't keep him long, just a couple of hours until he calmed down. That may have been because the paperwork involved for an overnight stay at the station was too tiresome or maybe someone took pity on Charlie, having deemed that whatever made him so distraught was punishment enough.

Charlie had caused a commotion on the street, shouting, 'Brenda! Brenda!' at the top of his voice after jumping out of his car. One of the police officers from the car following him threw Charlie against his own car and slapped on a pair of handcuffs.

'You're a danger to yourself. You been drinking, sir?'

Of course he hadn't been. If he was drunk, it was on emotions that fuelled him, charging him from head to toe. Fury. Worry. Anguish. Love. When the officers prevented him from going up to Brenda's flat, he saw red. All he'd wanted was to see Brenda, apologise for everything Ana had said to her. Brenda had to know of his decision. He loved her and he wanted to be with her. He was giving up everything he had for her. She was all that mattered in his life.

With a slightly clearer head, he left the police station only to discover that his car had been impounded. He had some cash in his wallet so waved down a black cab and asked the driver to rush him over to the street where Brenda lived.

His feet pounded the metal steps in the back alley behind the shops up to the flats. The iron creaked and clanged under his step. It wasn't quite dawn, and Charlie's heavy feet served as an early-morning alarm to anyone still asleep.

He rattled a large set of keys and found the little shiny one that fit the Chubb lock in Brenda's door and let himself in. He'd expected her to be sitting up, waiting for him. She must have heard him crying her name. He was sure she had, but of course, she'd be too upset with Charlie and his family to want to talk. Charlie would have to earn her forgiveness. He would apologise first of all for the way his wife acted, beg her to forgive everything Ana said that might have hurt her, pray that she could put any ugliness behind them. Secondly, he would go down on his knees and apologise from the core of his heart for not leaving his wife sooner. He had been a fool. He had loved Brenda the first night he met her. All night he'd chastised himself for not immediately admitting that there was nothing in the world he wanted more than to be with her.

He knew Brenda wasn't going to forgive him so easily. So often she had said, 'Charlie, it isn't love, it's lust. I'm a young woman. I sing in a club in sexy clothes. I'm not like your wife. I'm different. We all want something different, don't we?' Charlie always answered, 'You are so wrong. If you could feel what I feel, you'd know you were wrong. And one day, I will prove it.'

This was the day.

Charlie wondered why the flat was all in darkness. No lamp in the living room, no light on in the kitchen. He could smell something like burning but ignored it as he ran to the bedroom. He didn't care that she went to sleep. Brenda had every right to be angry.

'Brenda.' He whispered her name as he sat on the bed and reached for the lamp on the table. Before his eyes adjusted to the light, he ran a hand right across the neat bed finding nothing more to touch than a cold bedspread.

He sprang to his feet. The bathroom was empty. Rushing back to the bedroom, he slowly took in the way it had been left. The wardrobe door was wide open. Not one item of Brenda's clothing remained. Every surface had been wiped clear of any trace that this beautiful and vibrant woman once lived there. It had been the same in the living room and kitchen, but his brain had refused to acknowledge it. Now his mind allowed the fact that Brenda had gone to sink in until eventually his body did, too. It grew cold. It grew weak. His eyes couldn't stay open, they closed and flushed out warm, salty tears onto his cheeks. His hands shook as he raised them to his face, and his body gave way as it toppled to one side, landing with a soft thud onto the bed.

Several hours passed. He lay just like that for all of those hours, until the sound of a police siren woke him from a dark slumber. In the space between sleep and wakefulness, Charlie was confused. His eyes fully open, now, he realised where he was and why he was there.

He lifted slowly to a seated position. His neck racked with pain, pins and needles running down his arm. The sleep had done nothing to revive him: he was more wretched than when he'd arrived in the early hours. In the living room, he saw again the ironing board and unplugged iron, its silver metal stained a brownish black. Brenda must have been eager to get away, he thought, and left something burning while she packed.

He spun around in the flat, looking for clues. Where could she have gone? Why did it look as if she wasn't coming back? Charlie searched his thick head for ideas about her whereabouts. He realised very quickly that, apart from a mother who died and a father who went back to Jamaica when she was born, Charlie didn't know any of Brenda's family. In fact, she never spoke of them and it was implied that she had no living relatives in England. The only people Charlie ever saw Brenda with were the members of the band. He remembered her employer, downstairs in the dry-cleaners.

Stumbling back down the metal stairs, he rushed around to the dry-cleaners shopfront only to find it locked. It didn't open until eight-thirty and the time on the wall clock inside said six forty-five.

It's okay, he kept telling himself. I'll find her. I'll go home, pack, come back later and ask her boss for any information. If he didn't know anything, Charlie thought, he would ask each and every member of Brenda's band. One of them was bound to know. She might even be staying with one of them. That would be it. He began the walk home, catching a glimpse of himself in a shop window. Almost doing a double take because he didn't recognise himself, he rubbed his chin. He needed a shower, a shave, something to eat. To get his car out of the pound. Then he'd find Brenda and find a place for them to be together. It wasn't too late for him to make this happen. At last.

34

Ione

My next piano student, Katey, is due to arrive. Funny to say the words, 'next student', but I do have three now. Two are quite proficient piano players, and it's nice to hear the flat filled with music that I'm not making myself, either on my piano or from the player. The lonely, empty gaps disappear as the notes float into them: triplets, ornaments, legato lines and broken chords chime their way into the lonely spots and later, hours after the student has gone, the lonely spaces still ring with sound. I'm filled with the idea of possibilities with this new life I'm carving out for myself. For the first time since moving down here, I slept through the night. I didn't wake up frazzled, clenching my jaw or feeling bewildered. I'd often woken up wondering what the hell I was doing in London, in this flat, in this bedroom. But this is where I live now. It's new and it's mine. The bedroom belongs to me and I belong to it. This is no longer the place I had to run to.

I had to run, of course, to save my sanity and my life. One of the biggest feelings that I have, and probably the most important as I begin to settle in my new home, is that I'm not haunted by David anymore. I don't see him riding on the top deck of the bus. I don't see him in a mirror if I happen to be holding a dress up in front of me in a shop. I don't see that sneer on his face telling me with his eyes that I look ridiculous, that I should be ashamed of my appearance. I choose my own clothes, I make my own decisions. I have stopped flinching at loud bangs or sudden noises, and I don't stare at the phone if a number I don't know appears on the screen. I must have lost several potential students just because I was afraid to answer my bloody mobile. David doesn't have this number. David does not know where in London I am, and even if he did search me out, I feel ready to confront him. I will face him head on.

The doorbell rings, and I'm smiling to myself, standing in the living room with hands on my hips like a superhero. I run to answer the door only to see two figures standing on the other side of it.

Katey beams a smile at me. 'It's okay,' she says. 'You haven't double-booked. It's just my overprotective boyfriend insisted on walking me here.' She gives him a quick peck on the cheek. He is a tall, good-looking boy with short dark hair and a hint of olive in his skin. I smile to Katey as I close the door.

'Is that the musician you wanted to impress?' I ask as she leads the way to the living room, removing her navy donkey jacket as she goes.

'That's him. Nico.'

'Is it getting serious?'

Her sand-coloured cheeks fill with a pinkish glow. 'You could say that. He was just round at mine. My dad met him. Embarrassing or what. I wasn't expecting Dad to be home.'

'They're both musicians though, right?'

She nods.

'Well, it's an unspoken rule that musicians get on. We're easygoing people, generally.'

'It's true. I met my mum and dad's musician friends and they're all pretty chill. Come to think of it, Nico is, too. He's going through a hard time because his granddad is in hospital and he hasn't been able to see him yet.'

'I hope he'll be all right.'

'Me too. Sounds like a nice person. A bit senile, though.'

'Okay then. Shall we warm up with some scales?'

The lesson goes well. Katey has a natural flare for music, one she didn't explore when she was younger. More's the pity. She'd be flying by now if she had. But with a musical dad and boyfriend, she at least has people she can practise with.

'This is sounding great, Katey,' I tell her as she finishes her attempts at perfecting *Midnight Train to Georgia*. I've smiled all the way through as she has tried to master a song that was always a favourite of Mum's.

Several times, I found myself looking at the urn on the top shelf, wondering when I will eventually spread Mum's ashes. I decided that they have to be spread somewhere. They needed to blow free in the wind somewhere special, to be free like Mum's spirit. I had read that a person's soul is released in death, and I'd found myself waking up, perspiring on many nights, wondering if I'd trapped Mum's soul in that urn. I knew it was a silly thing to think, but I knew I couldn't scatter her ashes until the right place presented itself. It would one day.

There is a tap on the door as Katey closes the piano lid.

'Your next student?' she asks.

I shake my head as I go to the door. 'Maybe Nico hung around so he could escort you home.'

Katey giggles as she slips her arms through her jacket.

I open the door to another tall and good-looking man. Not Nico but one who seems to be lost and a little flustered.

'Um, yeah, sorry,' he says. 'I'm Katey's dad.'

'Dad? What you doing here?' Katey is at my shoulder, so I stand aside to let her out.

'You didn't have to come,' she says. 'I was going to walk.'

'I know, but the nights are darker and I've brought the car.'

'Nice,' she says and walks past him to the gate. She stops. 'Coming then?'

Her father hasn't left the outside doormat. He seems rooted there, a slight grin on his face. He swings around to face Katey and then back to me. 'I know you, don't I?' he says.

'Oh my God. Lame, Dad.' Katey opens the gate and barrels out. 'I'll be by the car.' I hear her loudly whisper, 'Embarrassing much,' as she walks away.

'I'm sorry,' he says. 'Katey can be a bit… This isn't a pickup or anything. I do know you, don't I?'

I nod and smile. 'I'll put you out of your misery. A couple of weeks ago, maybe three, a friend and I walked by your shop. Val's Music?'

His puzzled look turns into a grin. 'That's it,' he says. 'You wanted a piano tuner. Did you find someone?'

'I did. No. I didn't. Actually, it wasn't urgent. It's just that I'm new in the area and I was just wondering where to find things. A piano tuner. If I needed one.'

'Well, we need to be prepared for these things. Pianos can go out of tune'— he snaps his fingers—'just like that.'

'So true. I … um … I think Katey's waiting.'

He turns to face the street. 'She's actually waving me over. Better go. Thanks for the lessons. She's really loving them.'

'She's a great student. A fast learner.'

'Yeah.' He doesn't know what else to say, so he turns and leaves. He has a little trouble trying to unlock the gate and finally manages it. He keeps his head down as he mumbles, 'Thanks.' It's like his quota for flirtatious behaviour has expired and he has nothing left to say.

I hear him run to catch up with Katey, and from the living room, I hear their car start up and pull away.

I think I was flirting, too. Such a strange feeling but such a welcome one. Before I met David, I'd been single a long while. It seemed that as soon as I started to date him, I became the attraction of several men and David often became annoyed by the attention I got. I did the best I could to ignore any lingering looks, making sure I stayed close to David if we were out in public so that no other man spoke to or even looked at me. I look back now on how stupid that was on both David's and my part. That alone should have sounded alarm bells. But things turned out the way they did.

That was in the past, and I have a future now, not a dead end.

In my immediate future is a telephone call to Jeannie to tell her all about the man from the music shop. I still don't know his name. I don't know Katey's surname, either, so the man from the music shop remains a mystery. I take another glance at Mum's urn, and I reopen the piano and play her song.

35

Elliot

The drive home from Katey's piano lesson began in silence. The passenger side window was misted up and Elliot's view of the row of parked cars along Ione's road was a blur. He glanced at his daughter's profile against the dark evening. Though Katey was so like her mother in appearance, when she was this deep in thought, her bottom lip between her teeth, she reminded him more of himself.

Katey took her phone from her pocket releasing a heavy sigh that obscured the view through the windscreen further. Elliot directed the fan onto the screen and indicated left at the next junction. Katey sniffed her disapproval at the sudden waft of cold air and proceeded to Snap Chat or WhatsApp one or all of her many friends. He could imagine her message: *When your dad embarrasses you in front of your piano teacher*. Angry face emoji. She sent the occasional glare or frown in her father's direction. Elliot deflected them by turning the music up loud in the car and whistling along. Katey reached over and turned off the radio.

'What is it?' Elliot asked, a note of feigned exasperation in his voice.

'You know. Why were you moving to my piano teacher?'

'*Moving* to? If you mean chatting up, I was only being friendly.'

'Dad, I saw you.'

Elliot pulled in outside their house and turned off the engine. He put his hand on the lock release but turned to his daughter instead.

'I was only asking about your lesson, Katey-Kate. That's all.'

'You haven't called me that since I was four, and Ione is way out of your league.' She looked at her phone as it buzzed.

'Thanks a lot,' Elliot said, dipping his head to try to catch her eye. 'I thought you wanted me to have a girlfriend.'

'So you do like her?' She looked straight at him now.

'That's not what I said.'

Katey got out of the car and slammed the door shut. Elliot followed suit, clicking the remote to lock the car, a slight smile on his face which he wiped off the moment they stood at the door.

'Are we going in?' he asked. Katey had her key ready but didn't reach for the lock.

'I don't have a problem with you dating,' she said, her voice a lot less harsh. 'I just don't want you to embarrass me by asking her out. If she says no, I couldn't live with the humiliation of it.'

Elliot reached across to unlock the door, shaking his head, reluctant to engage in a teenage rant that centred entirely on how everything made Katey feel. He could do without a lecture from a seventeen-year-old about what he should or shouldn't do. Elliot was convinced that teenagers stressed too much about everything. He couldn't remember ever being like that. He remembered sitting in his room, playing music and letting his parents get on with their own life. Katey seemed hell-bent on telling him how to run his.

She had primed Elliot for a full hour before introducing him to Nico, telling him what he could and couldn't say, what to mention and what to keep quiet about. It hadn't left him with much to talk about. As it turned out, Katey's boyfriend, the first that he would know of at least, was a nice boy. Far less fussy and anxious than his daughter. Not once did he roll his eyes or shake his head at him for saying something that was 'lame'. So afraid of disappointing his daughter, when Nico appeared in their living room for the first time, Elliot barely said a word. He said so little that Katey bulged her eyes and tried to coax more out of him. It was Nico exclaiming, 'Nice guitar,' that broke the ice. Watched closely by Katey, Elliot talked about the guitar on the stand in the living room until she coughed and he quickly finished what he was saying.

Nico had been polite: he shook Elliot's hand, and Elliot was happy to leave them alone in the living room, retiring to the study where the rest of his instruments were kept. There he strummed tunes, quietly, until Nico left. Apparently, Nico thought Elliot was 'safe'. He'd passed the test.

As he and Katey got the dinner together, he thought about her piano teacher and the idea that someone like her could be in his life as a girlfriend. He had been flirtatious—Katey was right about that—but for him it had been more of an experiment to see if he could be like that with a woman who wasn't Val. Of course, he wasn't going to ask her out, he knew nothing about her: she could be a married woman for all he knew; she might not find him as attractive as he found her. He just wanted to sit with the idea for a while. Maybe one day he'd have the courage to follow up on his flirtations and actually ask someone out. Of course, he'd have to check with Katey whether she was in his league or not.

Once, when Val's time was close, he remembered sitting on the rug next to the bath. Val had just thrown up in the toilet and he was looking at the way the bones protruding from her shoulders jerked and shuddered with the effort of vomiting. Val wiped her mouth with a cloth he'd dampened and passed to her. She sat back against the cool radiator and looked at him, her hair piled in a messy bunch on the very top of her head.

‘Don’t take ages before you meet someone,’ she said. ‘You’ll be lonely.’

Val had already started to talk about what he and Katey should do after her death. She’d decided it was a given, agreeing the doctors knew what they were talking about despite him constantly searching online for miracle cures and trying to persuade Val that the power of positive thinking could get her through this.

‘If I do meet someone,’ he’d said, ‘I hope she doesn’t vomit all the time.’ He’d wanted to kick himself straight after saying such an idiotic thing at a time like that, but Val just grinned.

‘I hope she vomits all the time, on your shoes, into your guitar, in your dinner. Like the wedding party in *Like Water For Chocolate*.’

‘You know I haven’t read it.’

‘Read it and give it to Katey. In fact, give all my books to Katey. I don’t want her turning out to be a heathen, like you.’ She’d rolled towards the toilet bowl and was sick again.

The whites of Elliot’s eyes had turned pink. He blinked over and over, trying to clear them. Val hated to see him cry.

‘I do mean it,’ Val said. ‘Meet someone. Just make sure she’s a good person. I want you to be with a good person. When I’m gone.’

‘How you can be practical at a time like this, I’ll never know.’

‘Just promise me, El. It’s important.’

‘Okay, I promise. Now, let’s get you up.’

The timer for the broccoli clicked off, and Elliot continued to stare at the steam rising from the sides of the saucepan lid.

‘I think it’s done,’ Katey said. ‘I’ll dish out the pasta. You okay?’

‘I’m fine. Hungry. Let’s eat.’

All through dinner, he would wonder if Ione was a good person. As he cleared his plate, looking across at Katey, he silently agreed Ione was out of his league. Though, so too, he thought, had Val been.

36

Marta

To her relief, Louise came along to the Pilates class. There would be no awkward moments, her finger hovering over Louise's name on her phone, too shy to ask if she'd see her later. Marta had been looking forward to 'later' all afternoon. The October evening was mild, the streets were quiet and Marta felt a sense of calm. Everything was falling into place. Louise went over to chat to Callie as Marta and Ione said their goodbyes to a few of the other people from the class.

'Are we going for a drink?' Ione asked. Marta's eyes flicked quickly over to Louise. 'Oh, I see.' Ione smiled and nudged her elbow. 'It's back on then?'

'We met earlier. I think things will work out.' Marta lowered her voice. 'I think she's going through something and needs my help.'

'No problem,' Ione said. 'I'll get off home and leave you both to it.'

'Oh, no, I didn't mean—'

'Are we ready?' Louise jogged over to them, her yoga mat in its bag over her shoulder. She was wearing a red woolly hat that suited her perfectly.

'I'm not coming,' Ione said. 'I need to get back and sort some stuff out.'

'Are you sure?' Marta asked her.

'Oh. Absolutely. I might give you a call tomorrow.'

They left together, all three walking in the same direction towards The Plough. When they got there, Ione said goodbye and carried on up the road.

Marta and Louise settled at the table they always sat at. The Plough was never busy at that time of evening, and Marta went to the bar for a bottle of red wine.

'I'm not really a pub person,' Louise said when Marta arrived back carrying a wine bottle with a red and gold label and two bulbous glasses.

'You should have said before, we could have gone somewhere else,' Marta said.

'What I mean is, I like it here. Nice atmosphere.'

'How have you been since that accident?' Marta asked. 'I thought about you a lot. You must have been shaken up, but you seemed so calm.'

'Well, I was a nurse. It isn't the first time I've seen someone … watched a person slip away like that. I was thinking about her family. None of them would have been expecting that kind of news today.'

'It's awful.'

Louise searched the deep pockets of her padded jacket and pulled out two folded envelopes.

'I brought the letters. I wondered if you could read them with me. It was part of my training, you know, as a nurse, to respect people's property. Not that I wouldn't. I would now, but these letters…'

'You're troubled by them. I understand.'

'I did look inside, just quickly, and there isn't an address. I thought I'd get some clues if I read them.'

'Don't feel bad. Charlie trusted you. You said. He probably trusted you more than his family. At least you look out for him.'

'Sometimes he thought I was her. Brenda. You should have seen the look on his face when he talked about her. Oh no. I'm using the past tense. Like he's already gone. I'm going to see him tomorrow.'

Louise unfolded the envelopes, opened the first one and pulled out the letter, slowly, as if it were being held from inside by invisible hands.

The letter was dated February 1985. It read:

Brenda, My Love

I have been coming to the flat all week in case you changed your mind and came back. I am here. I am ready to start a life with you but I don't know where you are. I don't know where to go and I don't know what my life is without you. I came to tell you I love you. I came to tell you I know what they said to you and I'm sorry for that. But we can be together. We can. I just need you to come back. I just need you to call me and wherever you are I will follow you.

Charlie had signed it with love and kisses. The second letter was longer, more plaintive than the first. In it, Charlie proclaimed that he would sit on a bench in their park at the same time as they used to meet, every day, waiting for her to come back to him. The only reason he would stop was if she sent a note to say she did not love him anymore.

The women read the letters through blurred vision, the pain and anguish rising from the pages and into their very souls. They both knew what heartbreak was; they could feel Charlie's desperation.

'What can I do?' Louise asked. 'The letters don't tell me anything about Brenda. Charlie is as lost as we are.'

'Did you Google her name?'

'Yes. Loads of times. I knew she was a singer and sang in blues clubs in the West End. I already searched YouTube. Nothing. She was Brenda Mason then, what if she married and changed her name? What if she changed it anyway so Charlie couldn't find her?'

'It sounds as if she loved him, too. From what he says. And this park they used to meet at. I wonder which one it was. Someone in the family might know.'

'They were meeting in secret, so I guess not.'

‘My God, this is awful.’ Marta put her hand on Louise’s. ‘Now that you’ve read them, what will you do?’

‘I suppose, I’ll hang on to them. When I see Charlie, I’ll try telling him I found them. If he can tell me what to do, it would be better to try than to just give it to his wife or daughters. Looks like someone said something to Brenda, gave her a hard time, frightened her away. It was probably them.’

Marta nodded.

‘Oh, look, I’m depressing you.’ Louise tried to laugh, but the sound didn’t quite leave her throat.

‘Well, don’t worry about that. There are still some things I have to tell you about my life. Especially after talking to my sister. We can depress each other.’

Louise reached over and hugged Marta. A brief but strong hug. Before pulling away, she left a soft kiss on Marta’s cheek. ‘Let’s hope we don’t get depressed,’ Louise said, uncertainty in her voice, though her smile was wide. ‘Let’s hope everything works out. Not all love stories have to end like it did for these two.’

A wave which began in Marta’s stomach rose and swelled upwards to her heart. It rose higher until it filled the top cavity of her chest, cascading in her throat so that she heaved an audible sigh. It took all her might to keep this wave at bay, trying urgently to keep it lapping at her heart and to not allow it to choke her words away. She felt her breath deepen as she tried to calm herself but couldn’t stop the glow of redness in her cheeks as Louise’s words repeated in her head. For Marta, theirs was a love story that had only just begun. One tiny spark, unsteady at first and almost blown out before it could fully ignite. She wanted to believe that they were lovers with a future. But there was all this history to resolve. What if Louise changed her mind and thought better of trusting her love to Marta? If Marta were to talk about her sister to Louise, was there a chance Louise could run away, like Brenda, to a place where no one could find her? And hadn’t

Marta done the same thing to people she loved, run away so they couldn't find her?

There was so much for Marta to worry about, but instead, she allowed herself the feeling of falling in love. Her life had been devoid of this kind of emotion; she knew the only thing to do was to grab it with both hands. If it began to slip through her fingers, she could alter her grasp, hold it for as long as she could. If she didn't succeed, she would at least have this moment in time. A time when Louise was the present tense, her possible future, the best chance she had of knowing true love.

'I will help you,' Marta said, blurting the words out clumsily before even understanding what she was about to say. 'I will come with you to the hospital to see Charlie. I will help you find Brenda to see if she will come to him before he dies. This is too important to ignore. You're right, don't give the letter to his family. It'll get torn up, thrown away. That would be the worst thing that could happen to this love story. Can you imagine him sitting on that park bench, just waiting and waiting like that?'

'But if we find her, if she comes, he won't know her.'

'But she will know him. She might still love him. And the letters belong to her. No matter what she does with them.'

'I don't even know where to start.'

'Records? Births, marriages, deaths? I don't know. Maybe we get a private investigator.'

At this, Louise laughed. 'I thought we were the private investigators.'

'And we will find Brenda,' Marta insisted. 'I'm sure of it.'

Louise stared at Marta for a long time. Marta felt Louise's eyes searching her thoughts, even her heart. She wondered if Louise could hear it accelerate or the jaggedness of her breath as she tried to regulate it.

'I admire your tenacity,' Louise finally said. 'Let's go for it. I'll have a talk with someone I know who works in the council. Assuming Brenda was from around here, there will be official records somewhere. She might have gone away, but she might even be back. I'll see what I can dig up, and we'll start there.' Louise put a hand on Marta's thigh. 'Thank you. And I want to help you with everything concerning your family. Your sister, your husband, even your —'

Quickly, Marta placed her fingers on Louise's lips, resting them there briefly. 'We'll take my family a step at a time,' she said. 'Just at a pace that we can handle.' But by 'we' she meant herself.

'That's fair.'

'Should we go?' Marta asked. 'You could stay at my place.'

'I'd like that. No running off this time.'

'I hope not. I am a little afraid that I could lose you.'

'Like Charlie lost Brenda?'

Marta nodded, a veil of sadness falling over her eyes.

'I really can't see that happening,' said Louise. 'Not now.'

The women left The Plough, their fingers touching as they walked along the street. Display lights from shop windows lit their way, a car or van passed them at speed but they did not hold hands. Not until they were on the bus, on a journey of some three stops. Neither would remember who took the other's hand, but they would remember the warmth of skin touching skin. The image of white fingers intertwining with brown. The soft yet steady grip as if they held a secret in between their two palms. And they would remember how the idea of travelling forever, just like that on a never-ending journey, was all they permitted themselves to dream. Who knew what the future would hold for them and if they'd stay together until the end, or if they'd find Brenda, or if Brenda still loved Charlie.

At the end of the bus ride, they continued holding hands. They entered Marta's flat, knowing only this: that for one night, the future didn't matter at all.

37

Ione

Jeannie is the first person I speak to about Elliot. It would have been Marta, but she was off the grid for days. I sent a text, and she sent me a hurried one back saying that she was considering a trip before Christmas to Poland and should we meet for a coffee soon. I thought that if I met her for coffee after Pilates, she and Louise would lock me out of their bubble, and I seriously thought of not going because they'd be bound to want to pull me into it. With me along, the bubble would only pop, and I didn't want to do that to them.

I'm not even sure how I feel about Elliot. I just know that I liked very much that he was flirting with me, and I'd even tried to flirt back. It was the most amazing experience. I don't know when I last felt like it. I know Mum would approve of Elliot.

The whole of my insides have been churning away with this mix of excitement, anticipation and questioning. I was excited at seeing a glint of my wanting to embark on a relationship. I couldn't deny the idea that I'd like it if he were to follow up on his flirtations. I continuously questioned whether I could reciprocate in an appropriate way. I was out of practice and never was the *femme fatale* type.

'For goodness' sake,' Jeannie said. 'You don't have to marry the guy. Just go out with him, get laid once or twice, or three times, and see what happens. From what I saw, he seemed all right. But he'd have to pass my tests.'

Jeannie had proceeded to explain her so-called tests, making each of them up as she went along and succeeding, as always, at lightening my mood. I knew I was too serious at times, too heavy. I hadn't always been like that. I used to laugh constantly at one time. I was always happy. It came from knowing I had a strong foundation. A strong mother I loved and respected. I had forgiven her for dying, and long ago, I'd forgiven her for not letting me know who my father was. I decided that she'd had a bad enough time coping with being Charlie's lover. There had been times when I was angry at her for being 'the other woman'. I wondered how someone so strong could allow herself to fall into the trap. It's well documented, and even Mum should have been aware, that men very rarely leave their wives. Then, I wonder if she ever felt as vulnerable as I had when I fell in love with David. What had Mum been going through that she let her defences down? Then again, you can't stop yourself falling in love, even if it is with a married man.

'When can you see him again?' Jeannie asked.

'I have no idea. He could come and collect his daughter from her lesson again, but she was mortified by him showing up.' Katey had arrived the next week and apologised non-stop about her dad coming on to me. I'd told her it was nothing and I really didn't think he was doing that. She'd said she'd told him never to show up again. Just wait in the car. So I knew that option was off the table.

'You could go to his shop.' Jeannie bellowed this down the phone as if it was the greatest revelation of our times. Of course, I knew I could do that. I could casually pop in and see Marta on my day off and ask her to lunch. Jeannie had no idea I'd been dreaming up scenarios for seeing Elliot again because as quickly as I thought them up, I dismissed them as ridiculous and childish. I tried to tell her that it would be what it would be and if I never saw Elliot again, it wouldn't be the end of the world. I might meet someone else. Someone who wasn't connected to an embarrassed teenager who happened to be my piano student.

I decided I would do nothing. Let the future unfold in its way, and I'd go with the flow of things. That way, I didn't have to worry or have knots in my stomach about someone I didn't even know. I'd remembered, after this epiphany had landed on me, that Mum had said something similar about the time she met my father. She hadn't planned to fall in love with him, it happened before she knew where she was. He was impossible not to love. I knew I'd never had that feeling, not with David, not with anybody. To fall for someone who was impossible not to love was the ideal dream. I only hoped that if it happened to me, it would be with a good man. Not a married and not an abusive man. Just somebody good. Even while making this vow, the image of Elliot flickered across my mind, like a picture in a kaleidoscope, to the place where possibilities lie.

'I want to scatter Mum's ashes,' I'd said to Jeannie out of the blue.

'Are you coming to Manchester?'

'I think it has to be here, and I know exactly where.'

'The park?'

'Trust you to read my mind.'

'It's so obvious. The most romantic place in the world, or at least in Shepherd's Bush, where they exchanged love letters. Do you know where it is?'

'Yes, I do. I found it. It was just like she described. I went back to it one afternoon. I walked along the path, saw the school at one end, the benches along it. I wondered which one they sat in.'

'You'll want me to come down.'

'Of course.'

'Just let me know when, okay? And I'll be there.'

'Thanks Jeannie.'

Something changed within me that evening after speaking to Jeannie. For a long time, I'd struggled to lay down the past, my life with David. I'd been angry with myself for remaining in the marriage. I'd been devastated, hurt and ashamed. I'd bled, I'd wept and I never thought I'd recover. I'd felt alone when I was with David, and even when he'd gone and Jeannie never left my side, I couldn't shake the feeling of loneliness. With my counsellor, with Jeannie and on my own, I'd tried to get a handle of things, 'move on' as everyone says, and after one telephone conversation, I finally began to feel like I was moving on. It could have had something to do with being in the place Mum grew up, or that I'd talked about Elliot or the idea of a relationship. My chest swelled with the prospect of returning to my old self, and with each minute, I could feel it happening. No matter how slowly, I knew I could move on. I was facing a future with possibilities.

I know Jeannie offered to come with me to spread Mum's ashes, but I'd wished, deeply and quietly to no one in particular, that I would find Charlie so he could be there, too.

38

Louise

The corridors looked exactly the same in all parts of the hospital. No windows unless you'd walked a good ten minutes, the walls painted the same shade of watered-down apple juice, lots of locked doors and so few signs everyone got lost, even the people who worked there. No one spoke in the corridors, although there was always the faint drone of conversation coming from some waiting room or inside a room if the door happened to be open. You couldn't meet another person's eye if you tried. The doctors and nurses didn't want to be bothered, and the visitors didn't want to look as if they had no business being there, which many, Louise thought, looked as if they hadn't. One man in a long light brown raincoat with the hem unravelled, his pockets and collar stained greasy brown was eating couscous from a Sainbury's plastic container with a plastic spoon. As she walked past him, she could smell the streets, urine and stale socks. She knew those odours: people like him came into the hospital a lot, either to keep warm, to report that they'd been beaten up or to look for a friend who had been. He must be feeling the cold, Louise thought, and came in to keep the wind off his back.

She pulled the collar of her jacket up, the flowers in her hand almost slipped out and she righted them just in time. She was nervous of seeing Charlie. Silly, she told herself, she'd known him two years now. As she neared St Catherine's Ward, she told herself to be calm, but now she was no longer a nurse and she'd grown close to Charlie, she could be permitted to cry. She was afraid she would on seeing him. The flowers seemed petty. What was the point in bringing them? As gestures went, they hardly spoke of much. They only cost three pounds in the local supermarket but were all she could think of to bring. Those and the letters, of course. The letters stayed folded in the large square front pocket of her jacket. Again, she felt the twist of guilt, like a servant or employee stealing from their boss. It wasn't as if the letters were a packet of staples or a trinket that would go unnoticed, these letters bore Charlie's heart and his soul to a woman called Brenda. She had no business meddling. Except she couldn't help herself. Guilt was overshadowed by the sense of duty she felt to her friend, Charlie. He couldn't do for himself. She would have to do for him.

She approached geriatrics and pressed the admittance buzzer at the door to the ward.

'I'm visiting Mr Kàralos Manolis.'

The duty nurse was standing by a desk at the nurses' station. Louise asked her which room Charlie was in.

'It's Louise, isn't it?' the young nurse said to her. 'I was on your ward once, oh a long time ago, and only for a week or so. Do you remember showing me around?'

Louise had been so buried in her thoughts, it took a while to surface from them and put the pieces together. Heavily freckled, brown plaits knotted over the top of her head, a navy cardigan with a four-leaf clover brooch pinned to it.

'Yes,' she said. 'Maggie, right?'

'It's been a minute,' said Maggie.

'Oh yeah. I left the hospital a while ago now. I'm studying. I was actually Mr Manolis' carer before…'

'I see. Well, his daughters are in his room. Two of them. So shall I just check you can go in? His room is number four on the right.' She was pointing with a pencil along a dark hallway just round the corner from the main door, but Louise gently pulled Maggie's hand down.

‘No. I don’t want to see family. Just Charlie. I’ll wait.’

‘’Course. But visiting is almost over, unless it’s family.’ She pulled her lips down to a fake frown. Louise wondered if she used that face on the patients. They would tire of it very quickly if she did.

‘If I wait in one of the general wards, could you let me know when they go?’

As she said this, Louise heard voices she recognised, a set of high heels, accompanied by another, heading her way. She didn’t turn to face them. The door buzzed, and Charlie’s daughters were gone.

‘I guess you can go in,’ Maggie said. ‘They never seem to stay long.’

‘I see.’ Louise nodded to Maggie. ‘Thanks.’

‘D’you want me to find a vase?’

‘If you don’t mind.’

She handed the flowers, already looking in desperate need for water, to Maggie and went to Charlie’s room.

As a nurse, Louise had treated patients of all ages. She’d worked in A&E, paediatrics, maternity and on general wings, but dying in hospital always meant the same thing to Louise. No matter who the patient was, chances were that he or she would leave people behind. Those people would miss you for a lifetime. She knew this to be true of her memory of Charlie. She hated the fact that he would not see her, not know she was there, not know she was coming to say goodbye. Even the cheap flowers that Maggie would later place on his bedside table in a thin white vase would go unnoticed by Charlie. And if he glanced at them and Nurse Maggie said they were from your carer, Louise, he wouldn’t know what she was talking about.

So, when Louise pulled the letters out of her pocket and held them in her hand as she touched Charlie’s sleeve, she knew her intention was futile. How could Charlie ever say to her, yes, please deliver those letters if you find Brenda, or no, please destroy them, when he had forgotten all about them. Forgotten Brenda.

'Charlie? It's me. It's your Louise. I just wanted to see you. See how you were doing. Are they treating you all right? Do they make the ravioli the way I make it? I bet they don't, right?'

Someone walked past the door and went into the room next door. It was a nurse speaking so loudly to his patient, Louise could hear every word that he said.

'I just need to change your bag now. It's okay, I'll be quick and you can get straight off to sleep. Or do you want the TV on? Should I put the TV on for you? It's okay, Mrs Patterson, you don't have to move. I'll get someone to help me turn you. I just need to change your bag.'

The nurse didn't change the bag. Not that time. He was called away and came back ten minutes later saying, again, to Mrs Patterson that it was time to change her bag. Louise imagined the plastic bag dangling at the side of the bed, peeping out from beneath the covers, attached to Mrs Patterson by a catheter. The bag half-filled with yellow liquid. The nurse would have to check the colour, the amount and write it in Mrs Patterson's chart.

'You know what, Mrs Patterson? I don't think we'll worry about this bag. I'll mark the chart to come back in a couple of hours. Okay?'

Louise never heard a peep out of Mrs Patterson. With a trembling hand, she unfolded the first letter and read it to Charlie. He was sleepy: he hadn't looked up at her, save for a quick flick of his eyes in Louise's direction every now and again. His eyes fluttered open and shut, open and shut as she read, as if he blinked at each pause and opened his eyes when he wanted her to continue. Louise read the second letter and tucked it back into its envelope.

'I think I'll try to find her. Brenda. She was your sweetheart, wasn't she? You really loved her.' She put the letters into her jacket pocket. It rested on the back of her chair, and as she turned back to look at Charlie, he was staring right at her. He looked urgently at her as if he wanted something. Her eyes darted around the room to see if there was something he might need, but there was nothing obvious. Charlie lifted his arms, put them out to her. She knew instantly that Charlie was asking her to dance. She'd held his hands often and danced with him as he sat in his armchair by his living room window, smiling up at her, teary-eyed.

Louise bent forwards to hold his hands, but Charlie pulled her to him and enclosed her in a tight embrace. She wondered where he found the strength. She burrowed close to him, their cheeks touching, her face close to his pillow. He smelled of sleep and peppermint. He would not release his hold, not for a long time, and for a long time afterwards, Louise would wonder about the many reasons for the embrace. A goodbye? His approval for Louise to find Brenda to give her the letters? Maybe he was thanking her for looking after him. Perhaps he thought she was Brenda. It wouldn't have been the first time he'd mistaken her. The hug might be an involuntary reaction, a trigger from him hearing such endearing words to a woman called Brenda. Louise took it as her farewell to Charlie. She didn't know if or when she could come back. She hadn't wanted to run into any of Charlie's family. Guilt would have compelled her to give up the letters if she met the daughters, and how would it look that she'd had them for over a week? Open letters that she must have read. They would report her to the agency.

No, her mind was made up about the letters. If she was faltering before the visit to the hospital, she wasn't when she left.

Outside, she made a call to her friend in the council, the one who worked for the registrar. She made enquiries about how to begin a search for a missing woman—well, not quite missing but lost somewhere in Charlie's memory, plunged deep into his heart, an important chapter in his life. A story he could no longer tell.

39

Charlie

Brenda would have been fronting the band had she been there that night. But she wasn't. There was another girl singing in her place. A white girl who didn't have the voice that Brenda had, nor the moves. She had none of the fire Brenda had in her eyes, neither did she evoke the emotion of the lyrics as she moved on the stage. In fact, this girl never moved a muscle. She stood, looking over the tops of the heads of her audience like a deer looking down the barrel of the hunter's rifle.

Charlie recognised her as Geraldine, the girlfriend of the drummer who he'd seen several times in the sidelines or draped around the drummer any time the band members met at Brenda's house to discuss bookings and set lists. She was a nice enough girl but she was no performer. Charlie supposed that, like him, the band members were desperate. They needed someone to fill in for Brenda in a hurry because they had bookings and rent to pay.

In their break, Charlie questioned each and every member of the band, his hands squeezing their upper arms, asking, 'Where is she? Where did Brenda go?'

'Man, me nah know, y'know?' Jethro—the one they called Jethro Jamaica and who played blues guitar—had no idea. He looked sad that Brenda was gone, and he looked accusingly at Charlie as if it was all his fault. It was his fault. Charlie knew that. He took too long to leave his wife. He'd waited until his wife drove Brenda away, and for as long as he lived, he would regret it.

'I've been to the man from the dry-cleaners. She didn't leave a note. Just her key through his door. No notice. He said he didn't even pay her up for working the week.'

'Charlie, what can we say?' Edward the drummer was as equally upset as Jethro. 'She was here one minute. Gone the next. Never said a word to any of us. I swear to you. If we knew anything, we'd tell you. On the Friday night, we were all expecting her at Casey's Cave up in St Albans. She was meant to get a lift with me, but I assumed she arranged a lift with someone else because my car was going to be tight.'

'You didn't check?' asked Charlie.

'I called her house. No reply. So I just assumed.'

'But you never checked.'

'Charlie. We had to do the whole show without a singer. You know how much flack we got from the manager? We'll never get that booking again. Reputations can go up in smoke on this circuit. Me and Jethro were there the next morning, round her yard. Nothing. We're in the same boat as you. Sorry, Charlie, but we got another set to do, man.'

Charlie watched the musicians take to the stage. This time without Geraldine. She hung around at the side of the stage next to Charlie and rubbed his arm.

'Instrumental set,' she said, her voice soft, her Irish accent like a song. Not a blues song, that's not what her voice was cut out for. 'I don't know all the numbers, but they'll be holding auditions for a new singer.'

Charlie looked down at his feet. He shook his head and couldn't contain his anguish. Geraldine had looked away before the tear splashed to the floor.

'Charlie. Come here would you?'

Geraldine pulled Charlie out to a back corridor. She hugged him around his waist, resting her head against the lower part of his chest.

‘I’m sorry, Charlie. I wish I knew where she could have gone.’ She looked up at him as she pulled away. ‘Do you think she’ll keep the baby?’

A simple word. An implication of something sweet, innocent, tender and pure. The idea of a baby had not once entered Charlie’s thoughts. Not even when he dreamed about their future. There had never been a baby. A crease in the middle of his brow grew deep.

‘You didn’t know.’ Geraldine put both hands to her lips and shook her head. The boom of bass and the rolling fill of the drums vibrated the wall Charlie had fallen back against.

‘How-how did you know?’ Charlie’s eyes moved towards the door at the end of the corridor, on the other side of which the musicians played freely and loud.

‘I doubt any of them knew, Charlie. There would have been a song and dance. A celebration, anyway, until it hit them that it would have been it for Brenda. No more singing.’

Charlie said nothing, just felt the vibrations through his feet. His stomach roiled up at the thought that Brenda had kept this from him. Had run away with his baby in her belly and never told him.

‘Maybe she was waiting for the right time to tell you. But to be honest, I could be wrong about it.’

‘What do you mean?’

‘Well, I heard her throw up once. Only once. But I just thought she was different somehow. I followed her to the bathroom and put my hand on her tummy. All she did was nod her head, but that might not have meant anything. She never said the actual words, I’m pregnant, like.’

Slowly, Charlie walked away.

‘Charlie, when you find her, tell her I miss her. We all do.’

He didn’t turn back to wave goodbye to Geraldine. He bustled through to the noisy club, eyes straight ahead as he edged his way out of the place and into busy Piccadilly where buses passed oblivious to his mood and where a couple holding hands held their arms above Charlie's head so that the three wouldn't collide.

Charlie saw nothing but the yards of West End pavements rolling out ahead of him, unaware of anyone coming his way. He crossed at least one road without stopping first to see if it was clear. He kept his hands in his pockets and walked as far as Bayswater until he hailed a taxi and asked the driver to stop at his brother's house.

He remained in his brother's spare room, planning ways to find Brenda. He could contact the police, he could put an advertisement in the paper. Brenda had no family that she spoke of. Brenda had nowhere she could go that he knew of. He didn't know her birthday. He didn't know where she went to school. He knew her favourite colour, her favourite singer, the shoes she liked best for performing in. No real details he could give to the police. Brenda was gone, and without any clues to go on, he might never see her again. When she had the baby, he would never know if it was a boy or a girl.

Charlie spent all his days and nights at the restaurant. Ana had stayed away, refusing to see or to speak to him. He never knew which of his daughters' houses she was staying at. Not one of them let him into their home. He'd spent a great deal of time trying to apologise for upsetting his daughters, who found it difficult to look him in the eye. Then, one day, Ana showed up at the restaurant. She said they must make a go of their marriage for appearances.

For a whole year, each day, Charlie came and sat on a bench in the park for as long as he could, thinking of nothing else but Brenda. Hoping one day she would walk into the park, take his hand and they could begin again. This time with a child. This time with a future. But of course, she never came.

Five years later, Charlie and Ana divorced and Charlie moved into an ex-council house on Sundew Avenue. He continued to work at the restaurant until his daughters took over. He continued to dream about a life with Brenda and his child. He continued to dream until his memories became clouds billowing in a windy sky, moving away from him so fast he didn't know what memories were. Once in a while, a cloud would blow in again: a face, a voice, a song, a beautiful black woman singing and dancing before him. But one day, the clouds stopped coming.

40

Ione

It's late morning. Wrapped in a shawl, sitting in the kitchen with a cup of tea, I try to create a new flyer to advertise my piano teaching services. Marta said that someone had taken the old one away instead of noting down my number and that it happens sometimes. Katey advised I make it more eye-catching because I'm a 'sick' piano teacher and more people should get to hear of me. I knew for a fact she'd already been singing my praises to her friends. She would have given me a 'shout-out' on Instagram if I'd had an account.

'Is that something piano teachers do?' I'd asked the week before. 'Set up Instagram? I mean, I thought a website…'

Katey had looked at me as if I had no sense and said, 'If not Insta, then at least TikTok.'

I opted for a new flyer. It's not that I wanted to be inundated by students, I just needed a diversion from the quiet times, the lonely times, the times when a two bedroom garden flat can seem like a vast and eerie castle in the middle of a lonely forest. At least, that's how it seemed at first. Now I am more settled, more used to the flat, and I have a friend in Marta. Jeannie and I are in constant contact. We Skype, call or message each other on a regular basis. In the beginning, Jeannie called and sent texts on the hour every hour, or so it seemed. She was only worried for me, wanted to make sure I found my feet and started feeling more like I am now. Settled.

Finally, I'm happy with my creation, having found a website that practically designs the flyer for you: all I need to do is print one out. I decide I'll drop in at Val's Music Shop close to lunchtime, that way I might be able to persuade Marta to have lunch with me. Since the visit with Jeannie at half-term and lunch at the Caribbean restaurant, I'd been craving the food. It reminded me of Mum's cooking. Before I leave, I look at her urn, smiling because I know where I will scatter her ashes; I just need to decide on the day to do it.

I arrive at the music shop just a little before twelve. I don't look in the window first, I just go straight in, a big smile on my face, waving the envelope with my newly formatted flyer. Marta isn't in the shop. In fact, no one is, and I look around to the door as if I expect her to come rushing in after me or to see if I've missed a little notice that says, Back in Five Minutes.

'Ione?'

I turn around to the sound of a soft baritone voice. Elliot stands in the threshold of the back doorway, holding the neck of a guitar in one hand. He looks confused. He also looks expectant, and an embarrassed smile finds his full lips, the hint of white teeth disappearing quickly as he looks down at the guitar in his hand. He lifts a finger and runs back through the doorway, emerging seconds later without the guitar yet still with that puzzled look on his face.

'Everything all right?' he asks when the void of silence becomes almost impossible.

'Oh, yes, of course.' I hold up a gloved hand and shake it. 'It's all right. I haven't come about Katey.'

He finally steps further into the shop and stands by a row of bass guitars. 'No, I didn't think so,' he says. 'Is there anything I can help you with? Were you looking for Marta? You're friends with her, aren't you?'

'That's it, yes. I thought I'd see if she was free for lunch.'

‘Yeah, Marta took the day off today. She’s helping out a friend. Girlfriend.’

‘Right, I see.’ I look around the shop, aware that the last time I saw Elliot, he and I were positively flirting with each other. Here, in the middle of an empty shop, no one around to interrupt us, no impatient daughter waiting by the car for him, we are both behaving like shy teenagers with a crush. I didn’t think I’d actually see Elliot again, despite knowing I wanted to. Today, there is no evidence of the flirtatious side Elliot showed, and I wonder if I’d imagined it and he’d only been trying to be friendly.

‘Is that something you want to leave here for her?’ Elliot points at the envelope that I hold so tightly, the flyer inside is probably creased and illegible.

‘Actually, I could leave it with you. I had a card up on your noticeboard.’ I stupidly turn to point at the noticeboard as if he didn’t know such a thing existed. ‘But someone took it. Marta said. I decided to do a flyer, something bigger. More flashy. Katey said.’

‘I’m surprised she didn’t offer to do it for you.’ He seems to relax into a smile which goes some way to putting me at my ease.

‘Well, she did volunteer to give me a shout-out. But I thought a flyer would be better. Even if my artistic skills aren’t all that up to it.’

He holds out a hand. ‘Can I have a look? I can let you know. You know? If it’s any good.’ There’s a smirk on his face. He can’t help himself, and I can’t help but reciprocate. I hand over the envelope.

His fingers are long. The knuckles a darker shade of brown. His hands are steady and move with a confident dexterity that my hands, slightly shaky, slightly unsure, do not have. I look down as he studies my artistic skills. He draws his lower lip to the upper one and hums a sound of approval. ‘That’s pretty cool,’ he says.

'I'm glad you approve.' I attempt light and jocular sarcasm and Elliot walks over to the noticeboard. I follow.

'I'll stick it right in the middle here. Right where everyone can see it, Ione Mason. If I may call you that?'

'I'll settle for just Ione, and thank you for doing this.'

'No, no, I'm happy to. Katey will be coming for a lesson after school.'

I nod and I start to edge sideways to the door; sticking out a hand, I try and reach for the handle while still keeping my eyes on Elliot. He reaches across and puts his hand on the handle but doesn't pull open the door.

'You know,' he says, 'I just wondered if, now that I know your address, if I could pick you up from there one of these days, or evenings, and take you out for a meal. Or a drink. If you think that's okay.'

My hands are in my pockets now. I give him a serious look and say, 'I never date the parents of my students.'

'Oh.' He looks so disappointed, I can't allow him to think for a second more that I actually mean that.

'I'm joking,' I say and, involuntarily, I release a hand and tap Elliot's arm. His quick look at my outstretched hand causes a shift in my confidence and I cough, clearing my throat before saying, 'I'd like that. Actually.'

'Well. Good,' he says and then stares at my flyer again. 'So, I've got your number, so I can call you. Arrange a day, or evening, and a time?'

'Look forward to it.' I look at the door where his hand is still poised on the handle.

'So, good. That's good,' he says. 'Great, well, I'll er, I'll call you.'

'Elliot, you know you sound like you're regretting being so brazen.'

'Am I? Brazen? I didn't mean to be.'

'Again. Joking.'

'Sorry. It's been a while since I … you know?'

‘I know. So, I should go, and I’ll look forward to your call.’

His smile covers the whole of his face, his stance; the way he opens the door for me has an air of excitement and relief. He holds up the flyer with a smile, and I smile at him before leaving.

Not another word is exchanged, and I take a quick look back at the door to see Elliot still smiling, still seeming excited, like a child. I can sense a goodness about him. I know instantly that I don’t have to worry about him. I know there isn’t anything hidden, anything sinister about this man. He’s a good man. I just know he is.

As I walk in the direction of the Caribbean restaurant, I know he will call soon. I know we will see each other soon, and I know I will be seeing him for a long time to come.

41

Elliot

The days were long during that time, and the nights, always sleepless, grew in length. Elliot lay awake listening to Val breathing. Her breath drew in like a warm ocean wave, her exhale barely audible against his racing thoughts. What if this happens again? The doctor said there were no guarantees. Thank God I didn't lose her. He'd told himself, time after time, that Val was going to be just fine. She'd come through this. These were his hopes, his dreams, and it wasn't until Val had come home after the mastectomy that he finally believed it. Val had come through it. Yet, still, he couldn't sleep. He had to watch her, listen out for her, send prayers out to a place beyond the night that she would stay at his side.

As disquieting as the nights were, somehow they were easier than the days. During the day, he had to make conversation. Val was home, and he thought the best thing was for him to act as if everything was back to normal, they could just carry on as before. He pretended a lot. Tried to convince her he was fine. But his heart would break a little each time he watched Val moving around the house, her back stooped, the bandages tight around her chest while the wounds healed.

'It's all right.' Val spoke those words often to Elliot, holding his face in her palm while he blinked and blinked as he looked into her eyes. It wasn't okay to cry.

Months passed, and Val's physical wounds healed. A nurse arrived to change the drain, and she kept on coming so that she could change the dressing. This was something Elliot could and should have done for her when the wounds stopped seeping and there was no longer a risk of infection. But the nurse continued to call because an unspoken agreement had been made between Elliot and Val. Elliot was not to look at the cut. Elliot wasn't to see her body like this, yet. The time wasn't right.

As she recovered, Elliot noticed that Val had become a more dynamic model of herself. More positive, more chatty, more musical. Just more. He could hardly keep up with her. His mother, Corinthia, had stayed with them for the first two weeks. That had also been a challenge for Elliot. Knowing how much his mother doted on Val, he was aware he needed to be doing all the right things so he wouldn't let his mother down. She'd only stay longer if he wasn't proving himself. At the time, Elliot hadn't realised that no one expected any more from him than to be himself. Later, he would wonder if the reason Val's personality had amplified, why she was more mirthful, more likely to laugh, more inclined to chat, had inexorable energy, was because she needed him to relax. His mother told him, the day she headed back to Dalston, that he needed to find a way to adjust to everything and for goodness' sake, boy, get some sleep.

He'd begun to sleep. At first with an ear cocked in case Val woke up and needed anything. Eventually, he shut down for the night and slept for longer than three hours at a time. At some stage, his breathing was as deep and as calm as Val's. Each new day became easier. Val's colour returned to her face. She stopped walking with her shoulders drawn inwards towards her chest, and he was no longer afraid to hold her, hug her to him and tuck her into the curve of his body, the way they used to fall asleep some nights, before the cancer.

Months had gone by, and there had been no hint of anything more sexual than a heated kiss between them, late at night when they were in bed or they'd drunk lots of wine sitting on the sofa in front of the television. One evening, a kiss led to touching. Skin touching skin, hands beneath clothes.

'We should take this upstairs,' Val said.

'Are you sure?'

'That's what they say in films when someone is about to lose their virginity or they're sleeping together for the first time. "Are you sure?" Of course I am, El. Don't you think it's been long enough?'

He got up and reached to pull Val from the sofa. She stopped him by holding his arms.

'But I want you to want me,' she said. 'I don't want to do this because you think it's in your list of Things to Do For Val.'

He sat back down. 'Are you crazy?' he said. 'I've wanted you so much, you have no idea. It had to be the right time.'

'It is.'

They kissed again. They kissed more. They stayed on the sofa, the lights of the television illuminating the room but they neither noticed it nor heard one programme end or the next begin. Later, when the sound of the television filtered back into their scope of awareness, Val said they should go upstairs.

Elliot held her, carried her up the stairs, leaving their clothes behind on the sofa. She felt soft against his chest, and she held him tight around his neck, nestling her face against his shoulder.

'Look at me,' she said when they got to the bedroom. She stood in front of him, looking into his eyes. 'You still love me the same?'

'No, Val. I love you more every day. I always have and I always will.'

It began to rain then. Memories of their first night came to Elliot as he pulled back the covers and sank into the bed with Val, who tucked herself into the curve of his body before they fell asleep.

42

Ione

We hadn't asked for anyone's blessing before going on the date, but we got them anyway. From Marta, who passed them on to Elliot. From Jeannie, who passed them on to me by text and voicemail and a WhatsApp video call. And from Katey who gave her blessing to both Elliot and to me.

Elliot arrives at seven thirty on the dot. His shirt has two crisp creases down the chest. The same again across the upper and lower part of the sleeve. No amount of ironing can remove these little details from a brand new shirt, fresh from the packaging. Perhaps it was a present, perhaps he bought it especially for the date. It's cotton, mid blue and suits him perfectly. His jacket, on the other hand, is old and well worn. As it hangs over the back of his chair in the restaurant, the curves of his elbows are still in it and the shiny plastic covering one of the buttons is missing, lost somewhere in the jacket's history. His lucky jacket? I'll find out one day.

Tonight, for a change, I release all of my hair from the usual binds of a thick cornrow down my back or the stretchy hair band that normally holds my curls off my face. Tonight, my hair is as free as I feel. I wear black—sombre, I realise, but black works well on me. My coat is cherry red, the colour of my lipstick and the chunky wooden beads around my neck. I wear Mum's gold looped earrings. They are large, made and bought in the Caribbean, a present from the aunt she ran away to live with in Manchester before I was born.

Her aunt left the house to Mum, and Mum passed it to me, and now that chain is broken. I am a link, the last link of that chain, the only person left on my mother's side of the family.

I didn't know the name of the restaurant until Elliot and I made plans for the date.

'I know the place you mean,' he'd said on the phone. 'It's called Miranda's Oven. If we go on a Saturday, there might be music.'

'Sounds good.'

'Unless you think it'll be too much. Too loud.'

'I think it'll be perfect.'

Neither of us have dated in years, and the unavoidable conversation about ex-partners starts when we're halfway through the main course. I hadn't wanted to talk about David, not ever, so I skirt around that two-year period of my life and try to bring the conversation around to Mum. I talk about her cooking skills and about how she would have loved Miranda's Oven had it been around in her time.

'You miss her a lot, don't you?' Elliot asks.

'You have no idea. She had such a colourful life down here. She knew a lot of people, but when she moved away, she only had her aunt, and me, I guess.'

He smiles and looks at his plate briefly. 'It was hard on Katey, losing her mum. She missed her so much it was heartbreaking to watch. But she's been really supportive of me, even though I'm the parent. I don't think I would have coped with Val passing away if I didn't have Katey's strength and maturity to help me through it.'

I lean in. 'I love the way your voice softens when you talk about them. Katey and Val. Is it Valerie?'

'Valentine.'

'What a beautiful name,' I say.

Hearing Elliot say his wife's name fills me with a sense of comfort. It's as if I've known her, too. As if, had I actually met her, she and I would have been good friends. I even wonder if, had Mum not moved out of the area, she and I might have gone to the same school. It's an odd feeling, hard to vocalise, not that I have to. All I know is that I don't feel uncomfortable hearing about Val, neither does Elliot feel uncomfortable talking about her.

He's very interested in my story and my relationship with Mum. He's fascinated by the narrative surrounding Mum and Charlie and how Mum raised me on her own. He, too, came from a single parent family.

'Are all first dates like this, I wonder?' Elliot says as we sip coffee after our meal.

'You mean the obligatory airing of the past?'

'You don't mind, do you?'

'Of course not. And I wanted to know. I wanted to know what runs so deeply beneath that brow of yours, the seriousness in your eyes.'

I hope I haven't gone overboard with the psycho-speak, but Elliot is a man of layers. He doesn't appear to mind unravelling them before me. It's as important for him to talk about his past as it is for me to know. Jeannie had said, keep it light, don't mention your ex. That said, she would still be expecting a detailed rundown of Elliot's history, or at least the bullet points.

'Katey warned me to lighten up,' he says shaking his head. 'I know I have a serious exterior, but I'm having the best time I've had in a very long time.'

'Well, I don't know if it's such a compliment being as you haven't been on a date in so long.'

'No,' he said, 'believe me. This is the one I've been holding out for all this time. Thank you for making it special.'

'You know, for a serious man, you really have a way with words.'

'I'm just being myself. I'm being honest.'

'In that case, thank you. I'm having a great time, too.'

'So, we get to do it again?'

I nod and smile, and the waiter brings our bill. I know we will end up in my bed tonight. I think I knew this from the time Elliot came to pick me up in a taxi. I had smiled on the short journey to Miranda's Oven about how it was a real, old-fashioned type of date. Elliot wouldn't hear of me meeting him at the restaurant. I allowed him to pick me up, help me off with my coat. I watched as he remained standing until I'd sat down. He held doors open, and when we walked, he kept a hand in the small of my back. I know he will insist on paying. I'll offer but I know he won't hear of it. And I love this about him.

When we jump out of the taxi, its engine purring outside my door, Elliot stoops to ask the driver to wait.

'Why don't you let him go?' I say quickly. 'If you'd like to come in, that is.'

Elliot smiles, pays the driver and we walk to my door. I've left a lamp on in the living room but the hall light is off. We seem to mirror each other's movements from here. Two pairs of eyes glancing along the hall in the direction of the bedroom. Two pairs of feet making their way along the corridor, and two bodies forming into one on the bed, both eventually feeling the call of sleep and allowing it to pull us both, exhausted and satisfied, into its arms.

By Tuesday, Jeannie's notebook of questions about my date with Elliot is satisfactorily completed. I have also spoken to Elliot four times since Saturday. I've seen him briefly, waving from the gate when he picked Katey up from her lesson. She left, whipping her donkey jacket over her shoulders, saying to her father, 'Well, go on then, kiss her. But don't be all day because I've got to revise for a maths test.'

He had darted along the path, kissed me on the lips, held me so tightly I thought I might burst and left me at the door without either of us saying a word. We'll be meeting again on Friday. It's all arranged.

As the time for the Pilates class arrives, I put on my trainers, grab my yoga mat bag and leave the house. I decide to drive as the November nights have been brutal. I swear it's cold enough for snow, and it's worth taking the ten minute drive to save me a twenty-five minute drudge in the icy darkness. As I pass Mum's park, the gates already locked up, I wonder when a good day will be to scatter her ashes. I feel a tug at my heart because, in many respects, I don't want to say another goodbye but it feels right to allow Mum a place to rest.

Marta and Louise are already at the class when I arrive. At the front of the class, they lay out their mats and Marta gives me a little wave. She gestures the sign of having a drink, and I nod enthusiastically.

At The Plough, Marta tries to persuade me to have a small measure of wine and I have to remind her that I drove and I have to drive home again, later.

'Fine,' she says. 'Maybe next time.'

'Cheers,' I say.

They clink their glasses against my tea cup, and I notice Louise getting her phone out of her bag.

'Have you got assignments to do?' I ask.

'No, sorry, I hope you don't mind this. I was just going to show Marta some footage I found. It's all part of some research into someone's past that we've been doing.'

'Oh,' Marta sighs as she looks at me. 'You won't believe this so, so sad story about a man Louise was looking after.'

'Oh dear,' I say. '*Was*? Does that mean he's…'

Louise shakes her head. 'Oh no, no,' she says. 'He hasn't passed away, but it could happen soon. He's in hospital. In a critical condition.'

'That is sad,' I say. I blow into my tea as Louise plugs earbuds into her phone and hands them to Marta so she can listen to whatever it is they've found online. I don't feel excluded. In fact, I'm glad to see the way they are getting on. I look out of the window and think of Elliot. That kiss, the feeling of complete joy as he hugged me to him. He was wearing the old jacket. It has a particular smell, maybe of aftershave and certainly very pleasant. I sense it around me as I sit in the pub. Minutes after Marta has listened to the recording, Louise wraps the leads of her earbuds around her phone and puts them into her pocket.

'What was that?' I ask.

'It was the briefest video clip of a singer in a blues club that I wanted Marta to hear,' Louise says. 'She has such an amazing voice, and it's the only footage I've been able to find, but we're still no closer to finding her. She's beautiful. The picture is grainy and the sound isn't all that, but it's no wonder Charlie fell in love with her.'

'Charlie?' I ask in a stilted voice. There must be hundreds of men called Charlie, but how could I not ask after someone called Charlie?

'Oh.' Louise picks up her glass of wine and waves my question away as if she doesn't want to concern me. 'It's this search we've been doing. My client? Charlie? Well, he had written some letters to his lover. I found them when I was clearing his stuff out. It's a whole thing. But I don't think we can get much further with it. We were trying to trace her and give her the letters, but we don't have an address. Only her name.'

I stop for a second. Goosebumps tingle their way along the skin of my arms. 'What was Charlie's lover's name?'

Louise snorts a laugh. 'You think you'll know her?'

'Try me.'

'Brenda Mason.'

I'm stunned into silence. I start to shiver. I stare so hard at Louise that my eyes turn dry and I start to blink rapidly, shaking my head at her. Marta places a hand on mine.

'Ione? Ione, what's wrong?'

'I don't … I don't know. I'm even afraid to say anything.'

'It's all right.' Marta shuffles her chair close to mine and puts an arm around me. I pull away and look from her to

Louise. Is this Charlie and this Brenda Mason really who I think they are?

'She's my mother,' I say. 'Brenda Mason. Charlie ... she and he were lovers once. Back in the eighties, right here in Shepherd's Bush before Mum ran away and left him. Right before I was born.'

Now Marta and Louise are silent. Louise pulls the phone back out. Flicks buttons and swipes with shaking hands until she is making a mess of trying to find the footage she'd shown to Marta.

'Someone in the family helped me in the end. I needed to find an expert on London blues bands.' She is stumbling over her words. 'My mum's cousin. We finally got a band name. Found a fan page from all the way back then. Found a member. Got this footage. Look. Is this your mum?'

Now my hands shake as I hold Louise's phone. I see a scratchy picture and hear the sound of static from the loose earbuds. I don't put them in, but a close-up of Mum's face is now on screen. I see her and then I nod. Slowly, then faster, my head is moving involuntarily, and I begin to laugh at the same time that tears fall from my eyes. I put both hands over my mouth to dampen the volume of my laughter.

'It's her?' Marta exclaims. 'Your mother was *the* Brenda Mason?'

I nod again and ask Louise to play it back. Again. And Again. I watch it five times, the sound coming from the phone speaker because Louise pulls out the earbuds and we all gather around the video on her phone.

'Who sent you this?' I ask, sitting up.

'It was a band member. I've got his email if you want it. But he didn't know where your mother moved to,' says Louise.

'No,' I say. 'She never wanted to be found, and she never wanted me to find him. Charlie. I've never met my father.'

'Oh,' Louise says, remembering that she has already implied that Charlie is dying. A fact that comes back to me as I blink at the still image on the phone and watch it blink to black when the phone falls asleep. My heart is racing now. I've found him. I didn't even try. I never thought I'd stand a chance with so little to go on, and there he is, somewhere close by, my father. As Marta and Louise watch me in silence, it comes to me that it's not too late. I can go to him. Tell him what happened to Mum. Tell him who I am to him.

'It's okay,' I say to Louise. 'You weren't to know. But if you let me have the address of the hospital?'

'I could.' Her words are drawn out, and she keeps looking at Marta. Marta's cheeks are red.

'What is it?' I ask, anxious now.

'Charlie doesn't have long to live, like I said, but…'

'Just tell me.'

'He has dementia, Ione. He won't know what you're saying. I don't think he remembers your mum, if I'm honest. I just thought she might want to see him before…'

I slump in my chair, shaking my head, a fresh set of tears welling in my eyes.

'It's too late, then,' I say quietly. I look up at the women. 'Mum died of ovarian cancer. Nearly three years ago.'

Marta has already wrapped an arm around me. She knew about Mum dying, but it's news to Louise who gets out of her chair to hug me. Their words of consolation do nothing to abate my tears. I shouldn't be crying like this, but it all feels so hopeless. They would never have found Mum and I don't believe Mum would have come back to London, had she been alive. Her break was a final one. She wanted nothing to do with this life. She wanted to forget it and for it to forget about her. Now that Charlie can't remember her, I suppose she has her wish. Still, it does nothing to fill the hole that I'd always felt in my life. A feeling of incompleteness because I was always the girl with no father. I have him now, but at the same time, I don't. He will never know me, and he never knew I existed.

'I-I think I want to go home,' I say.

Slowly, Marta and Louise unravel themselves from me and I feel cold without their closeness. I have to go home alone and bring this feeling of alone with me. As the last member of Mum's family, I was alone. I find my father and now that he is dying it's still just me. I only wish, now, that I'd tried to find him while he had his memory. While he was able to complete the story for me. Now it's too late.

'Louise, could you text me the hospital name and ward that Charlie is on. I'd like to go and see him.'

'Of course,' she says. 'And I'm really sorry, Ione.'

I shake my head. Sniff. Dig a tissue out of my bag and dry my face. 'Don't worry,' I say. 'At least I can say goodbye if nothing else.'

As I get to the door, Louise runs to me and takes my hand.

'I've got the letters at home. Shall I drop them round? The ones from Charlie to your mum?'

'If you would, that would be wonderful. Thanks.'

Then I leave. The love affair had ended in sadness, but maybe the letters will tell me something about Charlie I don't already know. I'm hoping they'll tell me if he loved her as much as she deserved to be loved.

43

Charlie

Charlie would either be sound asleep or lying in bed, his eyes focused on the window in front of him. A screen that changed in slow motion as the day progressed. The blinds opening to the first picture of a winter sky. Clouds moved on invisible strings across a background streaked in red and grey. The soundtrack was the nurse's voice, shrill and bright as if she'd had lots of strong coffee before her shift. She attempted a conversation.

'How did you sleep?' Silence.

'You feeling okay?' Silence.

'Do you want some breakfast now?' Silence.

'Let's get you washed and changed, shall we?'

Charlie couldn't alter the volume on the soundtrack. The questions were relentless as if the speaker never expected an answer. As the questions came, the nurse bustled around the bed and blocked the red and grey. She filled the room with her perfume, filled in a chart at the foot of the bed and then she was gone.

Later, the red in the picture faded and the grey turned to fluffy white and the white moved a little faster and birds swooped and soared across the view and there was no soundtrack, even though there were two women in the room. They had nothing to say to Charlie until another nurse entered and asked more questions that he would never answer.

'How about some lunch?'

'Shall we try and roll you over for a bit?'

'Have you soiled your pyjamas?'

Very slowly, the sky darkened, but there was enough light in the room to see that a tray had appeared at the bottom of the picture and there was the smell of something like tomato sauce. There was a drink on the tray. A tiny plastic straw poked out of it and trails of white ran down the inside of it, and the vague recollection of someone trying to feed the white fluid to Charlie was like a montage against the ever-changing colour and movement of clouds. How much had he drunk? What had it tasted like? He couldn't remember and couldn't ask because he couldn't form the words. So he continued to stare at the scene through the window until a face appeared in front of it and he was filled with warmth, though he didn't say.

'Charlie, it's me, it's your Louise. I hope they're treating you okay.'

The owner of the voice picked something up from the end of the bed and she blocked the view through the window.

'I can see your levels have changed a little, but in a good way. I hope you're comfortable.'

Still blocking the scene outside, she sat at the end of the bed, continuing to add to the soundtrack of his day.

'I found someone I think you should meet. She's coming to meet you. Her name is Ione and, Charlie, you may not know this, but you two are related. She knew Brenda. She is Brenda's daughter and she's your daughter, too, Charlie. Imagine that.'

It was quiet in the room, but Charlie tuned in to the noises that came from outside of it. To the corridor where footsteps of all kinds moved up and down. Sometimes accompanied by the rolling of wheels: chairs, beds, trolleys and objects that rattled. Some things had a certain smell, depending on the time of day. Disinfectant, food, perfumes and bedpans.

The noise and smell kept up all day and echoed when it was quiet in his room.

Someone touched his hand.

'I wish you could understand. You have another daughter, Charlie, and tomorrow she is coming to meet you. She didn't know how to find you before, otherwise she would have come earlier.'

And then it was quiet in the room again. And then the picture outside changed and it became dark, and the hand touching his moved away, and he missed the warm feeling on his palm. He was compelled to reach out his arms, and someone he thought he knew leaned towards him, and he held her very tight because that felt like the right thing to do.

Some time later, and Charlie didn't know how late, the door opened and the noise out in the corridor droned on, and the person he knew was still in the room, so he smiled at her. Eventually, his eyes closed. When he opened them again, he could smell food. The scene from outside was gone, hidden by plastic slats.

A voice said, 'It's me, Charlie. I went for a sandwich, but I had to come back. Oh, you didn't eat your dinner. I would stay longer, but I really should go. Good night, Charlie, sleep well.'

Charlie reached his arms out again, only this time he knew exactly who he was holding in them. It was hard to let Brenda go because he knew it would be the last time he'd see her, to smell the perfume she bought from the market, to feel her soft brown skin against his as it touched his chin. He wished he had shaved. He wished he could look better for Brenda, but there was no time to prepare for her visit. He'd waited a long time. And now, they both had to go, so he released the strong hold he had around her upper body, and slowly, Brenda moved away. She smiled before she closed the door, and he heard nothing else, not even her footsteps along the corridor.

44

Ione

It's two thirty in the afternoon when I arrive at the hospital. I'm exhausted from crying and from talking about finding my father to both Jeannie and Elliot. I was so afraid to go and see him yesterday, so I told Louise to go without me and I'd go on my own. The sad truth, as I tried to explain my trepidation to Elliot and Jeannie respectively, was the pain of watching another parent die. Jeannie said that was a natural reaction, to do whatever I was comfortable with, as long as I didn't have regret later.

'I can come with you, for support,' Elliot had said. 'You might need somebody after you've seen him.'

'If I do, can I call you?' I asked him.

'Of course you can. In fact, why don't we see each other anyway?'

I nodded at the suggestion, but I had no idea how I'd feel after seeing Charlie. I had no experience of anyone with dementia, let alone that person being my estranged father.

The hospital is big, enormous in fact, and reminds me so much of the one Mum spent months in before I brought her home. I find the ward easily enough, but I have a strange feeling in my body. My limbs are lifeless and I am not aware of a heartbeat, the sensation of drawing breath in and out or the feeling of the stone painted hospital floors under my feet. I've heard the saying, I felt numb, but never really experienced it before, not until now.

I try to analyse why I have this numbness—surely I should feel something. Anxiety, joy, relief. I don't know. Not just numb.

At the door to the ward, I have to press the button and announce myself. What on earth do I say? I'm visiting my father? I have no time to come up with a plan before a nurse, who I can see through the little window of the door, is holding the phone and looking right at me. I falter, um and ah for a second before I speak.

'I'm … I'm visiting Mr Manolis. I believe he's on this ward.' I can hear a very formal voice coming from my lips, but it is convincing enough for the nurse to release the lock. With a loud buzz, the door slowly opens and I walk through. I rub antibacterial gel onto my hands, standing at the dispenser, stalling for time. I look around at the doors to the various rooms: two are wide open and I can see rows of beds and patients sitting or lying in them. I have no idea what my father looks like. The nurse who let me in is walking towards me; I attempt to move out of her way but realise her eyes are fixed on mine and I'm the one she's aiming to talk to.

'You're here for Mr Manolis?' she asks, a crease forming between shaped eyebrows and heavily made-up eyes.

'Yes, but I'm a little early for visiting. I could wait outside if…' I angle my body to the door that has closed behind me with automated precision, but the nurse rests a hand on my arm.

'No, you can wait in here. Just follow me.'

I follow her, my eyes trained on the patients on the open wards. The corridor brightens just past the nurse's station, and the nurse walks purposefully into a side room where there is a businesslike desk and chair by the window and a low sofa along the wall opposite. The light isn't on in here, and she looks behind me for the switch. I sit on the sofa, perching myself on the edge to wait for visiting time and for the nurse to disappear and leave me. She doesn't go, however, she props wide hips onto the back of the upright chair on my side of the desk and looks at my shoes. I shuffle my feet, smiling up at her and wondering if it's customary for nurses to wait with visitors. I'm the only visitor here but the one-to-one attention is excessive and suddenly quite unnerving. I can tell she is gearing up to tell me something.

'Are you family?' she asks. As I thought, I'm not allowed to see Charlie. He's critical and I'm not family, so she'll turn me away. Then I remember. Of course I'm family. Charlie is all I have left, but I don't tell her that.

'Actually, yes. I only just found out.' I look straight at her now, realising that I'm faltering and might not be able to convince her of my relationship to her patient. 'But he's my father.'

'Oh, I see. It's just that … well, we had to call the family in last night. You see, Charlie died. I'm so sorry you weren't told. His daughters were here. I mean, the other daughters, the ones that came to see him. Sorry.' She holds up her hands then puts them to her face. 'Obviously, you would have come to visit sooner had you known before.'

But actually, I did know sooner. A whole day ago, and I couldn't bring myself to come. I missed seeing my father by one day, and I can't believe I've let that happen.

'Wh-what?' I ask. But I don't give her time to answer. 'I was afraid to come. I was told he wasn't lucid, that he wouldn't know me. It was a shock, you see, to find out, just like that, that he was here. I didn't … I should have…'

'Well, that's two shocks you've had in quick succession.' She pulls two tissues from a box on the desk and hands them to me before I even realise I'm crying. Tears fall from my eyes, but I'm not sobbing. I have no voice in my throat. It is dry and I'm afraid I'll sound hoarse even if I could find any words at all.

The nurse sits beside me on the sofa and puts a hand on my back. 'I think a nice cup of tea might help. I'll put lots of sugar in it. You wait here.' She gets up hastily and spins quickly back because she has forgotten something. Something else from the nurse's code book for visitors who are in shock. 'Would you like to speak to Charlie's doctor? I'm not sure when he'll be back on the ward, but he could tell you more than I can. I wasn't here, but I believe he slipped away very quietly and with no pain. It's usually the way it goes in circumstances like Charlie's. He was a sweet man.'

'I won't see the doctor. I won't have tea, but thank you. I'll go in a minute. If I can just sit here?' I'm drying my eyes, my cheeks. I need to blow my nose, but I'll wait until she's left the room.

'You sure? It's no trouble? Could do you the world of good.'

'Really, I don't think I could drink it anyway. My throat … I don't know, it's…' Now I'm rubbing my throat and sniffing so that my nose won't run. I want her to leave so I can blow my nose. All of a sudden, it's of the utmost importance and I couldn't say why. Surely I'm permitted a runny nose. I found my father and he died before I could meet him. I'm allowed a runny nose.

From somewhere within, a sob leaps from my throat. It echoes in the room, and the nurse closes the door and comes back to sit with me. She rubs my back. She gets more tissues. Rubs my back again. I blow my nose and I sob aloud because I don't have a mechanism within me to make myself stop. Mum always swore by a good old cry. 'Let it all out, and who the hell cares, can care. You just do it, and you'll see how much better you feel after.'

The only time I ever saw Mum cry was when she spoke of Charlie. Even then, those times were rare. Mum's most important remedy for a broken heart, for good news, for bad news, for when she had the blues, was to sing and dance. I can hardly do that here, so I opt for the big cry. I let it all out until I find I'm slumped against the nurse, my head on her lap and she strokes my hair. Someone pops their head in the door but promptly leaves. I sit up.

‘They probably need this room,’ I say.

‘No, you’re all right. It’s all yours.’

I dry my face again. I hope for the last time. I need to pull myself together. I can’t bring Charlie back, and everything I don’t know about him, about his version of my parent’s affair, will remain unsaid.

‘Do you have the telephone number for the family?’ the nurse asks. ‘I imagine the funeral will be soon. You’ll get a chance to say goodbye to your father.’ The nurse looks tearful herself. As she’d sat and comforted me, she must have wondered how I came to know Charlie was my father. I suppose my skin colour makes it obvious that Charlie’s daughters are my half-sisters and most likely unaware of my existence. Maybe she hopes for a reunion, a happy ever after. But I know there won’t be a happy ever after with my half-sisters. They’ll hate me as much as they hated Mum, and now that their father is dead, they can put his relationship with Mum to one side and just get on with their lives.

I leave the ward, and the doors close behind me. At the landing, I stop to get out my phone. I call Elliot as I hold onto the banister rail.

‘I was too late,’ I tell him. ‘Charlie already passed away. Yesterday evening. I should have gone with Louise. I should have.’

‘Stay there, I’m coming to meet you.’

‘I’ll get the train back to Shepherd’s Bush. I’ll meet you at the station. Maybe half an hour?’

‘I’ll be there.’

It’s forty-five minutes later as I emerge from the station and I see Elliot’s anxious face bobbing above the passengers ahead of me. He runs to hold me, and I fall against him. I rest my head on his chest and touch the rough surface of the button on his jacket that’s missing the shiny coating. Elliot strokes my hair.

‘I’m so sorry, Ione,’ he says. ‘How are you feeling?’

He hooks his arm around my shoulder and we begin to walk. I don't know where we're going, but I want to get off the main road. I feel as if people are looking at me and judging me and wondering why I hadn't rushed to the hospital the second I knew I'd found my father. I was being ridiculous, and I hate myself for being so weak-willed.

'Don't do it,' Elliot says as he guides me off down a side street, away from the busy Uxbridge Road.

'Don't do what?'

'What you're doing right now. Blaming yourself.'

I stop. We're opposite The Queen Adelaide on Adelaide Grove, the road that leads to Mum and Charlie's park.

'Why do you say that?' I ask Elliot.

'Because that's what we do, the ones they leave behind. We ask ourselves what we could have done differently. We ask ourselves if we did all the right things or all the wrong things that lead up to the time they die. We can't let them go without some sort of guilt about something which starts to nag away at us.' Elliot leads me in the direction of the park. 'But the thing is, it was coming. It was going to happen, and you just have to allow that it happened the way it did.'

'But I could have said goodbye. I could have seen him.'

'You might never have come to London. You might have always been too late. You just don't know, do you, Ione. All you can be sure of is that beating yourself up about something you can never change isn't going to help. If you're sad, just be sad. I'll be here to hold you, to dry your tears. To talk about it, if you want to. To sit quietly with you, if that's what you want. But don't punish yourself. You're a good person, Ione. Never forget that.'

At the gates of the park, I take a deep breath and turn to Elliot. 'Thank you for being here. Thank you for being you. I just want to sit in the park. Will you sit with me?'

'Of course.'

It isn't the first time Elliot has listened to the stories of Charlie and Brenda and how they met in this very park. How they sat on a bench together on a day they felt bold. How she and Charlie passed letters to each other along the long path that ran from one gate to another at each end.

'It's a beautiful story,' Elliot says.

'And sad.'

'I know.' Elliot strokes my arm and pulls me to him so that my head leans against him, and he wraps a strong arm around me. 'It's sad but it did bring me you. I'm glad you came here, or we would never have met. I can feel my life changing for the better because of you, Ione.'

I sit up and look into his eyes. 'That's a beautiful thing to say.' I smile and have to catch my breath because of how he looks at me.

'It's true, though,' he says in his serious way. 'Something big is happening here. I know it comes out of a lot of tragedy, but you and I are heading for a really good place. I hope you feel it, too.'

I nod my head because I do. The breath releases from my throat in a pant. Blinking, I try not to cry. 'I do feel it.' I shiver, not because of the biting wind that circles its way into the sleeves and collar of my coat but at the thought that Charlie and Brenda began a love story that ended abruptly, but that Elliot and I are about to continue.

'Are you cold?' Elliot asks.

'Freezing.'

'Let's go back to mine. I'll cook you dinner. Marta is locking up the shop. Katey might be late from school. She's meeting her boyfriend. He's just lost someone, too. His granddad.'

'I'm sorry to hear that.'

At Elliot's house, the lights are on in the living room.

'Looks like Katey beat us to it.'

He calls to her as we enter the house, and she comes to give me a hug. 'Dad told me about your dad and everything,' she says. 'You remember, Nico?' As we enter the kitchen,

Nico stands and nods. He puts his hands into the front pockets of his jeans. 'We came here because there are tons of people at Nico's house. Is that okay?'

'Of course,' Elliot says as he puts the kettle on. 'Ione's staying for dinner. How about you, Nico? Staying or will you need to get back?'

'To be honest, I don't think I'll be missed. They're talking about funerals and stuff, and they don't need me. It's like a circus round there.'

'I'm sorry to hear about your granddad, Nico,' I say.

'Ione's dad died,' Katey says before he can respond. 'She only just found out she had a dad and now he's dead.'

'Oh, sorry,' says Nico.

'Ione knew she had a dad,' Elliot says with a slight shake of his head. 'She only knew his name was Charlie and only just found out he was in hospital a couple days ago.'

'*Another* Charlie,' Katey blusters. 'Nico, your granddad was Charlie, too.'

Nico blushes. 'They called him Charlie, but his Greek name was Kàralos Manolis.'

I stop and stare at Nico. I knew I had half-sisters, but I didn't even consider that they would have families, children. I never thought for one moment that I could also be an aunt. Nico and I are related, and he doesn't know it. Elliot hands me a hot cup of coffee and gestures for us to go back to the living room. I can't take my eyes off Nico, though, and it's obvious to him that I'm staring. He blushes again.

'Nico, I'm sorry,' I say. 'It's just that, well, I've found out a lot of things all in the last few days, and the thing is, I don't know if you know this, you probably don't, I don't think anyone does, but…' Now they are all looking at me, confused. 'Look, forget it. I don't know what I'm saying. I shouldn't have said anything.' He's just a boy. It's not for me to talk about his grandfather's lover. Not even his mother will know of my existence, so I can't reveal this to a boy. Not out of the blue like that.

‘Is this anything to do with Brenda?’ Nico looks hard at me.

‘You knew about Brenda?’ I say.

‘Some things. I knew they had an affair. How do you know Brenda?’ Although he asks the question, I can tell he has worked out the answer.

‘Brenda was my mum. Charlie was my dad.’ There. It’s out. I can’t take it back. ‘The thing is. He never knew I existed. No one in your family does.’

‘And you don’t want me to say anything to my family. My grandmother.’ Nico is more mature than I’d thought.

‘Well, you know, now,’ I tell him. ‘It’s up to you what you say.’

‘He won’t say anything if you don’t want him to,’ Katey puts in. ‘Will you?’

Nico shakes his head.

‘Katey, this isn’t up to you,’ says Elliot. She tuts.

‘No, I get it,’ says Nico. ‘They didn’t like her. I wouldn’t tell them anyway. They don’t need to know, and they don’t deserve to.’

‘Thanks Nico. And again. I’m so sorry about your grandfather.’ I look at Elliot, and he holds open the kitchen door for me. We leave the teenagers in the kitchen and sit in the warm living room. I stare ahead at the floor, my coffee cup in my hand. Elliot is quiet, too. The whirlwind of the last few days begins to settle, and the pieces of a jigsaw come together. I don’t feel annoyed at myself for not going sooner to find Charlie. I couldn’t have changed anything that came; all I have is what comes next.

45

Louise

Louise woke early and listened to the peaceful sound of Marta asleep on the pillow beside her. Marta, facing away from Louise, continued to dream, unaware of Louise having had a disturbed night. Louise lifted onto an elbow and pulled the veil of dark hair from Marta's face. She watched the tick of the pulse on her neck. Outside, a light rain had begun, tiny dots speckled the window pane. The room was cold, the chill in the air making contact with her arm, the rest of her body warm beneath the duvet. So cosy, she could sink back underneath it and try to make up for the hours she'd spent awake. But today was Charlie's funeral and she had to get up, leave the warm bed and leave Marta after spending a whole weekend in her arms.

Louise had taken Charlie's death badly, and she'd insisted on going over to Ione's house the minute she'd found out that Ione knew about her father's passing. She could only imagine how she must feel. Up until that point, she hadn't given Ione the two letters that were intended for her mother, Brenda. Head bowed, Louise had stood at Ione's door and handed her the letters, the last two love letters that Charlie wrote to his lover long before accepting that all hope of finding her was gone.

Louise had explained to Ione the process, the links, the beauty of coincidence that led her to finding that piece of footage of Brenda singing in the nightclub, and they had played it over and over again.

'That's her, that's Mum, that's her voice,' Ione said, and each time, her smile grew wider.

Louise's contact at the council couldn't shed any light on the identity of Brenda Mason. A little while after that disappointing discovery and several days of trawling the internet with a scant number of clues, Louise paid a visit to her mother. She happened to talk about the letters. She told her the whole history about Charlie and Brenda, everything she knew from where she lived to the only name of the West End club she knew of that Brenda sang at. By some miracle, Louise had recalled the name of Brenda's band, plucked it from a memory of a day Charlie could remember names and places. She said she'd been looking up blues singers for days. The mention of the word blues caught her mother's attention. Louise's mother had said, 'Why you don't ask cousin Frederick if he know anything. You know he's a big blues fan. He knew a lot of people in bands and clubs and whatnot. And he lived in Shepherd's Bush.'

Cousin Frederick turned out to be a good source of information. He'd discovered the internet late and reluctantly, like most people of his generation, but his son had showed him how to access music and how to do searches. Long ago, he'd discovered a fan page for Nightingales in London and saw the pictures that fans had placed there. A member of Nightingales, the drummer, had posted the video of Brenda. Louise had tracked down the very drummer of the band. He was either apprehensive or genuinely clueless because he had no idea where anyone could find Brenda Mason. She had disappeared from Shepherd's Bush without a trace, and there, Louise's journey had come to a standstill until Ione saw the video.

'I felt so guilty,' Ione had told Louise.

'About what?'

'That I didn't do a proper search for my father. That I didn't find him sooner so that I could tell him what happened to Mum.'

'You can't punish yourself for that.' Louise had tried her best to console her. 'Look, you've found him now. Come with me to his service, it might be helpful to at least see his send off.'

'Will they mind?'

'It's a church. You just walk in. You've come to pay respects, and they don't need to know who you are. The sister knows I'm the carer, you could just as well be another of his carers. They're not even going to notice. Their noses are always up in the air. We'll sit in the back and then we'll leave before everyone else.'

'I will come. I don't want to speak to any of them anyway, and it's best if they never know anything about me, from what Mum said and from what Charlie says in his letters.'

They'd spent the rest of the evening talking. Louise told Ione all she could about Charlie, and Ione told Louise what she knew about their relationship. The talk helped them both to understand more about the two lovers. Louise left Ione's house tired and talked out.

Now, looking down at Marta's face, so peaceful and serene, she wished she didn't have to face the day ahead but she resolved to be strong for Ione. After all, she was the one who was saying goodbye to her father.

Marta stretched and rolled towards Louise. Slowly, her eyes blinked open and she looked up to see Louise looking thoughtfully at her.

'Is it time for you to go already?' Marta said in a sleepy voice. 'What time is it?'

'Almost seven thirty. The service is at nine.'

'That's too early.'

'It's probably convenient for his daughters so they can go back to their restaurant and not lose business.'

'Don't be angry with them. This isn't anyone's fault.'

Louise rolled onto her back and looked at Marta. She found her hand under the quilt. 'I know, but it's all just so sad.'

'Funerals are sad. Full stop. You sure you don't want me to come?'

'No, you stay. Enjoy your morning. We'll meet you later, at the park.'

When Louise peeled her body from the bed, she saw Marta pull the quilt up to her neck. She smiled at Louise but rolled over again. Monday morning, the shop was closed and Elliot would be at the park later, too.

St Nicholas' Church stood on the corner of the residential Godolphin Road in Shepherd's Bush. Externally, it was unassuming with neat manicured hedges and sand-coloured bricks; the arched doorway was old and the building could be mistaken for a school. Outside, around the solitary plane tree, members of Charlie's family gathered. They chatted loudly on this damp and grey day, waiting for the hearse to arrive, catching up on family they hadn't seen in a while.

Two women with black hats and shiny, patent shoes dabbed their cheeks with white cotton handkerchiefs, and Louise wondered who they were to Charlie. They were the only two whose mood suited the occasion. She linked Ione's arm and guided her towards the entrance. Beneath the stone carved cross above the door, they were met by Nico. He looked handsome in his suit and tie, his hair neatly off his face. He smiled at Louise and bent to whisper to her.

'Mum said it is impossible to play *Midnight Train to Georgia,* but she thinks I might be able to play it at the house. I'm sure she'll say no then, too.' He gave her a quick wink and gestured for them to move along the front yard, away from the door. He looked at Ione. 'The coffin is coming and we'll follow the priest in.'

'What do we do?' Ione asked. A group of middle-aged women came to stand by the gates and the small crowd gathered to take turns to deliver some sort of greeting to them. The women, all dressed in black designer coats, nodded and shook hands. An older, wiry woman in a large black hat, a thick black shawl around her shoulders, nodded at each greeting but never once looked up from her feet. She looked shaky, and one of the well-dressed women in black put an arm of support around her shoulder.

'I better go and stand with the others,' Nico said. 'I'll see you both at the park.'

Louise and Ione watched as the priest, carrying a censer, recited a hymn and walked into the church. Close behind him, the pallbearers carried a modest mahogany casket decorated with a sheaf of white flowers. The family followed in next and then the rest of the mourners. Ione and Louise slotted in behind the last of them, some thirty to forty people, collected the lit candle that was handed to them by a sombre man in a suit and found an empty pew a few rows from the back.

Inside, candles and lights illuminated the ornate carvings, the intricate paintings on the ceiling at the front of the church and the statues along the walls. The carpet glowed furnace red but it was cold inside the church. That December morning, a draught whipped around their ankles, the doors remaining open for some unknown reason. Louise and Ione would keep their coats and gloves on during the entire ceremony. About an hour later, after prayers, hymns and a few words spoken in Greek by a portly man with silver hair, the mourners got up and walked to the open casket near the altar. Each kissed Charlie's forehead while whispering a message or a blessing and left the church by the centre aisle. Louise pulled Ione to the side aisle, and as the mourners left, the two walked slowly to the front of the church. They saw a paper band tied around Charlie's forehead as he lay in the casket. An altar server leaned towards them, saying, 'Now you pay your last respects before we leave for the burial.'

The women looked at each other. Ione leaned into the casket. She recognised the plump, unreal skin of the deceased in her father's face, frozen into a half-smile. Between his folded palms was a tiny wooden cross. He wore a black suit and tie, his thin white hair neatly swept back from his forehead. Over her shoulder, Louise whispered, 'Bye Charlie.' Ione turned briefly to her, then to the altar server and the pallbearers waiting patiently for the women to leave. Looking back at her father, Ione drew closer. She whispered, 'Goodbye, Dad. Goodbye, Charlie.' Then she left a soft kiss on his cheek.

'Let's get to the park,' Louise said as she held Ione around her shoulders and led her out of the church.

46

Ione

We sit on the park bench, the one in the central lane, right in the middle of the park. We are six figures: four seated and two standing. Everyone is waiting for me to make a decision. Katey persuaded Elliot to let her call in sick at school —she was determined to join us at the park, insisting that she had so few lessons on a Monday it would be easy to catch up. Nico, already granted compassionate leave, found it easy to slip away after the casket was lowered into the ground. He'd begged a lift from his cousin from the cemetery in Hammersmith to the park where we all waited for him. Elliot, Katey and Marta were already at the park when Louise and I arrived.

I haven't been able to feel my toes since leaving the church, save for the two seconds spent indoors picking up the urn from the shelf in the living room before heading back out again.

It's grey and dark in Mum's park. It's only eleven o'clock, but it's been a long morning and seems so much later. Nico said it was forbidden to cremate a body in his religion, but it would have been great to scatter his grandfather's ashes alongside Mum's, even just a few.

The next thing we do is walk around the park. I'm trying to find somewhere symbolic to scatter Mum's ashes. I'm not sure if this is even legal, but no one can see us, save for the man sitting on his own at the far end of the park. In less than an hour, the local school will break for lunch and the sounds of children spilling out onto the playground will filter into the serenity of the morning. I must make my decision.

'We'll walk over to that tree,' I say. The sturdy sycamore has lost all of its leaves, but there are hundreds of branches on which a rich array of green will grow in the spring. It's the proudest looking tree in the small park. The leaves have been cleared, and the soil above the roots is dark and rich and feels perfect to me.

Everyone stands, waiting for me to say something. I didn't prepare a speech, and I don't know an appropriate prayer. Maybe a song, but I can't bring myself to sing.

'Thank you all for being here,' I say. 'I wish you could have met Mum, she would have charmed you and she would have loved you all.' I open the urn and take out a handful of ash. I begin to scatter it around the tree and watch as it coats the dark earth in silver grey. Small motes of ash lift from the ground and find their way to the dewy lawn, patchy now, but I'm sure it will be beautiful in the summer. As I turn the box on its end, emptying the last of the ashes into my palm, a breeze picks up and takes the remaining grains on its back. I watch the spray of ash, rising and spreading itself in the direction of the central path. I imagine Mum standing there, holding Charlie's hands as he spins her around, the ash swirling around them. They release their hands and Mum dances the way she did when she stood in the living room, coaxing me to join her, singing her invitation to join the dance. The ash settles in their clothes and on the path around them, and they hold hands again and leave the park together.

'I don't know about you guys,' I say, opening my eyes and looking at them all, 'but I'm freezing and there's hot coffee and breakfast at my house if you want to come with me.'

Everyone is quiet as we leave the park. Elliot has his arm around my shoulders, and I lean into him, hugging his waist and hugging the urn to my chest. In front of us, Marta and Louise walk side by side, their fingers interlaced, their arms swinging together between them. Katey and Nico lead the way. At one stage, she jumps onto his back and he carries her effortlessly some of the way until she jumps down and beckons for us all to keep up.

I look up at Elliot. 'It's the perfect send-off. Nico wasn't allowed to play his grandfather's song at the funeral, so we should all go home and play it now. For Charlie and for Mum.'

'I'm not much of a singer,' Elliot says as he leans down to kiss the top of my head. 'You have been warned.'

'I'll be the judge of that.'

At the end of the path, just by the gate, Elliot stops to hand me something. It's a folded piece of manuscript paper. I take it and look curiously at it.

'It's the first sixteen bars of a song,' Elliot says.

'*Ione's Tune.*' I read the title and, below it, the handwritten notes on the staves. 'You wrote me a song?'

'It was for today. Well, not just today. It was inspired by you,' Elliot says. 'I will finish it, but I wanted to give you something today. Is that all right?'

'Of course it is? I look forward to hearing it.'

Katey shouts for us to get a move on, and I fold the piece of paper away, tucking it into my pocket before I take Elliot's hand.

I look over my shoulder before we turn the corner and before the park is out of sight. I will come back to the park many times in the years to come. One day, I'll bring my daughter to play there. One day, I'll tell her all about her grandmother, her grandfather, some love letters and a song.

Thank you for reading Lovers! If you enjoyed this book please leave an online review with the retailer and any social media platforms you use. I'd love to hear your thoughts.

Holding Paradise Book 1 of my upcoming Island Secrets Series is out February 2024. Join my Mailing List and get the prequel **FREE**!

Connect with me

Twitter @FranClarkAuthor

Instagram @franclarkauthor

Facebook www.facebook.com/FranClarkAuthorPage/

My website www.franclarkauthor.co.uk

Email: franclarkauthor@btinternet.com

Join my mailing list for a Free Read! Grab a preview copy of my next book and be ahead of all my news and updates!

The Island Secrets series:

Holding Paradise

A Prayer For Junie

The Long Way Home

When Skies Are Grey

About the author

Originally from London, Fran Clark moved to the English countryside with her musician husband. A musician herself, Fran teaches vocals and leads a choir. She has two sons.

Her first novel was published by Indigo Dreams in 2014. In the same year she achieved a Distinction in her Creative Writing MA from Brunel University. In 2016 she was shortlisted for the SI Leeds Literary Prize.

Fran also writes under the pseudonym, Rosa Temple, writing contemporary fiction and published by HQ Digital and Simon & Schuster UK.

Printed in Great Britain
by Amazon

36666926R00158